CEMETERY ROAD

*The new novel from a critically acclaimed
and award-winning author*

When Errol 'Handy' White returns to his
native Los Angeles to attend the funeral of
his old friend R.J. Burrow, who has been
brutally murdered, a terrible secret threatens
to reveal itself. Twenty-six years earlier,
Handy, R.J. and O'Neal Holden pulled a
heist that went horrible awry, and Handy's
been waiting for it to come back and haunt
them ever since. Was the murder linked to
the past? Handy knows he can't leave until
he finds out for sure.

CEMETERY ROAD

Gar Anthony Haywood

WARRINGTON BOROUGH COUNCIL	
34143199998483	
Bertrams	14/02/2011
AF	£19.99

Severn House Large Print
London & New York

This first large print edition published 2011
in Great Britain and the USA by
SEVERN HOUSE PUBLISHERS LTD of
9-15 High Street, Sutton, Surrey, SM1 1DF.
First world regular print edition published 2009 by
Severn House Publishers Ltd., London and New York.

British Library Cataloguing in Publication Data

Haywood, Gar Anthony.
    Cemetery Road.
    1. Criminals--Crimes against--California--Los Angeles--
    Fiction. 2. Los Angeles (Calif.)--Fiction. 3. Detective
    and mystery stories. 4. Large type books.
    I. Title
    813.5'4-dc22

ISBN-13: 978-0-7278-7914-1

Severn House Publishers support The Forest Stewardship Council
[FSC], the leading international forest certification organisation. All
our titles that are printed on Greenpeace-approved FSC-certified paper
carry the FSC logo.

MIX
Paper from
responsible sources
FSC® C018575

Printed and bound in Great Britain by the
MPG Books Group, Bodmin, Cornwall.

For the stubborn few who continued to believe, long after the lights went out. You know who you are. God bless you and keep you well.

ACKNOWLEDGMENTS

Many people offered me invaluable assistance in the writing of this book, but the following individuals deserve specific mention:

Alexis Moreno, Los Angeles historian

Eddie Muller, writer and pal

Joe Rein, boxing journalist and historian

Lt Ken Thomas, Public Information Office, Pelican State Prison

Patricia Medina, Executive Director, Crescent City Chamber of Commerce

Ray Mooring, US Bureau of Engraving and Printing

Winter, 1979

What I've always remembered most about my last day in Los Angeles is the smell of burning tar.

A neighbor across the alley from O's mother's garage was having his roof redone and the stench of molten tar hung in the air like a hot, black cloud.

'Goddamn, that shit stinks!' R.J. kept saying.

O' was late as usual and all the waiting around had R.J. going through Kools like a chocolate junky through Kisses. By the time O' finally showed up, over forty minutes after the agreed-upon hour, the floor of the garage was littered with butts, R.J. having crushed them underfoot with an animal-like ferocity to assuage his terror.

'What the fuck kept you?'

It was a curious thing. R.J. was tighter with O' than I had ever been, but it was he who seemed afraid our friend was gone forever, that O' had changed the plan and decided not to come. I had entertained the idea myself, but only briefly. We were all going to be running soon enough; leaving without making this final, farewell gesture would have surely been too foolish an improvisation for O' to even consider.

'I thought somebody might be following me, so I had to drive around a while till I was sure nobody was.'

O' tossed the big canvas bag he'd brought with him on to a workbench overrun with hand tools. It landed with the sound of a fat man jumping on a hardwood floor.

'You don't trust me enough to know I was still coming, you probably don't trust me enough to believe it's all here.' He opened the mouth of the bag, kept his eyes on R.J. 'You want to count it?'

'Goddamn right we want to count it.' R.J. flicked one last cigarette toward the floor and moved to the bag, never giving me so much as a backwards glance. He reached in, retrieved a pair of dog-eared bundles of green, and flipped them over to me. 'Check it out, Handy,' he said.

I ran a thumb across the bills as he rifled through the bag's full contents, O' watching us both with the detached demeanor of an innocent man in a police line-up. I wasn't as concerned about O's dishonesty as R.J. was, but I scrutinized the two stacks of tens and twenties closely enough to make a rough estimate: 'Looks like fifteen hundred, give or take.' I underhanded the money back to R.J., who returned it to the swollen belly of the canvas bag and proceeded to flip through two more bundles of his own.

'It's all there, R.J.,' I said.

He looked up.

'And we don't have time to get in his ass even if it's not. We're on the clock here.'

'Fuck the clock. A hundred and forty grand is a lotta bread, Handy. How do we know—'

'Because we know the *man*,' I said. 'That's how.'

R.J. thought about it, giving O' the hard look his unabashed suspicion demanded, and closed up the bag.

'Let's do this, then,' O' said.

He had rolled an old black, steel-drum barbecue grill to the center of the garage earlier that day, hours before R.J. and I had arrived shortly before noon, and now he brought the canvas bag and a can of kerosene over to it, acting as high priest of the dark ceremony we had all come here to take part in. He poured the bag's contents over the grill's open maw, drenched the mountain of emerald paper liberally with kerosene, and produced a book of matches. He started to strike one, but I put a hand out at the last second and said, 'I'll do it.'

My two friends looked at me with equal surprise.

'I'm the one who wanted this. I'm the one who should have to live with it.'

I took the matches from O's hand and snapped one to life, tossing the yellow flame into the grill before regret had any chance to take over the room.

We watched the money burn in silence for a

long while, our eyes thick with smoke and our hearts heavy. This was only part of the price we had to pay for absolution, and it wasn't going to be anywhere near high enough.

'It wasn't our fault,' O' said, his gaze fixed on the fire.

'Hell, no,' R.J. agreed, speaking a lie he knew he would never truly be able to believe.

I didn't say anything. I didn't want the debate to begin anew.

'I'm gonna miss you niggas,' R.J. said.

O' and I nodded our heads in silence, though I was already certain it wasn't O's and R.J.'s friendship I was going to miss most in the years to come.

It was the hope I used to have for my eternal soul.

ONE

It's not a problem young people have to worry about, but right around the time he hits his middle forties, a man starts giving serious thought to dying well. In his sleep in his own bed, or in the course of a street fight meant to settle something meaningful. His end doesn't have to be poignant, just devoid of indignity. You wouldn't think that would be too much to ask.

But how a man leaves this world, much like the way he comes into it, is almost never his own call to make, so evil men die on satin sheets in 400-dollar-a-night hotel rooms, while good ones breathe their last lying face down in cold, dark alleyways, their bodies growing stiff and blue on beds of rain-soaked newspaper.

Robert James Burrow didn't deserve to go out like royalty, perhaps, but he didn't deserve the ignoble exit he made either, shot four times and left to rot in the trunk of a stolen Buick LeSabre, down by the Santa Monica Pier in Los Angeles where we both grew up.

Twenty-six years earlier, a more fitting death for the hardnosed brother we all knew as 'R.J.' could hardly have been imagined. Back then,

13

like me, R.J. and trouble went hand-in-hand, so relentless was his pursuit of it. But this was two-and-a-half decades later, and the weight of all that time should have slowed him down some. The man was closing in on fifty, just as I was myself, and four bullets was at least two more than his killing should have required.

I learned of my old friend's murder via telephone. His widow had somehow tracked me down in Minnesota and invited me to the funeral, talking to me like someone who hadn't last seen or spoken to her husband in over twenty years. I allowed her to say goodbye and hang up believing I intended to come, when in fact I had no such compulsion. It didn't matter that R.J. and I had once been as close as two men not bound by blood could possibly become, nor that I literally owed him my life. He was a reminder of what I had always considered my darkest hour, and I wasn't going to stop avoiding him now just to answer the quixotic call of loyalty and unpaid debt.

Or so I thought.

Squeezed into an overpriced coach seat on a flight from Minneapolis/St Paul to Los Angeles, two days after receiving the Widow Burrow's call, I tried to tell myself I was making the trip simply to close the book on R.J. forever. I wasn't going out there to see anybody, or to ask any questions. R.J.'s death had nothing to do with me, and I had nothing to gain by trying to behave otherwise.

Had I only found the strength to stay home, I

14

might never have learned how wrong I was. I would not have gone rooting around the city of my birth for people I had no reason to make enemies of, and I would not have seen what a pitiful corpse my old friend made, gray and silent in his fancy burial clothes. A few words of bad news taken over the telephone, that's all R.J.'s murder would have been to me. Something to be saddened and shaken by for a day or two, then slowly set aside like a faded letter I no longer cared to read.

There are times I almost wish things had gone down exactly that way. But then I remind myself of the remote possibility that R.J.'s soul rests a little easier because they didn't, and I leave all my second-guessing for another day.

TWO

R.J.'s service was mercifully brief.

It was a hushed and somber Catholic affair that somewhere in the neighborhood of twenty people attended in the chapel at Holy Cross Cemetery in Fox Hills. The young white priest who called my friend's soul to rest did not know him, and everyone else only thought they did. I stood in the back of the chapel for the duration of the proceedings, cold marble walls on all sides, then followed the throng out to the

15

treeless hill where the priest said a few last words over the body before it was dispatched to the earth. I intended to leave right then, my duty to a man I hadn't seen in over twenty years done, but before I could peel away from the crowd, someone behind me dropped a hand on my shoulder to thwart my cowardly escape.

'Need a ride to the repast, Handy?'

I'd been dreading the sight of O'Neal Holden all morning, and now that the fear of finding him had finally left me, here he was, grinning like the joke was on me. He'd added a few pounds around the waist and his clothes were befitting a man who gave more orders than he took, but other than that, he looked like the same old O'. Big, gregarious, and as prone to pounce upon the vulnerable as a cat in the high weeds.

Without thinking about it, I offered him my hand, too overcome by nostalgia to do anything else. 'O'. What's goin' on?'

He gripped my hand with both of his and drew me into an embrace. 'Not a thing. Damn, it's good to see you.'

We were fast becoming the last ones standing at the gravesite. R.J's widow Frances and their only child, a lovely and statuesque daughter named Toni who'd been at her mother's side throughout the service, had long since been loaded into the lead car of the funeral procession and taken away, and with the sky overhead turning an appropriate shade of gray, everyone else was rushing to follow.

16

'I didn't think you'd come,' I said. 'But then, I didn't think *I* was coming, either.'

'Yeah, I hear you. I wasn't sure I was coming myself until I got in the car. But hell, it was R.J. What else was I gonna do?' He gave me the once-over, said, 'I damn near didn't recognize you. I was expecting big changes – gut like mine, male pattern baldness, a mouth full of false teeth. But hell, man, you might look better now than the last time I saw you! What, they don't have red meat and cheese where you come from?'

'Red meat costs money and dairy wreaks havoc on the blood pressure. Weight's not much of a problem when your income and your doctor have you eating apples and oatmeal.'

'Yeah, but what doctor where? What part of the world you call home now, exactly?'

'Minnesota. St Paul,' I said, accepting the fact that I was either going to give him this information, or hear him ask for it in a dozen more, and increasingly indiscreet ways.

'St Paul, huh? Damn. What line of work you in up there? Something mechanical, right?'

'I own a repair shop, yeah.'

'Let me guess: TVs, computers, vacuum cleaners...'

'A little of all that, but mostly I just fix junk. Things too old and obsolete for anyone else to be bothered with.'

'I like it. It suits you. Now – you wanna guess what business *I'm* in?'

'You're a city mayor. Down in Bellwood, I

17

think it is.'

'"Where LA business goes to work." That's right.' He flashed his discomfiting grin again. 'You like that? "Where LA business goes to work"? I came up with that.'

I nodded to be kind.

'Hey, come on, brother, let's go. We'll run by the repast for a hot minute, then drive out to my fair city, finish catching up over a big, fat-and-cholesterol laden dinner. What do you say?'

'I'm not going to the repast, O'. My flight home's at seven, I'm going back to the motel before I miss it.'

'You're going back tonight? You came for the funeral and that's it?'

He'd been working on my nerves for a while now, but I'd finally reached my limit. I set my jaw and said, 'I don't feel particularly safe out here, to tell you the truth. Call me a victim of an overactive imagination.'

'Say what?'

'My thinking what happened to R.J. might have had something to do with us, I mean.'

He let out a small laugh, said, 'You aren't serious?'

'They shot the man four times and left him in the trunk of a car, O'. You gonna tell me you haven't been thinking the same thing?'

'Man, that's bullshit. That's *crazy*.' He checked to make sure we were alone, then lowered his voice anyway. 'What happened to R.J. was all about R.J. He was doing what he always did, looking for trouble where you or I wouldn't

18

even think to try, and he got hurt. End of story.'

'You sound awfully sure of that.'

'I am sure of it. But before you ask—'

'Had you seen him recently?'

'—the answer's no. I hadn't. We had a deal, remember?'

'I remember. But deals change. People change. Agreements get renegotiated.'

O' shook his head.

A pair of groundskeepers were busy setting R.J.'s casket in the grave, apparently in a race to beat the oncoming rain. It wasn't much of a distraction, but I let my eyes drift over in their direction as if it were.

'It was good seeing you again, O'. If you go on to the repast, offer the family my condolences, will you?'

'Handy, Jesus Christ...'

I turned to walk away and he let me go, down the hill toward the taxi I hoped was still waiting for me at the chapel.

'You can stop running now, Handy,' O' called out after me. 'Nobody's chasing you, and nobody ever was!'

I wanted badly to believe him. He had charged me with cowardice in this way once before and I was still trying to convince myself he was right, that all my reasons for being afraid were nothing more than smoke. But I couldn't. Just as I had the first time, I fled Los Angeles hoping to never see it again.

Unable to shake the absolute certainty that it was either that or die.

THREE

One of life's greatest mercies is the impermanence of memory.

Some memories lose their shape and form faster than others. Details dim and disappear, forever out of reach of the conscious mind. Settings shift and grow vague, while the people in them perform all nature of tricks, morphing into others and moving about at will, either imposing themselves upon a time and place in which they played no part, or vacating one that holds little meaning without them. Six men in a room become two, three become five. The variations are endless.

Other memories, meanwhile, prove themselves to be indelible.

The smile of an old girlfriend; the sound of a car crash; the pain of a knife wound at the very instant the blade invades your flesh.

For me, it has always been a voice.

It is the voice of a child. Small, female, infused with dread. When she comes to me in my sleep, she never utters more than a single word, yet the inflection she places upon it is something I have been unable to shake for going on three decades:

Daddy.

It is a plea for mercy not intended for me. I am not the child's father. But I am the only one there to hear her, and to see the flames of a raging fire threatening to engulf her, so I am the one she is left to implore.

Her name is Sienna.

She has fair skin and dark brown hair that radiates in curls around her face like silken ribbon. Her eyes are wide, the color of a golden sunset, and her cheeks are aglow with youth and untested innocence. She is the most beautiful black child I have ever seen, and she is only four years old.

Daddy, she says.

She is not my responsibility. I have never laid eyes on her before, and her father is all but a stranger to me. If I reach out to save her, I am as doomed as she, because the fire is not the only danger such an act will require me to face. I know this, and I am paralyzed by the thought. But I eventually go to her nonetheless, diving into the white-hot halo surrounding her with arms outstretched, fingers beckoning.

Then, suddenly, smoke floods my lungs and fills my eyes, and the girl is no longer there to be rescued. I am alone in the fire, and it has me in its full and immutable grasp before I can even open my mouth to scream.

It is all a false memory, of course. The fire is of my own invention.

Still, even with my eyes wide open, I can sometimes feel its tendrils peeling the flesh off my bones just the same.

On the street in Frogtown, the St Paul community I call home, people call me 'Handy', exactly as they did in what was then called 'South-Central' Los Angeles over twenty-five years ago.

I can no longer recall exactly how or when I got the name, but it refers to the penchant I have always had for fixing things others have declared either beyond all hope or unworthy of repair.

Growing up, I was one of those kids who like to take things apart just to see how they work – toys and clocks, bicycles and radios – and this habit has followed me right into middle-age. My gift, if you can call it that, is an innate comprehension of machines and the mysteries they present, the cause and effect of levers and switches, motors and drive belts. It is a talent which has never earned me anything approaching wealth, to be sure, but it has at least managed to be sporadically profitable.

For the past nine years, after leapfrogging from one dead-end job and ungrateful employer to another, I have made a meager living working for myself, juggling small jobs almost anyone else could do with larger ones few others can or will take on for themselves. The small jobs, I perform in great number and on the cheap – rewiring old table lamps, installing cards and upgrade components in home computers – but the big ones I take on selectively, and for a considerable fee. The people who bring me the simple stuff are generally lazy individuals who lack the initiative to read a user's manual, but those who hire me to tackle more challenging projects almost always have nowhere else to turn. I am the only person they've been able to find with either the expertise or patience the work they want done requires.

The objects of these latter exercises tend to be old and mechanical: manual typewriters and wind-up alarm clocks, belt-driven turntables and telephones with rotary dials. It is not always clear to me why their owners prefer to have them repaired rather than replaced, but I suspect they are motivated more by sentiment than common sense. There is a magic in old-school devices that newer, more technologically advanced versions of same do not possess, and sometimes, just the sounds these machines make alone are enough to render them irreplaceable to their owner.

Such as it is, I ply my trade out of a little storefront on Rice and University I share with 'Ploitation Station, a video and memorabilia shop that specializes in the movies of the 1970s Blaxploitation era. Under a constant, period-appropriate soundtrack of Motown, Stax and Sound of Philadelphia R & B, Quincy Hardaway rents out copies of *Cleopatra Jones* and *Black Gunn* on the east side of the shop, while I tinker with things that are broken on the west side. Quincy is a very fat and effeminate black man in his early thirties who would starve in a day if he were dependent upon the shop to eat, but its proprietorship is really just a hobby for him; the business was a footnote to a large estate he inherited from a wealthy aunt many years ago, and he keeps it going at no small expense primarily as a gesture to her memory.

Ordinarily, I pay little attention to the ebb and flow of Quincy's business, especially when the object of my day's work holds a certain fascination for me. Consumed by the challenge and nostalgia of some projects, I can sit at my bench and listen to Quincy jabber without actually registering a word he's saying, both of us laboring to the accompaniment of the music of my youth, the hours slipping by like a train on greased rails.

It should have been this way for me with Andy Loderick's mini-bike. When Loderick first wheeled the home-made, motorized two-wheeler in for me to see, I almost took the job of refurbishing it for free. He said he had built the thing himself over thirty years earlier when he was just fourteen, using an old bicycle frame and a Briggs & Stratton lawnmower engine in accordance with some mail order plans he'd ordered from an ad in a comic book, and now that his mother's passing had brought him home from Pennsylvania where he'd gone off to college and remained, he'd hauled the stout but rusted little bike out of her garage in the hopes that I could recondition it for the entertainment of his two sons.

I told him I would do exactly that, or die

24

trying.

Unfortunately, the bike had come to me less than twenty-four hours after R.J.'s funeral, and O'Neal Holden's final words to me at the cemetery were still rattling around in my head. I *was* running scared, and I had been for a long time.

O' thought I had no reason to run, any more than he did. He had always been steadfast in this opinion, and I had never been able to decide whether that made him the smartest man I knew, or the most oblivious. Either way, before I'd picked up the phone less than a week ago to hear the news of R.J.'s death, I'd been capable of acknowledging the possibility, however remote, that O' was right and I was wrong. It was the only hope I had worth living for.

But no more. Now, R.J. was dead, murdered in a cruel and gratuitous fashion that reeked of malice, and I had come home from Los Angeles with renewed confidence in both my right to be afraid, and my need to run farther still.

For three days, I strove to go about my normal business, barely able to concentrate on the work I had before me. My distraction made mild annoyances out of things I usually have no quarrel with – Quincy's choice in music, the smell of oil and solvent that always lightly permeates my side of the shop – and heightened my awareness of the people entering and exiting my peripheral vision. For this reason, it was I who looked up first when two young bucks sauntered into the shop just before noon, moving with the leisurely pace and unsettling silence of encroaching death.

The older and larger of the two couldn't have been much more than seventeen. He had jet-black skin and a head crowned with a white Yankees cap over a red bandanna, the cap's visor turned at a right-angle to his slitted eyes. His younger, fair-skinned homie wore a mushroom cloud Afro and a giant ski jacket festooned with logos on the back and along the length of both sleeves. Both boys were otherwise dressed in the standard urban uniform of oversized baggy pants and sports jersey, gleaming white tennis shoes barely visible beneath pant legs that scraped the ground in a dozen folds of excess material.

None of this by itself was cause for alarm, of course; the clothes and the attitudinal gait, even the big kid's sneer were all too commonplace for young people today. But the younger boy, the one with the big hair and benign facial expression, had brought a distinctive aura into the shop along with his shadow, and I knew what it was even before the door had completely closed behind them.

Quincy did too. He watched the pair slink around between his racks of precious videos for a full minute, Yankee-boy fingering through the cases as if he actually knew who the hell Fred Williamson was, then said, 'Can I help you boys?' Asking the question in that way salespeople always do when what they really want to know is, *Why the fuck did you pick* my *place to jack?*

'We just lookin',' the big kid said.

His friend said nothing, but both of them continued to inch along their separate aisles, patiently and all-too conspicuously working their way toward Quincy and the counter he stood behind, right beside the cash register.

The boy with the Afro was just slipping a long-barreled revolver out from under his jacket when I eased up behind him and jammed the snout of an old .38 Beretta into the back of his left ear. He and his older dog never saw me coming because they didn't think I could move that fast, or would care to even if I were somehow capable. They'd given me a passing glance at the door and seen little more than a sad-eyed, middle-aged black man with a salt-and-pepper beard sitting at a workbench, a meaningless screwdriver in his hand. I knew that was all they'd seen, because that was the man I often saw myself, gazing out from the mirror while brushing my teeth, or reflected in the glass of a storefront window as I passed. I couldn't blame them for not expecting much.

'Give me the gun, youngblood,' I said, and I made a point of saying it like something I only had the patience to say once.

While he thought the order over, and Quincy stood there staring at me in mute astonishment, I watched the larger boy to see how much killing was about to be forced upon me. If he was armed too, and made a move to prove it, I'd have to shoot both boys in rapid succession: first the one near me, then his dark-skinned companion. Anything less would have been foolhardy.

Three seconds went by, and I still didn't have the boy with the Afro's answer.

'Don't try me, junior,' I said, and I screwed the Beretta's nose harder yet into the side of his skull, my eyes still fixed upon the kid closer to Quincy. When the latter boy suddenly came unfrozen, bringing me within an inch of committing the double-homicide I'd been contemplating, his only intent was to flee. He was at the shop's door and out of it in the time it takes most people to blink, his incredulous accomplice crying out his name in a senseless attempt to order his return.

'Tommy!'

But Tommy was good and gone.

I finally snatched the revolver from the younger boy's hand while the shock of his abandonment was still setting in, and then it was just him and me and Quincy, and the .38 I continued to jam into the back of the kid's left ear.

'Call nine-one-one,' I said to Quincy.

As my landlord slid to the phone on the wall behind him, I told the boy with all the hair to turn around, and make sure he took his sweet damn time doing it. He did.

I don't know what I was expecting to find on his face when he showed it to me – fear, anger, amusement – but what I got resembled none of these things. What I got was a stare as vacant as a paneless window in a gutted building, a little boy gazing at a television set tuned to a non-existent channel. I had a loaded gun aimed at his head, and the wild-eyed look of a man he might have just pushed close enough to the edge to use it, and he didn't care. I could do with him as I pleased; whatever fate I chose for him now, he was willing to accept without question or quarrel.

He was fourteen years old at the most and, already, life and death to him were but inter-changeable, equally valueless sides of the same coin.

At this particular moment in my own life, he could have cursed my mother in her grave and not enraged me more.

Quincy had been stunned by the show of reckless bravado I'd just put on, without a doubt, but I knew it was the sight of the gun in my hand alone that he had found most in-credible, because he had never seen me with such a weapon before. In truth, I'd had the Beretta in the shop with me for four days now, after not having touched it in almost twenty-six years. R.J.'s murder had changed the world for me in such a way that I preferred to have the gun close at hand over dying for the lack of it.

Quincy would say later that God had spoken to me that morning four days ago, when I'd gone up to the attic and withdrawn the Beretta from the old liquor bottle sack in which I had banished it, and that was why it was there on the bottom shelf of my workbench when our two would-be thieves stepped in on us, perhaps intending to do more to enhance their street cred than just take Quincy's money and run. But I knew God had had nothing to do with it. God would not have put that gun in my hand knowing how close I would come to emptying it into the head of a child whose most egregious crime was his resemblance to another young fool I once knew, many years ago.

In reality, the two boys looked nothing alike. In height, weight, even the color of their skin, they could hardly have been more different. But deep inside, behind their eyes, they had one thing in common I couldn't help but take note of: the apathy of the dead. A cool, inalterable kind of indifference that winds itself around the heart like a shield and chokes the soul down to the size of a small stone. Such inurement is the fuel of great folly, and it can sometimes lead a boy to do harm to others in ways he will eternally, and altogether uselessly, regret.

'Handy! Handy, *don't*!'

Hanging up the phone, Quincy must have seen a change come over my face, my fear and mild irritation giving way to something far more combustible and impossible to contain. I slammed the butt of the Beretta across the forehead of the teenage boy before me, hard enough to leave an imprint on his skull, and he dropped to the floor like an empty coat. I stood over him and watched a wide rivulet of blood run from a fresh scalp wound down the side of his face, and put everything I had into finding all the satisfaction possible in the sight, before my rage could spur me on to greater and far more unforgivable things.

'Jesus Christ, Handy, you didn't have'ta do that!' Quincy cried, forcing his great girth between me and the motionless body on the floor. 'You might'a killed the boy!'

He wanted to disarm me, but was too afraid to try. I wasn't Errol 'Handy' White anymore, or anyone else he thought he knew; I was just a crazy man with two guns who might be capable of anything. In the midst of his indecision, I walked back to my side of the shop and sat down at my workbench again. I put the two firearms down on the bench where the uniforms could see them when they eventually responded to Quincy's call and braced myself for their arrival.

As tired of being alive as I could ever remember being.

FOUR

The difference between a good man and a bad one often comes down to nothing more than the quality of his judgment. In making life-altering choices, his conscience may speak to him, but it is the voice of reason he ultimately adheres to, the basic math of what he has to gain versus what he stands to lose.

The two close friends I made for myself as I entered into manhood – O'Neal Holden and R.J. Burrow – were no more inherently evil than I. We took little pleasure in the distress of others, and put no effort into feigning indifference to it. But we were all brash and foolish and drunk with the power of youth, and serious consequences for our actions was a concept we scoffed at like a ghost story. We saw ourselves as invulnerable, and could not imagine how we could bring any real harm to others when we could not possibly bring harm to ourselves.

We first came together as a trio in our junior year at Manual Arts High School, where I essentially affixed myself to the pre-existing duo of O' and R.J., who had been best friends since the third grade. O' was a tall and beautiful ladies-magnet offhandedly involved in two sports, while R.J. was a comic with a mean streak nobody ever crossed without losing teeth. Each was fascinating in his own way, but O' was the real draw, a beacon of future stardom I was powerless not to admire and idolize. I expect R.J. felt much the same.

O' was born to be a mover and a shaker, a force of nature wrapped tightly if precariously in human form. No one who ever met him came away wondering what he would eventually become, because only one vocation offered him wealth and power to the extent he seemed to deserve them. Politics was O's unavoidable destiny, and the only thing open to question was what *kind* of elected official he would choose to become: the kind whose wisdom and compassion for his constituency marks him worthy of their trust, or the kind, far more common than the other, who wields that trust like chips on a poker table for his own personal enrichment?

The O' I grew up with was equally capable of evolving into either animal, and it was this quality of unpredictability that always made it so exhilarating – and terrifying – to know him as a friend.

R.J., by comparison, was not nearly so complex. If any of us was predisposed to a life of crime, it was him. R.J. was short and lean and forever on the lookout for any sign of disrespect, and there was no fight or challenge he would not take on with the zeal of a man possessed. His father was a closeted gay man who, in a drunken stupor, liked to beat his wife unconscious to minimize his sense of emasculation, and R.J. came to school most days relishing the opportunity to either make people laugh or make them bleed, the choice was entirely theirs. He had fast hands and quick feet, and he came at you like a blur, throwing punches you couldn't see while deflecting all your own. Had there been an ounce of bully in him, he would have been the most feared man at Manual; as it was, he was simply the most vigorously avoided.

As for myself, I was the wildcard, the consistent middle ground between O's lethal charm and R.J.'s brute force. Some people probably thought of me as the 'brains of the outfit', but brains were a non-issue. What I had over my two friends was restraint: the unremitting need to question and second-guess any action before daring to take it. O' always equated this inclination to a shortage of courage, but it saved our asses on enough occasions that he came to grudgingly appreciate it over time.

We were petty thieves. That was the simple truth of it. Larceny was not our constant occupation, just an occasional one, something to do with all our excess testosterone until we could find more constructive uses for our time. We all had big plans for the future, and with varying degrees of effort, we pursued them beyond high school, O' at UCLA, R.J. and I at Los Angeles City College. O' was going into politics, I was going to be a mechanical engineer, and R.J. had ambitions toward sports writing. None of us expected to be stealing televisions and car stereos forever.

In the end, however, a little more than three years out of high school, we were still players in the game when we committed one crime too many, and only O' had the wherewithal to survive its repercussions. It was just another rip-off, a bit larger and more complicated than most of the others we'd pulled over the years, perhaps, but like the others, it should have incurred no casualties.

That R.J. was the one who predicted otherwise still haunts me to this day.

'Excel Rucker? Man, are you crazy?'

'No. What's crazy about it?'

From the other end of the couch I was slouched across, R.J. took a long, expansive drag on the blunt pinched between his thumb and forefinger, his face taking on a scowl of deep concentration. 'That's some dangerous shit, that's what. Jackin' dope dealers.'

'It ain't dangerous if we do it right,' I said.

I stole a furtive glance at O', fishing for his reaction, but all he did was sink even deeper into the red leather beanbag chair he was sitting in and stare further yet into space, happy for now just to smoke a joint of his own and listen in.

We were all hanging at O's crib, our official base of operations in those days. It was a one-bedroom bachelor pad way out in Playa del Rey, big and clean and architecturally futuristic, and it sat just close enough to the beach that we could smoke dope and talk strategy with the illusion that we were doing so in style.

'What you mean, "right"?' R.J. asked.

'I mean we find one of his safe houses and watch it for a while. See who goes in and out, and when.'

'And then?'

'And then we figure out a way to take it down without anybody getting hurt. Same as we always do.'

''Cept we ain't always rippin' off drug dealers. Drug dealers got guns, nigga!' He passed me the joint, holding a lungful of smoke down tight. 'And what about the dope? We don't know nothin' 'bout sellin' cocaine, how we gonna move it without Excel findin' out?'

'We wouldn't try to move it. We'd flush it. The only thing we'd keep is the bread.'

'Say what?'

'He'll be looking for the drugs to show up on the street, but they never will. So all he'll be able to figure is that it had to be another dealer who ripped him off and just rolled the product into his own inventory. 'Cause nobody else would boost the shit and not even *try* to sell it, right?'

R.J. thought about it, looked over at the man in the beanbag chair. 'You hearin' all this, O'? What's this fool talkin' about?'

O' turned, glassy-eyed, and smiled. 'He's talkin' about payback,' he said.

'Huh?'

'Man's got a good idea, but it ain't about the

36

money and it ain't about the drugs. It's about Olivia Gardner. Ain't that right, Handy?'

I took a good long while to answer him because his insight into minds not his own always galled me. 'Yeah, that's right. It's about Olivia,' I said.

She was my brother's girl, not mine. Like Chancellor, Olivia Gardner was five years younger than me, almost a child at seventeen when I last saw her alive. She had almond-colored skin and big brown eyes, and a small, girlish body that was not ordinarily to my taste. I don't think I was ever in love with her, but she had my attention from the first time Chancellor brought her around the house.

She was the poorest person I knew. Her family lived in a little two-bedroom house just outside the northern perimeter of the Jordan Downs housing projects, and every meal they ever ate there had been scraped together with Welfare money. It was Olivia, two brothers, one sister, and their mother, all getting by on fumes and, in her mother's case, alcohol. One look at the dirt yard out front and you knew all the dresser drawers inside were filled with clothes even the second-hand stores didn't want, and the bathroom had a toilet that only flushed when it was willing.

Still, Olivia was a girl with the potential to escape it all. She was smarter than my brother by any form of assessment, and she had the will to fight, to make any sacrifice necessary to rise above the conditions she'd been born into. Left to her own devices, she was destined for greater things.

But lives as tenuous as Olivia Gardner's can all too often be derailed by a single mistake. The margin for error is just too small to tolerate the kind of miscues the rest of us survive routinely without suffering any ill effect. All she did was go to a party and do a little blow, the first she ever tried, and when she left, it was in the back of a red ambulance that killed its sirens halfway to the hospital because it wasn't worth diverting traffic for a dead girl.

It wasn't Excel Rucker's party, but the coke it was running on was. He was in the house himself that night, passing the shit out like a servant with a tray of hors d'oeuvres. People said later it was Excel personally who laid the white line down on the mirror in front of Olivia, but this, in my opinion, was a pointless accusation. Olivia did the blow of her own free will; she made a choice to duck her head down toward the man's white powder and take it into her body, and the consequences of that decision were hers alone to bear.

No one would have thought to play on Excel's conscience regarding her death until it became obvious that her family couldn't afford to bury her. Interred in a mass grave provided by the county morgue, with not so much as three words said by a man of God to recognize her passing, wasn't how anyone who knew her wanted to say goodbye; something had to be done. Somebody had to step forward and buy her a decent plot somewhere, and put the money up for a funeral, and my brother Chancellor got it in his head that this somebody should be Excel Rucker.

Unlike myself, Chancellor knew exactly how he felt about Olivia. He was madly in love with her, and when she died, he was wracked with guilt for not having been there to see it. Without consulting me first, he sought Rucker out to formally request that he honor the dead girl's memory with the price of a decent burial. None of Olivia's survivors would go in his place. My brother was careful to avoid any suggestion of culpability on Excel's part; he simply stated the fact that it had been Excel's cocaine that had caused her heart to seize up in her chest, and no one else had the means to spare her the indignity of having the county dispose of her remains.

According to Chancellor, Excel laughed in his face upon hearing this argument and had him forcibly shown to the door.

My brother took the rebuff badly, but I took it worse. A kinder and more sensitive man than I, Chancellor had humbled himself before God and man to solicit the dealer's aid, to respectfully ask for something that should have been freely given, and Excel had answered him with a playful kick in the teeth. Up until then, I'd been willing to hold the dealer blameless for Olivia's death, preferring to chalk the tragedy up to the precariousness of youth, but now I could see how unworthy he was of my absolution.

If he didn't want to spend a few thousand dollars to clean up one of the countless messes his business made, that was his prerogative. Liability coverage is never part of the deal anyone makes with a purveyor of illicit narcotics. But Excel was not within his rights to be cheerfully indifferent to the untimely death of someone as beautiful and vibrant as Olivia Gardner. If she didn't warrant his sympathy, she at the very least deserved his respect, and one way or another, she was going to get it.

I was going to see to it.

FIVE

R.J.'s widow Frances owned a nice home up in Ladera Heights. It was a white, single-level number with a pseudo-Asian motif that seemed to scream its 1960s origins out loud, and the clean, quiet street to which it was anchored had nary a parked car upon it when I arrived, back in LA less than a full week after R.J.'s funeral.

I was left to stand on the porch for a long time before somebody answered my persistent knocking. I had never been formally introduced to the young woman who eventually came to the door, but I recognized her as R.J.'s daughter nonetheless. She was the same bronze-haired beauty I'd seen glued to the side of Frances Burrow throughout the funeral, the product of a mixed race union that had blessed her with the smooth, oval face of her Latina mother and the brown-sugar flesh tones of her African-American father. There was no genetic explanation for the large brown eyes, however; those were all her own.

'Yes?'

'I apologize for just dropping in on you like this. But my name is Errol White. I was an old friend of your father's.'

'Of course. I remember seeing you at the funeral.'

She waited for me to explain myself.

'If I've caught you at a bad time...'

'No, no. Please, come in.'

She pulled the door open for me and I stepped inside. The house was all white walls and ancient furniture: antique lamps and mirrors, velvet upholstery and Indian throw rugs. It was a decor that created a sense of time travel back to the days of six-digit telephone numbers and Packard automobiles. Over five days had come and gone since the repast, but I would have sworn I could still smell all the plates piled high with sliced ham and potato salad those who had attended had no doubt carried from room to room. I was almost sorry now I hadn't come.

At the young woman's insistence, I took a seat upon the embroidered rose petals of a heavily cushioned couch, then watched as she

41

lowered herself into a matching armchair directly opposite. There was no sign of her mother.

'You're the one Daddy called "Handy",' R.J.'s daughter said, smiling.

'Yes. And I believe your name is Toni.'

'With an "i".' She nodded. 'Mr Holden said you missed the repast because you had urgent business back home. You didn't go?'

'I did go, yes.' I told the lie I'd been rehearsing all morning: 'But I had to come back to see your mother. To offer her the personal condolences I should have offered her – and you – last week.'

She smiled again, surprised. 'That really wasn't necessary.'

'I think it was. Business or no business, as close as R.J. and I once were, it was wrong of me to run off the way I did, without paying my proper respects, and it seems I won't rest easy until I do. Is your mother in, by any chance?'

She hesitated. 'She is, but I'm afraid she isn't up to seeing visitors. Daddy's death has hit her quite hard, as I'm sure you can imagine, and she spends most of her time these days in bed. I'm sorry.'

'I understand,' I said, nodding as if I did. 'The way R.J. died, from what I heard at the funeral, it all must have come as a great shock to her.'

'It did.' She was biting her lower lip to steady herself.

'Do you mind if I ask a question?'

'Not at all.'

42

'How did you and your mother find me? I haven't talked or written to your father in almost 30 years, and all my contact info's unlisted.'

'Oh. I'm afraid I took the liberty of looking you up on a few private databases I have access to at work. I wouldn't have done it, but you and Daddy had once been so close, mother was convinced you'd want to know about his passing.'

'What kind of databases?'

'The kind the police use,' someone behind me said.

Toni and I turned to see Frances Burrow standing in the archway between alcove and living room, a faded yellow bathrobe tied loosely around her waist. She was a powerfully built, steel-eyed Latina who had mourned at R.J.'s funeral with a dignity that approached surrealism, but only a fraction of that dignity was in evidence today. Today, she just looked tired and angry, braced by R.J.'s sudden death for years of potential loneliness.

'This is Errol White, Momma. Daddy's old friend from high school,' Toni said, both of us quickly rising to our feet.

'Handy White?' R.J.'s widow shuffled into the room to get a better look. 'We were told you went back home to Minnesota.'

'I did. But—'

'You're curious too. Of course you are. Bobby didn't die the way they say, and we all know it.' She smiled at her daughter. 'Didn't I

43

tell you?'

'Mother...'

'My daughter actually believes there could be some truth to what the police say about what happened to her father, Mr White. That he stole a car and drove it down to that beach to make some kind of drug deal that "went wrong". Can you imagine?'

'I never said I believed it, Mother. I only said it's doubtful that the whole thing is a lie.' Toni turned to me. 'He was shot two times in the back, and twice more in the head, and his fingerprints and cocaine residue were found all over the car's interior. What does that sound like to you, Mr White?'

I hadn't seen much of R.J.'s spirit in her up to now, but this was it all over: Her glare could have sliced cast iron into ribbons.

'Well,' I said, feeling like a man about to step on to a minefield, 'it sounds like a drug-related homicide, I suppose. But that could be only because somebody wanted it to look that way.'

'Exactly!' Frances Burrow said. She took a seat at the end of the couch I'd been sitting on and gestured for Toni and me to return to our own. 'Toni, have you offered our guest something to drink? What can we get you, Mr White?'

I told her I wanted for nothing, and it was just as well that I did, because Toni Burrow didn't look like she had any interest in serving me anything. I'd been drafted by her mother as an ally into whatever feud it was they were engaged in, and the young woman now clearly viewed me as a member of the enemy camp.

'Toni is a licensed private investigator up in Seattle where she lives now,' Frances Burrow said. 'And she's going to stay down here and talk to people until she gets some answers.'

I turned to Toni, who only looked back at me with the burning resentment of an indentured servant.

'I'm not sure that would be a very good idea,' I said.

'No? And why is that?'

'Because the police aren't going to like it, Mother. I've explained that to you,' Toni said.

'I don't care what they like or don't like, and neither should you. They think your father was a common drug dealer, and as long as they have that ridiculous idea, they're never going to find the animal who killed him. Never!'

R.J.'s widow set her jaw and waited for her daughter's rebuttal, but Toni Burrow didn't offer one. I gathered my nerve and spoke in her stead, again about to tread on dangerous ground.

'I hope both of you will forgive me for asking this, because I'm certain you'll find it a ridiculous question. But it's been over twenty-five years since I last saw R.J., like I said, so I don't know.'

'Yes?'

'Is there any way he *could* have died the way they say? That is, is it possible—'

'No.'

45

'If things weren't going well for him lately, or if he was in some kind of serious money trouble—'

'No! He wasn't out on that beach making any drug deal!' Frances Burrow was livid, her eyes tearing up now. 'You didn't know him. How far he'd come, how hard he'd worked to change.' She looked over at Toni. 'Neither one of you knows.'

'That isn't fair, Momma.'

'What isn't fair is what they did to him. He didn't deserve to die like that, I don't care what he was doing that night!'

She finally broke down, sobbing into her hands, body heaving. Her daughter went to comfort her, but was waved away.

'I'm going back up to my room,' Frances Burrow said, rising on unsteady legs. 'I'm tired.' I stood up again and watched as she slowly made her way to the door. 'Goodbye, Mr White. Bobby always spoke very highly of you, and it was kind of you to come by.'

I opened my mouth to apologize but she was gone before I could get the words out. Toni Burrow and I endured an awkward silence for a moment, then she put us out of our misery. 'I'll walk you to the door,' she said.

Back out on the porch, in lieu of a simple goodbye, I said, 'She's a very headstrong woman and she obviously loved your father a great deal. But I don't think your mother understands how much trouble you could get yourself into, trying to find out who killed R.J. on your

46

own.'

'No. She doesn't.'

'At the very least, I expect the LAPD would threaten to arrest you for interfering in an ongoing investigation.'

'Actually, it's Santa Monica PD, but your point is well taken.'

'You really a private investigator up in Seattle like she said?'

'Yes. But not the kind she thinks. I work for a law firm up there, Hubble and Kleinman. The majority of what I do is conduct interviews and collect evidence in paternity cases.'

'Then homicide investigations aren't a big part of your practice.'

'They aren't *any* part of my practice. But trying to tell that to Mother is pointless. She thinks my license to operate in Washington State is as good as a detective's badge anywhere in the world.'

'Well, you can't really blame her, can you? Convinced as she is that the police are all wrong about R.J. and the way he died, what else would she do but expect his daughter to set them straight?'

If she heard the question, she didn't answer it.

'Or maybe you don't think they *need* to be set straight,' I said, probing.

'It was good of you to come back and see us, Mr White,' Toni Burrow said. 'I hope you have a pleasant trip back home.'

It was all the farewell she was going to leave me with before closing her mother's front door.

47

SIX

Bellwood, California, is a small and quiet incorporated city in the southern hemisphere of Los Angeles County that is roughly 11 square miles in size and serves a populace of just under 30,000 people, most of them black and Hispanic. It is primarily a stronghold of commerce, laden with business parks and corporate headquarters, and you tend to see its name in the papers only when the Bellwood Monarchs have further solidified the city's long history of high school athletic supremacy.

How O'Neal Holden had come to be the overseer of such a tiny and unimposing fiefdom, I couldn't say, as disconnected to him and his fortunes as I had been for the last two-and-a-half decades. But from what little I had read and heard about him from time to time, he seemed to be enjoying the role. He was always smiling brightly when cameras were around, and the sound bites from his public appearances were consistently upbeat. If he was at all concerned about the accusations of misappropriation and malfeasance that were beginning to stir all about his office, it didn't show in the face he had perpetually turned toward the public. O' was a rock. As always, he had no time for fear, and no need to pretend otherwise.

I knew it would not be a simple matter to receive an audience with such a man, even for me. The mayor of any city is invariably busy, beholden to obligations that make impromptu meetings difficult to arrange. But I went calling on O' just the same. My digging into the mess that was R.J.'s murder was going to draw his attention sooner or later, and I decided it would be best to go knocking on his door first, rather than wait for him to come sniffing around mine.

For a brief moment, I considered taking the conventional route of engagement, calling his office to see if he could see me on a moment's notice. But then I imagined all the evasions that tact would afford him, should he feel the need to study his lines before we met, and I chose to take another, somewhat more direct approach.

An ambush.

'Goddamn, Handy. You haven't missed a trick, I swear.'

We were having lunch at an upscale Italian restaurant on the outskirts of Bellwood called Antonio Z's. O's name wasn't on the booth in the back we were occupying, but I could tell it belonged to him just the same. The officious young hostess who'd greeted us out front led us to the spot without a word of instruction, and the staff as a whole was treating the mayor like the first Pope to wear a cream-colored suit and 300-dollar Stacy Adams shoes.

'How do you mean?'

'Hell, you know what I mean. Walking into a Council meeting in mid-session to take a front-row seat right under my nose. You couldn't have made yourself more conspicuous if you'd been pulling an elephant along on a leash.'

'It got your attention, didn't it?'

'If you wanted to see me, Handy, you could have just called my office for an appointment.'

'And waited three weeks for you to clear a date on your calendar? I needed to see you today, O'.'

I'd found Bellwood's City Council chambers on the second floor of the City Hall building, in the heart of a two-block stretch of commercial real estate the locals ambitiously called 'down-town'. Wood-paneled and brightly lit, the chamber room had held all of fifteen people upon my entrance, including the mayor and four members of his Council. I could have stood in the back by the door and still given O' little choice but to eventually acknowledge my presence and deal with it.

Which, to his credit, he did sooner rather than later. In the process of delivering an enthusiastic and highly persuasive argument in favor of a Main Street beautification project, Bellwood's large and charismatic mayor noted my arrival and registered it with a wink and a smile, never missing a beat of his oratory. It was classic O'Neal Holden. When you pinned the big man into a corner from which there was no escape, he didn't waste a whole lot of time resenting you for it. He simply resigned himself to the space you'd hemmed him up in and commended you for having had the foresight to corner him first.

'I knew you'd come back,' he said to me now, ivory smile beaming with self-satisfaction. 'I just didn't think it'd be so soon.'

'What can I say? Guess I'm still the fool you've always said I am.'

'Not a fool. Just an alarmist. We've got nothing to be afraid of, Handy. R.J.'s murder had nothing to do with us.'

'And you know that how?'

'I know it because I've talked to people familiar with the case who've told me so, that's how. Have you?'

He paused for me to answer him, forged ahead when I didn't. 'Look, I can't be getting involved in this thing, all right? I stuck my neck out farther than I should have just by going to homeboy's funeral. The press ever puts me and R.J. together, they're gonna go back to where the three of us began and start digging. And I think you and I both know where that could lead.'

I didn't have to tell him that I did.

A waiter came around to ask for our order, and we used the interruption to get all the unavoidable small talk out of the way. We asked each other about wives and kids, O' confessed to having one of the former and two of the latter, and I told him what little there was to tell about Coral. He took the info in without much

51

visible reaction, but I was certain the story saddened him all the same, because it saddened me just to relate it. A forty-nine-year-old man who'd never married but had a grown daughter he rarely saw and barely knew, turning screws on broken toasters and washing machines just to eat ... The only thing that could have made my life more disheartening to describe was its belonging to someone who deserved better.

'So when was the last time you'd seen him?' I asked, forcibly steering our conversation back toward the business that had brought me here.

'R.J.? Brother, *I* was gonna ask *you* that. I hadn't seen R.J. in a hundred years.'

'That right?'

'Come on, Handy. I just told you: I couldn't get anywhere near R.J. Burrow. And even if I could have—'

'We had an agreement. Sure we did. But what if R.J. tried to reach you all the same? Twenty-six years is a long time to stay away from people you used to look upon as family, O'.'

Bellwood's mayor shook his head. 'Didn't happen,' he said.

'But if it had. What would you have done?'

'I'd have taken his call, same as I would have taken yours. Hell, what are you getting at here? You don't think *I* had something to do with his murder?'

'If one of us was ever going to talk out of turn, it would have been him,' I said. 'I think you and I have always known that. Nobody had a harder time dealing with what we did than R.J.'

52

'We didn't "do" anything,' O' said tersely.

'You really still believe that?'

'You're goddamn right I do.'

I shouldn't have been surprised, but I was. I had thought his sense of denial on the subject would wear down after twenty-six years. Instead, its edge seemed as keen as ever.

'OK, how's this,' I said. 'Nobody took what "happened" to us harder than R.J., and maybe after wrestling with his conscience all this time, he found the need to vent.'

Just as I sometimes do myself, I thought, but did not say.

'Vent to whom? The police?'

'There wouldn't have been much point, but the impulse would have been a natural one just the same. Only, R.J. wouldn't have wanted to go to them alone. He'd have wanted one or both of us to go with him.'

'And you're suggesting that, if he'd come to me, I would have killed him to keep him quiet. Shot his ass full of holes and left him in that car to die down by the pier.'

I didn't say anything.

O' shook his head at the ceiling and chuckled, deriding the absurdity of my thinking. He leaned hard across the table toward me, said, 'Listen to me, Handy. I'm going to tell you the same thing I told you two fools twenty-six years ago, and the same thing I would have told either one of you if you'd asked me about it since, but didn't: We made a mistake. We made a play that turned bad, and some innocent

53

people got hurt. It was fucked up, but that's how it goes sometimes.'

Our server chose this moment to deliver our meals, and O' seemed to find some relief in his timing. He was starting to lose his cool, and the respite gave him a chance to regenerate before any real damage could be done.

'Tell me something, O',' I said. 'Has R.J.'s daughter been around to see you yet?'

'Toni? No. Why should she?'

'Because she's a private investigator by profession up in Seattle, and she and her mother aren't going to take R.J.'s murder lying down. I was just up by R.J.'s place to see them and they're both frothing at the mouth over all the rocks she's going to turn over searching for his killer on her own.'

'So?'

'So you're going to have to talk to the young lady eventually, brother, and lies aren't going to fly with her. You want to hand me some line about it being twenty-six years since you last spoke to R.J., fine, but if you try that shit on *her*—'

'OK, OK. Take it easy, Jesus.' I'd deliberately let my voice rise above that of mere civil conversation and he took the bait, finally betraying some aggravation for all the effort I'd been putting into provoking it. 'R.J. called me once or twice over the years, sure. The *Times* runs a picture of me on the City Hall steps every other month, and he's three months behind on his mortgage – who else was he going to ask for help? You?'

'I thought you couldn't afford any contact with the man.'

'I can't, and I've never had any. The two times I loaned him a few dollars, there were two people between me and the bagman who actually handed him the money.'

'How long ago was this?'

'The last time? Two, maybe three years ago, I'm not sure.'

'And how much was a "few dollars"?'

'Ten bills the last time, and six before that, about fifteen years ago. Look, Handy, this is ridiculous. Why in the hell should you, or R.J.'s daughter, or anyone else be trying to connect his murder to people he last knew almost thirty years ago? R.J. was always a magnet for trouble, and he'd had a hell of lot of time to find more since we all said our goodbyes to each other. Even if he didn't die exactly the way the police think he did, it's sure as hell safe to say one thing about their theory of the crime is dead-on: However all that blow got in that car that night, some of it went up homeboy's nose. That sound like a man who wasn't asking for what happened to him to you?'

'Waitaminute. You're saying he was loaded when he died?'

'Damn straight.'

'How do you know?'

'It's in the coroner's report. I've got a man close to the investigation. You're making me repeat everything I tell you twice, Handy, damn.'

Neither R.J.'s widow nor his daughter had said anything to me that morning about cocaine being found in R.J.'s system, only that traces of the drug had been discovered in the car in which he died.

'Don't look so damn surprised,' O' said. 'You said it yourself: The man always took what happened back in the day harder than us. If somewhere down the line he got in the habit of doing a little blow to help him forget now and then, it wouldn't have been entirely unlike him. And R.J. under the influence of an illegal narcotic, well ... If that's not a formula for disaster, I don't know what is.'

He was right. I couldn't envision any scenario in which a combination of R.J. and blow would not have eventually resulted in either his death or incarceration, no matter how much he might have mellowed over the years.

'I want to talk to him,' I said.

'Who?'

'Your man "close to the investigation". I want you to set up a meeting.'

'Forget it. He'd never talk to you. You're a Maytag repairman, Handy, not a cop.'

'If you made it worth his while, he'd take the meeting. I'm asking you to make it worth his while.'

My old friend shook his head again, preparing to hand me another line of excuses, but before he could open his mouth, I said, 'It's bullshit, O'. Fifty-year-old man steals a car, fills it up with cocaine, then drives it out to the beach to try and sell it? You can buy that if you want, but not me.'

'Handy...'

'I'm not going back home until I'm sure this time, all right? I've been running for twenty-six years, just like you said back at the cemetery, and I'm tired of it. If I'm next on somebody's shit list, they're going to have to do me right here, right now, before I find a way to do them first.'

'That's crazy talk,' O' said.

'Maybe. But if I'm not crazy, it might be in your best interests to give me all the help you can. If you follow my drift.'

He did. The math was too simple to ignore. There once had been three of us to hold accountable for the decades-old crime we had committed, and now there were only two. Unless that was a mere coincidence, O's life was just as much at risk now as mine.

'I'll see what I can do,' he said irritably, waving our waiter over to collect the bill. He drew a platinum credit card from his wallet and laid it down in the tray. 'Where can my man reach you?'

I gave him my mobile phone number and the name of my motel, and he input the info into a cellphone that probably cost more than the rental car I was driving.

'Anything else?'

'Just one. Allow me to pay for lunch today. From what I heard at that meeting this morning, you don't need to give Councilwoman Madera any more quote-unquote "business" expenses to put under her little microscope.'

O' snorted. 'Angie? Please. I've left her on the short end of too many Council votes for her liking lately, and that was her idea of payback, making a big show of sniffing around my every move for some sign of impropriety.'

For the sixty-plus minutes I'd spent in chambers waiting for the mayor to get free, I'd thought nothing would ever raise the dialogue above a tepid drone until Madera – a short, stern-faced Latina I figured to be in her early forties – tried to enter an item to the floor that was not on the day's agenda. As near as I could tell, it had something to do with a trip to San Francisco the mayor and an aide had taken the previous month on the city's dime, which Madera failed to see as relevant to the business affairs of Bellwood.

'This aide you took up to San Francisco – it wouldn't be that pretty young thing you were talking to after the meeting?'

She'd been a stunner, late twenties or early thirties, caramel complexion, wearing a tailored brown business suit that looked tight enough to leave imprints of its stitches on her skin. Just the sort of younger woman to whom a man like O' might assign the duties of a mistress. She'd conferred with O' for a quick minute, delivering some papers for him to sign, then he'd sent her on her way, post-haste, as if he knew I'd be asking him the very question I'd just asked about her now.

'Get your mind out of the gutter, Handy,' O'
said, either miffed, uncomfortable, or some
combination of the two. 'That was Brenda's
daughter Iman. She works for me.'

'Your sister Brenda?'

'Iman was her second husband's oldest
daughter. And for the record, no – she wasn't
the aide who went up north with me. That was
Gerald Coker. You wanna make something
dirty out of that?'

'No, but I bet Angie Madera sure would.'

'Yeah, well, she's out of luck. Same as
always. Take this little conference you and I
just had, for instance.' He flashed me a grin and
winked his right eye. 'You're an old dog of
mine, Handy. If the lady wants to find the
money for your lunch where I plan to hide it,
her fat ass is welcome to try.'

And with that, he threw his head back and
laughed, the way he used to in the old days
whenever he'd sold a lie to somebody just for
the thrill of proving he could.

SEVEN

It all went down exactly the way we planned it. That was the greatest irony of all. No one was supposed to get hurt, and technically, no one did. Our intended victim was Excel Rucker, and we were only after his money, not his soul.

We took our time putting everything together. We were in no hurry to act. For four weeks, R.J., O' and I took turns shadowing Rucker until his routine made his safe houses evident, and then we watched the safe houses themselves. We did our own census of occupants and visitors, tracking every movement and habit, and compiled careful records of the hours in which lights went dim in windows and doors were dead-bolted shut. We knew who and how many, what they drove and, in some cases, how well they were armed, and eventually, we knew exactly where we wanted to take Excel down.

It was an ordinary little duplex apartment out in Inglewood, several miles west of the dealer's normal scope of operations. The apartment was home to a woman and three men, a quartet we broke down to a supervisor, his wife, and a pair of male soldiers. The supervisor was obese and

60

non-threatening, and the soldiers were typical of the breed in their interminable projection of menace, but it was the woman who may have spooked us the most. She was a wild-haired crazy who flew into spontaneous rages, the kind of rages that precipitate many a prison yard killing, and in partnership with the en-forcers who catered to her every whim, she was arguably the most intimidating of all the guard dogs under Excel Rucker's employ.

More than the people who occupied it, however, it was the Inglewood apartment itself that made the site ideal for our purposes. Excel's three other safe houses were either apartments in large complexes or single-family homes crawling with children. They were all crowded and cramped, in buildings that seemed to be separated from their neighbors by the breadth of a chalk line, and none of them offer-ed easy entrance nor exit to a thief. Conversely, the Inglewood duplex sat on a short, quiet block outside the chaos of the 'hood proper, with room to breathe on all sides, and there was rarely very much in the way of vehicular or foot traffic around to disturb it. Though it had bars on all its windows, and a pair of relative inno-cents lived in the unit adjacent to Excel's, these were minor drawbacks easily trumped by the additional access of an alley out back and an uncomplicated, single-story layout its exterior made all but obvious.

We watched the place for twenty-two days. During that time, it was Rucker's routine to visit twice a week, on Monday and Thursday nights, and always around ten thirty p.m. We were never able to determine which night was for deposits and which was for withdrawals, nor what, exactly, was the currency involved – dope or cash? – but based upon what few clues the dealer and his crew gave us, we eventually concluded that our biggest take awaited us immediately after one of his Thursday night appearances.

The plan, as I've said, was to enter, grab the cash and dope, and get out, without bloodshed of any kind. We had no experience in gunplay and did not intend to resort to any now. But Excel Rucker was not our typical mark, and certain concessions had to be made. If something went wrong and we weren't prepared to deal with it, we could all wind up dead, and even I wasn't ready to take that risk.

The day R.J. showed O' and me the three guns he had secured for our use, the three of us all sitting around O's dining room table, I was given my first clue that what we were about to do could only end badly.

'This one here,' R.J. said, bouncing a black, .45 caliber Colt around in his right hand like a kid with a new baseball, 'will take a motherfucker's head off from across the room. This right here is *mine*.'

O' and I looked over the two weapons remaining – a 9 mm Smith & Wesson semi-auto, and an old, badly scarred .38 caliber Beretta revolver – with equal disinterest.

'Do you care?' O' asked.

'No. Why should I? They're only going to be for show.'

'Shee-it,' R.J. said, laughing.

I turned to face him directly. 'I say something funny?'

R.J. looked first to O' – '"For show", the man says.' – then back at me. 'You think that's all we might have to do? *Show* them niggas a gun?' He shook his head at the sheer stupidity of the idea. 'You need to stop trippin', Handy.'

'Trippin'? Who's trippin'?' I could feel my face burning red.

'Take it easy, Handy,' O' said.

'No, no, fuck that. We've already had this conversation. We aren't firing a goddamn shot that we don't have to fire. This fool here doesn't like that, we can forget this whole thing right now.'

R.J. frowned as if amused. 'Who you callin' a fool?'

'Nobody. He's not callin' anybody a fool. Both of you niggas chill out,' O' said.

'Only fool around here is you,' R.J. said, mad-dogging me, 'if you think we gonna go in there and take Excel's shit without fuckin' somebody up or gettin' fucked up ourselves. It's a drug dealer's safe house, dumb-ass, not a furniture warehouse! We're in the big leagues now.'

He was grinning from ear to ear. I turned to O', demanding his intervention.

'Put the gun down, R.J.,' he said.

'What? This?'

'Yeah, that. Put it down.'

R.J. did as he was told, but the grin stayed where it was.

'Homeboy's right. Ain't nobody here gonna be pulling the trigger on any of these pieces. And I'm gonna tell you why, just as soon as you wipe that ignorant-ass smile off your face.'

This time, it took R.J. a little longer to comply.

'Because if we do, it means somebody fucked up. Forgot what the plan was, or did something stupid. And ain't none of us are gonna do that, are we?'

'O', all I'm sayin'—'

'I said, none of us are gonna do that, are we?'

R.J. sat there for a long minute, burning. No one had the influence over him O' did, but sometimes, even O' could push him too far. One day they were going to throw down on each other and R.J. would have O's neck in two pieces before he remembered who he was sparring with.

'No. We ain't,' R.J. said.

It was O' who had asked the question, but R.J.'s sneer was directed at me.

I tried to make peace with him later that evening, as we walked out to our cars to drive home. He'd had little to say to either of us after O' called him out, and I didn't want his foul mood to carry over into the critical days ahead.

'Look, brother,' I said, 'I'm sorry about getting in your face about the guns. But you were freaking me out. Talking like you're actually *hopin'* to shoot somebody, or something.'

R.J. looked at me in a way that left no doubt that he found my naivety pathetic. 'I ain't gotta hope,' he said.

'What the hell does that mean?'

'It means jackin' Excel Rucker was *your* idea, nigga, not mine or O's. You the one got the hard-on for him, not us.'

'So?'

He got right up in my face, nose-to-nose. 'So I ain't gonna let neither one of us get killed tryin' to do this shit your way, Handy. I told you from the get-go, fuckin' with a playa like Excel ain't no joke. You wanna go up in his house and rip him off, you gotta be ready to lay a mother-fucker *out*.' He stuck a finger in my chest. 'And that's exactly what I'm gonna be.'

He gave me one last jab to cast me aside and walked away. I thought about going after him, but I couldn't see any point.

I had a chance right then to call the Excel Rucker job off and I didn't take it. The memory of Olivia Gardner was still a call for revenge too powerful for me to ignore. To put myself at ease, I told myself we had devised a plan that even R.J.'s volatility could not impair. All we had to do was follow it to the letter, avoid all improvisation and error, and our success would be assured.

What I failed to understand is that no plan is ever impervious to chance. No matter how scrupulously rehearsed or executed, the designs of mortal men will always be as prone to the unexpected as cloud patterns in the sky.

It was a lesson I was doomed to learn the hard way.

EIGHT

My brother Chancellor was the only family I left behind when I fled Los Angeles for good in the winter of 1979. Our mother had died of ovarian cancer three years earlier and our father had disappeared six years before that, allegedly with a fat woman who had money. We were our parents' only offspring, and as far as my brother and I knew, we had no other living relatives west of the Mississippi.

I cannot say we parted on the best of terms. Olivia Gardner's death had shaken Chancellor badly, and he was already on the downward spiral that would not bottom out for many years when I told him I was leaving. My reasons were all hollow and fabricated, and he knew it, but all he did to let on was accept them in silence, as if they weren't even worth the breath it would take to discount them. Like our mother, he had never cared for R.J. and O', and had always been able to see the trouble my association with them would bring me, so there was nothing about my sudden need to put some distance between us he could find particularly surprising.

My leaving hurt him nonetheless.

We kept in contact for the first year or so strictly by telephone, calling each other after months of avoiding it just to keep the illusion of interest alive. Then we just stopped. Chancellor's descent into alcoholism became too pronounced for him to disguise anymore, and I couldn't keep the ring of pity out of my voice. I had never before seen the loss of a woman drag a man that far down into despair, and in my ignorance of the phenomenon, I decided it would be better to abandon my brother altogether than to bear witness to his resounding weakness.

I have no actual knowledge, then, of the depths he eventually reached. I only know that the woman who answered his phone late one night in 1989 could not stop weeping long enough to properly explain his absence, and that was the last time the number I had for him worked at all. I had given him up for dead until he resurfaced four years later, ending our estrangement not with a phone call but a letter, written from a hospital bed. It was an invitation to resume contact and little else, sprinkled with allusions to his recovery from a personal nightmare he would not name.

Whatever had prompted his disappearance, he came out of it a new man, equally laconic, perhaps, but stronger and less self-absorbed. Gradually, and with considerable caution, we returned to our routine of intermittent phone calls, and in the course of our reconciliation, Chancellor went back to school and married the weepy woman who'd answered his phone that night in 1989. He earned a degree in Journalism from Cal State Dominguez Hills and eventually parlayed it into the steady job he continued to hold today, staff writer for the *Los Angeles Guardian*, the oldest black-owned newspaper in the city.

I hadn't bothered to look my brother up when I'd come out for R.J.'s funeral, having only planned to be in town less than a day, but now that I'd returned with the idea of staying for a while, I couldn't see my way around to not getting in touch. He invited me to dinner at his home in Carson early Monday night, and I accepted, anxious to see how much of his re-habilitation was of my own invention, and how much was real.

Like O'Neal Holden had a week before, Chancellor lied and told me I looked good, but he was the one who showed marked improve-ment from the last time we had met. Gone was the little brother who had always been smaller and less muscular than me; the only physical advantage I held over my sibling today was in height, and that by only the merest of margins. He was hard and chiseled from head to toe, and his every movement transmitted a message of power and vitality that belied his age. Now he had smarts *and* good looks, and I couldn't help but envy his incredible transformation.

'You could have stayed with us, you know,' he said after dinner, as his wife Andrea did the dishes in the kitchen and he and I sat in the quiet of his living room, absently watching a muted television. 'We have plenty of room.'

I shook my head. 'I'd be too much of a nuisance. Coming and going at all hours of the night. I'm better off at a motel.'

I had told him I was here on a rare parts search for a repair job I'd taken on back home, and if he had any doubts about this explanation, he had yet to let on.

'I think you forget we have two teenage boys,' he said, laughing. 'People come and go in this house twenty-four-seven.'

His wife chuckled from the kitchen, having overheard the joke. Andrea was a tall, big-boned Filipina with the face of a child's doll, and I could picture her standing at the sink, her whole body trembling with genuine mirth. She too had made a transformation of sorts, in that I imagined the crying, grief-stricken woman I first met over the phone sixteen years earlier was also a thing of the past.

'Where are the boys now?' I asked. I had seen photos of my nephews but we had never actually met, and I'd been looking forward to finding out how their individual personalities meshed with the stoic, almost surly countenance they had in common.

'In the street. Where else?'

'It's after ten. They don't have curfew?'

'Eleven o'clock, same as the one Momma

69

gave us. But it's flexible. Byron's sixteen and Garrett'll be fifteen in three weeks. Their mother and I figure as long as they keep bringing As and Bs home from school, it doesn't much matter what time they get in.

'So tell me again what you're doing out here,' my brother said, seemingly eager to dispense with all the small talk. 'You said you're looking for parts of some kind?'

'Pieces to a set of lamps I'm refurbishing,' I said, repeating the story I'd concocted on the drive over. 'A company called Modeline made 'em back in the sixties, and most of the few lamps still in existence are out here in LA where they were originally manufactured.'

'The company's no longer around?'

'They went out of business years ago.'

'You try looking on the Internet?'

'I've tried everything. The things are all wood and brass with canvas shades, so units in any kind of decent shape are rare as hell. Hollywood seems to have a fondness for the brand as movie props, though, and if I'm lucky, I might be able to find one or two in shops that cater to that kind of business.'

After a long pause, studying my face throughout, Chancellor said, 'I see.'

I had put a lot of time and effort into developing a lie elaborate enough to fool him, and in the end, I could have saved myself the trouble. He took a swig from his canned soda, turned to eye the silent television, and, keeping his voice down for the sake of his wife, said,

'What happened to R.J. is none of your business, Errol. Why do you feel the need to get involved?'

I went right on lying. 'I don't know what you're talking about.'

'I think you do.'

And then I gave up. 'We were friends, Chance, and I owe him. Those are the only reasons I've got.'

'You don't think the police can solve his murder without your help?'

'Not if they're unwilling to look beyond the obvious.'

'Meaning?'

'Meaning you don't shoot a man one year shy of his fiftieth birthday four times if all you want is his coke or his money.'

'You think it was personal.'

'At least in part. Yes.' I took up my own water glass and drank, my throat suddenly dry. 'O' told me today the coroner found cocaine in R.J.'s system, so the blow can't be completely ruled out as a motive. But there had to be more to his murder than that.'

'Why? Because he was shot four times instead of two? People who deal in drugs don't need a reason to be crueler than necessary, Errol. One bullet or twenty, guns get emptied into old men over drugs every day.'

'That's true enough,' I said.

'You want to do us both a favor? Keep your nose out of this thing and let the authorities handle it.'

'I'm not planning on doing anything danger-ous. I just want to cover some of the ground the cops might miss, before somebody else tries first and makes a complete mess of it.'

'Somebody else? Like who?'

I told him about R.J.'s daughter Toni. 'Appar-ently, she's a private investigator back home in Seattle and her mother's pushing hard for her to start an investigation of her own.'

'So? Let her.'

'She's not that kind of PI, Chance. She pushes paper for an insurance company, the girl doesn't know the first thing about criminal law.'

'And you do?'

'Let's just say I like my chances better than hers of poking around in this thing without getting hurt.'

My brother fell silent again, weighing his need to protect me from myself against his almost nonexistent chances of success.

'Is there anything I can do to help?'

I sensed, more so than saw, his wife appear in the kitchen doorway to one side of us, where she stood and waited to hear how I would answer her husband's question.

'The stories you write for the *Guardian*. Are any of them ever political?'

'Political?' He shrugged. 'Some. Not many. Why?'

'The picture I've been getting of O' as a public servant isn't all that attractive. Corrup-tion, in particular, seems to come up a lot when people talk about him.'

'You think O' had something to do with R.J.'s murder?'

'No. Not at all. But the business he's in is the dirtiest one around, and if the man's anywhere near as crooked as some people think he is, it's at least conceivable that he might've got R.J. killed just by accident.'

Chancellor thought that over, said, 'Bellwood isn't my beat, so I can't say I know for sure. But if I had to guess, I'd say the rumors about the mayor almost have to contain a fair amount of truth. He's gotten a lot done in Bellwood in a short period of time, and it doesn't seem logical he could have done it all without bending a law or two along the way.'

'Bending or breaking?'

'I can't answer that, but I know a woman who probably could. Jessie Scott, she's a writer on staff at the local paper down there. Would you like to talk to her?'

'Absolutely.'

'All right. I'll call her tomorrow and give her your number. Anything else?'

'Nothing else,' his wife said, finally stepping into the room. 'I don't want you doing anything to get mixed up in all this murder business, and neither does your brother.' She trained her steady gaze on me. 'Do you, Errol?'

'Andrea...' Chance said.

'No, she's right,' I said. 'I don't. One of us acting the fool is enough.' I stood up. 'Thank you both for dinner. Tell the boys I'll catch up with 'em at least once before I leave.'

I made it out to my car without either one of them trying to stop me.

Without much trouble, I talked myself into stopping for a drink somewhere between my brother's home and my motel. I was staying at the Holiday Motor Court Inn, a ten-unit cluster of dirty white bungalows on Adams and Western, and I had yet to discover how being a guest there could accurately be described as a 'holiday'. The motel was cheap and clean, and the big, mumbling Nigerian behind the front desk was the closest thing to a roach I'd seen since checking in, but my room was perpetually cold, its walls painted the color of sour milk, and I didn't care to spend a minute longer on the premises than I had to.

It was just after eleven when I found a bar I remembered from the old days on the 2700 block of Western Avenue. The name it had gone by in my youth was no longer visible out front; a small, nearly illegible neon sign over the entrance now referred to the place as 'Moody's'. Almost thirty years had passed since I'd last dropped in, but it seemed little more than the bar's name had changed. It was still small and pitch black inside, strewn with cheap round tables and listing chairs, and the only business it was doing was courtesy of a few lifeless scarecrows at the bar and one loud, toothless drunk at a distant table. The latter might have been Moody himself, I didn't ask.

What I did do was plant myself on a stool at the bar and ask the tiny, dark-skinned girl standing behind it for a beer off the tap. I watched her draw it into a tall, clean glass and, while Marvin Gaye tried to make the best of a bad stereo, assessed my fellow patrons in the mirror, even as they did the same to me. A new face always requires some study, the more conspicuous the better, and not returning the favor can too easily be taken as a show of disrespect. What I saw was a woman and three men, all black and middle-aged like me, each of them just sober enough to keep their chins off their chests and their eyes halfway open. The woman was big and pretty, and her reflection smiled at me in the mirror. I just nodded back, not wanting either of the brothers flanking her to confuse simple courtesy with wanton desire.

I paid for my beer and took a long draw from it, looking for a mild state of inebriation in which to organize my thoughts. I was no closer to knowing why R.J. had been killed now than I had been at his funeral, but my long day of amateur police work had established one thing to my satisfaction, at least: O'Neal Holden knew more about it than he was telling. If he'd been loaning our old friend money from time to time as he claimed, it was for certain he knew precisely why R.J. needed it, because R.J. in financial straits would have instantly raised the mayor's antenna for trouble, as it would have mine. Just as we'd admitted to each other over lunch, O' and I had always expected that R.J.

would be the one responsible if the lid ever came off the secret we had all once sworn to keep, so O' would have responded to R.J.'s desperate loan requests with all the investigative powers at his disposal, needing to assure himself that R.J.'s problems weren't somehow about to become his own.

Why Bellwood's mayor had chosen to be less than forthcoming with me about the exact nature of our dead friend's money troubles, I couldn't say. I could only imagine that he had done so to protect his own interests, which were probably too varied and clandestine to list. The omission didn't mean he had somehow been complicit in R.J.'s murder, but it did seem to reinforce the possibility.

Reflecting upon all this, it struck me that the light buzz from a domestic beer or two was not going to be anesthesia enough. I called the little bartender over and ordered something more debilitating: a J & B neat. The glass of amber liquid was barely in my hand when our party got bigger by a factor of one, a brother in paint-spattered work clothes and boots who entered the bar like a man who'd been given the wrong address. Younger than everyone else here but the bartender by at least a decade, he stood just inside the door and gave his narrow, wide-set eyes more time than they should have needed to adjust to the dark. He looked tired and angry, the victim of a day that had subjected him to more insult than he deserved.

'Can I help you?' the girl behind the bar

asked.

By way of answer, he turned on his heel and vanished into the night again.

'Know him?' the bartender asked me.

'No. You?'

She shook her head. I could see her trying to determine just how worried she should be.

'He comes back and asks you to empty the cash register, don't even stop to think about it. Just do it,' I said, throwing back a long swig of scotch. 'The money's not yours, is it?'

'No. But—'

'You've got something back there for people like him and your orders are to use it. Yeah, I know. The thing is, if it goes down like that, he's either gonna have to run, or you're gonna have to kill him. Did he look like the kind who'll run to you?'

'No,' the girl said, without hesitation. I had her thinking about playing it safe, but I could see she was still conflicted. She had a job to protect, and maybe even a couple of children to support, and women have their pride too. Just giving the man Moody's money if he asked for it would be both a violation of her duties and a humiliating act of capitulation.

This was assuming, of course, that the man in the paint-spattered clothes had any intention of coming back just to order a drink, let alone jack the place. I didn't know if the girl's instincts about him were right or not, but I did know mine were questionable at best. I had been primed to sense trouble in every direction since

I'd stepped off the plane at LAX this morning, and this was probably just the latest example of my finding it where none actually existed.

Still, for nearly an hour, I sat there at the bar waiting for the front door to reopen with the same degree of dread as the little bartender, until time and another two shots of scotch finally eased my mind. Maybe the brother with all the paint on his clothes was just biding his time, waiting for last call to reappear when the girl with the keys to the cash register might be the only one around to see him shove a gun in her face, but if so, I was no longer sober or paranoid enough to consider the possibility. I had enough real monsters to worry about; there wasn't room in my head for any imaginary ones.

When at last I was feeling marginally less pain than a man about to get behind the wheel of a car probably should, I raised myself up off my bar stool and paid my tab, giving the bartender a clumsy nod as I tossed the bills down on the counter to let her know I wasn't as wasted as I appeared. She didn't buy it.

'You gonna be OK?'

I treated the question like she'd thrown it at someone else and shuffled out on to the sidewalk, where the cold night air wrapped fingers of ice around my face. All was quiet as I found my rental car in the deserted parking lot and ran a hand through my trouser pocket for the keys. When I had them out, finger poised over the alarm button on the fob, a voice behind me said,

'Open it up and get in.'

He'd found a gun somewhere; other than that, everything else was the same: the scowl, the paint-dappled pants, and the trouble he seemed to advertise like an odor he couldn't scrub from his skin. I tried to play stupid.

'Say what?'

'I said open the goddamn car and get in. Back door, too, for me.'

My eyes couldn't be completely trusted in the lot's paltry light, inebriated as I was, but the gun in his hand looked like a short-barreled .38, weapon enough to put a hole in my gut he could put his fist through once the bullet was done tearing it open.

'You want the car? Here...'

I tried to offer him the keys, but he stepped back, said, 'I ain't gonna ask you again, old man. Open the motherfuckin' car!'

I hit the button on the key fob and the car doors came free with a loud chirp of the alarm, but I made no move to get in. Afraid as I was, there was a limit to how complicit I was willing to be in my own demise. I knew that if he wanted me to play driver while he sat in the back, pointing the snout of his piece at the nape of my neck, it wasn't because he needed a ride somewhere and the buses had all stopped running. He had a destination for me in mind and, if I was fool enough to actually help him get me there, I'd probably pay for it with my life.

'I'm not getting in the car, son,' I said.

It was an insane thing to say, and he had to

study me closely for several seconds before he could bring himself to believe I wasn't joking. Incredulous as well as furious now, he shook his head and said, 'I don't wanna hurt you. But you ain't givin' me no choice. If you don't get in that mother fucka right now—'

He stretched his right arm out to aim the .38 directly at the sweet spot between my eyes.

'—you're a dead man.'

Which, as far as I was concerned, I was doomed to be either way. I held my ground and said nothing.

'Have it your way, then,' he said.

I don't know what I was thinking, other than that I didn't have anything to lose, but I threw my left hand up to knock his arm to one side and ducked down low, throwing myself at him with all the controlled movement my intoxicated state would allow. His gun went off once only inches from my left ear and, after that, things played out exactly as I would have expected. He retreated a couple of steps, turned to one side as I came in, and then tossed me to the ground like an overcoat he'd just shaken off.

I lay there at his feet, breathing hard and heavy, and watched him swing the .38 around to finally get the job done right. I heard a loud bang and jumped, like a toddler at the sound of a popping balloon, and the back window of the car above me exploded into fragments, showering my head with glass.

As I brought a hand up to shield my eyes, I turned to see Moody's little bartender standing nearby, pumping another shell into the chamber of a shotgun that looked like a cannon in her doll-like hands.

Whether her second shot would have been any better than her first, I never found out, because it quickly became unnecessary. When I turned to find him again my friend in the paint-spattered clothes was gone, having decided against testing the girl's aim or resolve more than once. From the look on her face, I had to believe he'd made the right move.

'I knew that asshole would be back,' she said.

NINE

I spent the better part of the next morning alone, learning my native city all over again. I'd almost been shot to death the night before and I needed some time in the enclosed space of a car to turn the experience around in my head, looking for proof that it was a chance occurrence and not something I had brought upon myself by being too curious about R.J. Burrow's murder.

A great number of things had changed since I'd last made Los Angeles my home, and the most glaringly obvious was the seismic shift in the kinds of people who had taken my place. Neighborhoods that had once been all white or all black were now either diluted or overwhelmed by Asians or Hispanics of one geographic origin or another: Koreans and Vietnamese, Guatemalans and Salvadorans. Mexican-Americans in particular seemed to have made inroads everywhere.

The freeways I remembered from the old days were wider yet more intractable, and a few new ones had been added to distribute the city's trademark gridlock across a broader area. Los Angeles even claimed a light-rail transit system today, though I never saw a line that seemed to be going anywhere I would have wanted or needed to go.

Some positives: The air was cleaner and the cuisine more diverse. Either dished out on wax paper by street vendors in Compton, or served with soup and salad by celebrity-owned restaurants in Century City, culinary delights from all around the world were on the menu: Cuban, Thai, Jamaican, East Indian. Chicken alone came in dozens of variations, most with a distinctly Latin flavor.

The once diminutive downtown skyline, too, had changed, maturing into something less laughable when compared to those of New York and Chicago. Business had finally decided to put down roots in the heart of the city, rather than at its outer reaches. Thick clusters of commercial high-rises had sprung up in my absence like sunflower fields, and people were now actually living among them, making their homes not on the Westside or out in the Valley, but in downtown apartments and loft complexes that until only recently had not existed.

And then there were the gangs. Banging had been a disease threatening to expand beyond the economically depressed shores of South Central and East Los Angeles long before I ran off to Minnesota, but now it was a beast grown as wild and unstoppable as a Santa Ana-fed brushfire. Gone were the simple affiliations of Crip and Blood, black and brown, eastside and westside. The homeboys and the vatos had seen their monopoly on tribal warfare crashed by young thugs of every color and nationality, from Armenian crews in Glendale to Cambodian ones in Long Beach. Tagging that had once been the exclusive eyesore of places such as Watts and Monterey Park now seemed to adorn every corner of the city, blooming on walls and bus benches, traffic signs and billboards, in rich and poor neighborhoods alike. If the messages were just as illegible as before, it was not without good reason: They were written in a host of different languages.

All Tuesday morning, as the memory of my near-death experience at Moody's bar the night before continued to unnerve me, I drove my faceless blue rental car from one end of my abandoned home to the other, making note of all the things twenty-six years had either altered, erased, or built completely from scratch. Theaters, shopping malls, schools, parking lots, even whole city blocks – nothing was exactly as

I remembered it, and yet everything was exactly the same.

Beneath the skin, it was all still Los Angeles. Benzes and Caddies ruled the roads like locusts and all but a few of the people who drove them – more international in origin or not – were too beautiful to be real. Los Angeles has always been a metropolis fueled by a single dream – becoming the Next Big Thing – and the weight of that wonderful, desperate hope looms over every inhabitant of the city like a pending death sentence. White, brown, rich, poor; musicians, actors, busboys, attorneys – no one is immune to the Dream. Outsiders often describe LA's collective mood as 'laid back', but what it really is is a form of shock, a seemingly lifeless state the mind retreats to when the pain of wealth and fame deferred has become too great to bear.

My exile to Minnesota had inured me to all these things, but they were fresh in my mind now. I had taken this self-guided tour of my old city believing it would better equip me for the job I'd come here to do, but I felt no smarter at the end of it than I had at the beginning.

I was just happier to know I had someplace else to call home.

While I was cruising the streets of Los Angeles that Tuesday morning, I succumbed to a life-long obsession. Most people would think of it as no more than dumpster diving, rooting around among the discards of strangers to pull something out of a trash bin before the sanitation department can rightfully dispose of it. But this is a woefully short-sighted view of what I do. In my mind, the exercises I engage in are rescue operations, mercy missions intended to save imperfect but salvageable objects from a premature, and therefore wasteful, death.

It is not an easy thing to do well. Separating those things that can and should be saved from those that are not worth the trouble requires a keen eye and years of experience. Sometimes I make mistakes. I snatch an old sewing machine or electric typewriter from the clutches of the gallows, get it home and open it up, only to discover internal organs no surgeon would dare touch. It happens. But these are the exceptions to the rule. I choose the subjects of my charity too carefully to err in this way very often, so usually what I gather to my breast as a prize to polish up and return to a purposeful existence proves itself deserving of my effort.

Today, my find was an old reel-to-reel tape recorder, a Sony-made portable with only one empty reel on its right spindle, that somebody in Culver City had set atop a garbage can out in front of their home. Its fake woodgrain case was battered and scratched, and the lens cover on one of its VU meters was cracked like the shell of an egg, but at first glance, I could see no reason why it shouldn't function as it had originally.

I wound the machine's power cord into a neat bundle, deposited it into the trunk of my car and drove off, feeling the way I always did on these occasions: like a kid who'd just plucked the hubcaps from the wheels of a neighbor's car.

You might wonder why I bothered. Surely the complicated business of playing detective should have superseded any need to tinker with a new toy. But tinkering clears my head; it is what I do to make space for my best thinking. When I would find the time to work on the recorder over the next few days, I didn't know.

I just had a feeling I'd find a use for the distraction.

By ten a.m., my cellphone had yet to ring, and the desk clerk at my motel said the same was true about the phone in my room. I was disappointed but not surprised. I had called Toni Burrow at her mother's home just before embarking upon my impromptu tour of the 'new' Los Angeles, and Frances Burrow had told me she wasn't in. She promised I'd get a call-back as soon as Toni returned to the house, but I hadn't really believed I'd get one. Less than twenty-four hours earlier, I had sent the elder Lady Burrow scurrying back up to bed in tears and prompted the younger one to all but slam her mother's front door in my face, so I had little reason to expect either woman would place much importance on my need to speak with Toni again.

I tried her a second time anyway.

'Hello?'

I'd gotten lucky. This time, it was Toni herself

86

who answered the phone.

'Toni, this is Handy White. I hope I haven't caught you at a bad time.'

A brief silence, then: 'What can I do for you, Mr White?'

'I'd like to talk to you. Over lunch. Do you think you could meet me in about an hour or so?'

'I'm afraid not. What exactly did you want to talk about?'

'The same thing we talked about yesterday, only a little more directly: Who killed your father, and why.'

'I don't see where that's any of your business, Mr White.'

'Frankly, I'm not sure I do, either. But whether it is or it isn't, I'm going to do whatever I can to try and answer those two questions.'

'You? You're no more a criminal investigator than I am.'

'That's true. If I could go home right now and forget the whole thing, I would, believe me. But I tried that once and it didn't work, so...'

'I don't understand.'

'It's like this: For reasons I won't get into right now, I owe him. Too much to simply assume the cops will get this one right on their own.'

'So what do you propose to do?'

'Talk to people who knew R.J. Try to find out if somebody other than a buyer or seller of cocaine could have wanted him dead. And I was hoping to start with you.'

I was left to count the seconds before Toni Burrow spoke again. 'Tell me where you want me to be, and when,' she said.

It was my idea to have a late breakfast at a place called Pann's. Unlike the Ship's coffee shop in Culver City, my first choice among the handful of space-age style pancake houses I loved to frequent in the old days, I'd found Pann's that morning still standing where I'd last seen it, on the south-west corner of La Cienega and La Tijera, in the lowlands of Ladera Heights. A thickly landscaped, glass-predominant en-closure capped by a triangular, tortoiseshell roof, it was the only building in the area I truly recognized; everything else – bistros, shopping malls, drive-thru restaurants – either bore new names and facades, or had sprung up out of the ground during my absence. Sometimes, it was hard to tell which.

R.J.'s daughter was already sitting at a booth when I arrived around ten thirty. She was wear-ing a sleeveless, white cotton blouse and cream-colored slacks, and her hair was pulled back in a simple French braid behind her head. She looked anxious, as if she had some reason to dread what was coming, but she raised a small smile from somewhere within as I sat down to join her.

'You haven't been waiting long, I hope,' I said.

'No. I just sat down. Mr White—'

'Call me Handy, please.' I took up my menu and opened it. 'Have you ordered yet?'

I made her wait to make conversation until a broad-shouldered Latina waitress had taken our identical orders of ham and eggs, sloshed some coffee into our cups, and disappeared.

'I don't understand the point of this,' Toni said. 'You told me yourself only yesterday I should leave investigating Daddy's murder to the police.'

'I know. I did. But that was before O'Neal Holden told me the car in which R.J. died wasn't the only place the police found traces of cocaine.'

'What do you mean?'

'I mean the coroner's report says they found the drug in your father's body, as well.'

The woman seated across from me said nothing, though her eyes conveyed a host of conflicting messages all at once.

'O' also said R.J. had called him at least twice in the last fifteen years to ask for money. He loaned your father sixteen hundred in all, he said. Were you aware of that?'

The wounded expression on her face was all the answer I needed, but she offered me one anyway: 'No.'

'The police didn't tell your mother they found cocaine in R.J.'s system?'

'They might have told *her*. But she didn't tell me.'

'What about the money?'

'I didn't know anything about that, either.'

I let a moment pass before asking my next question. 'Why do you suppose she didn't tell you?'

'I imagine because she knew what I would have said.'

'"I told you so"?'

'Something like that.'

'Then R.J. and drugs were nothing new to you.'

'No.' She let out a deep breath, trying to keep her emotions in check. 'He'd been a steady user for over fifteen months, just before he hired on with Coughlin Construction. But that was eighteen years ago. He couldn't find work, he was an ex-con without a degree—'

'Whoa, hold on,' I said. 'R.J. was an ex-con?'

She nodded, face coloring with shame. 'He served three years in the mid-eighties for armed robbery at Lancaster State Penitentiary. I was only a year old when he went away.' She shook her head. 'I'm sorry, but I can't do this. I have to go.'

She tried to bolt from the booth, but I caught her wrist before she could fly past.

'Wait!'

'I'll say it again, Mr White: This is none of your business. Go home.'

'I didn't mean to upset you. I'm just trying to make sense of it, that's all. I need your help. Please.'

She snatched her arm free but remained where she was, the black light of her gaze trying to bore right through me. Our waitress and several patrons had stopped what they were doing to watch, no doubt hoping for an ugly scene they could recreate for friends and family later, but Toni Burrow let them down. Instead of capping our little drama by storming out, she fooled us all by returning to the seat across from me.

'You have no idea what he put Momma through,' she said. 'How hard he made things for her.'

She backhanded a tear from her right eye, infuriated by her need to shed it, and paused as the big woman in the blue uniform set our plates down in front of us, scowling at me now like a sheepdog eyeing a wolf. The quarrel I'd just had with my dining companion had apparently left our waitress with an unflattering impression of me, and she didn't leave Toni alone with me again until she was satisfied I was all through putting my hands on her.

'He was a wonderful husband and father for the most part,' R.J.'s daughter said when we were finally alone again, 'but something inside him wasn't right. He had everything a man could want – wife, family, career – and he was never at peace with any of it.'

'How do you mean?'

'I mean he'd go months and months acting as if everything was fine, then out of nowhere, he'd disappear for a weekend without explanation. Or lock himself up in the bathroom at three in the morning just to cry himself to sleep. It was all typical behavior for a drug abuser, of course, but he swore to us that wasn't it. Coke had only been a crutch for him when he could not get work, and he'd given it up the minute he hired on at Coughlin. Or so he always said.'

'You didn't believe him?'

'I didn't know what to believe. All I knew was that he needed help, and he was too selfish and stubborn to ever get it, no matter how much his behavior hurt my mother.'

'When you say he needed help – you're talking about psychiatric help?'

'Of course. Daddy was deeply disturbed. He was either doing coke again or, as Mother suspected, something else was slowly driving him insane. I always believed it was the former, and I still do. His story that he used for fifteen months, then quit cold turkey as soon as the Coughlin job came along, has never really flown with me. But Mother's never doubted it for a minute. She thinks something happened to Daddy in prison, that he was haunted by something he saw or did there that his conscience wouldn't allow him to forget.'

It was not an unsound theory. R.J. had been as hard as nails, to be sure, but his heart was as soft as they came. If during his three years in lock-down he'd witnessed more than a few senseless acts of violence against people he considered friends, it would not have been unlike him to drag the memory around behind him like a burlap sack filled with lead.

There was at least one other explanation for the depth of despondency in her father Toni

Burrow was describing, however, and the fact that she made no allusion to it now could only mean that she was unaware of it. She doesn't know, I thought, finally allowing myself to stop fearing otherwise, and my sense of relief was almost too overpowering to conceal.

'What about his job?' I asked. 'Could whatever was troubling him have been connected to something he was dealing with at work?'

'Well, we wondered about that, certainly. But whenever we'd ask him about it, he'd just say things at work were fine.'

'Exactly what did he do for Coughlin?'

'He was a security guard, primarily. But they had just made him a consultant about a year ago.'

'A security consultant? With a criminal record?'

'It does seem strange, I know. But the man who got him in the door there had some serious pull in personnel, the way it was always explained to me, and Daddy's duties the first few years were too innocuous to make trusting him much of a concern. Watching the lobby in empty satellite offices, or the gate at small construction sites – he couldn't have stolen anything worth stealing if he'd wanted to back then.'

'So who was this man who got him the job?'

'I don't know. I never met him.'

'You don't have a name?'

'I think his last name was Allen, but that's just a guess. Mother would know for sure. All I ever heard about him is that he was a rep for the company Daddy met through a work training program Coughlin used to sponsor at the prison.'

'Do you know if he still works there?'

'It's possible. There were several people from the company at the funeral, but as far as I know, he wasn't one of them.'

'Can I get you two anything else?'

The waitress's name was Rosie. I hadn't seen it stenciled to the white plastic tag pinned to her blouse until now.

I looked to Toni, who shook her head, and I did the same for Rosie. 'We're fine, thanks.'

The big Latina laid the bill down in front of me, not quite smiling, and shuffled off again.

'I seem to have given her a reason to dislike you,' R.J.'s daughter said, almost smiling herself. 'I'm sorry.'

I shrugged and smiled back.

'Look, Mr White—'

'Handy.'

'Handy. I appreciate what you're trying to do. Really. But you were right to tell me yesterday we should leave Daddy's murder to the authorities, and I'd like to give you the same advice. Before you just make matters worse.'

'Worse? For whom?'

'For my mother, mostly. And for me, as well. By doubling the efforts of the police like this, there's a chance you could open a can of worms that nobody needs to know about.'

'Maybe you'd like to explain that.'

'I'm talking about drug abuse, for one thing. Infidelity. Homosexuality. Complicity in one form of felonious activity or another. Do I need to go on?'

'You're saying R.J. was guilty of all that?'

'I'm saying he told my mother too many lies over the years not to be guilty of something, and the less she knows about whatever it was, the better off she's likely to be. The better off *I'm* likely to be.'

'And if your mother wants to know anyway?'

'She doesn't. She only *thinks* she wants to know. You heard her yesterday. She thinks it's all a frame-up, that Daddy was some innocent victim of an elaborate plot to discredit him. She only wants to know the truth because she can't believe the truth will be all that terrible.'

'And you? Don't *you* want to know the truth?'

'Honestly? Sometimes I do, and sometimes I don't. But mostly, I don't.'

'You're afraid to know.'

'Yes. I am afraid. If you could have seen what he was like, when whatever it was he was hiding from us had him acting like a frightened child...' She shook her head. 'I've always had the feeling, if we ever found out what it was, it would change our view of him forever. And I don't want that to happen. I just want his killer found and put away, that's all. I don't care about the reasons for it, and neither does my mother, whether she realizes it or not.'

She had no idea how close the two of us were to wanting the exact same thing, if for totally different reasons. She was looking to minimize the damage all my questions might do to protect her memory of her father; I was only doing so to protect myself.

'I understand how you feel,' I said. 'Nobody ever really wants to know just how dark the dark side is in people they care for deeply. But—'

'You're not going to stop asking all these questions.'

'If I had the benefit of your recent perspective on R.J., maybe I could. It sounds like the man you knew in recent years could have been exactly what the police are saying he was, just one old coke addict who got wasted by another. But that's not the R.J. I remember, and my memories of him are all I have to work with.'

'But you said so yourself: He had cocaine in his system. He drove that car down to the beach, his prints were all over the steering wheel. Jesus, I don't want to believe the police's version of Daddy's murder any more than you do, but when you do the math, what else can you believe?'

'Maybe nothing. Maybe they're right and all this second-guessing is just a waste of time and energy.'

'Then leave it alone. You last knew Daddy thirty years ago. No matter what you owed him then, paying him back now can't possibly serve any purpose. Can it?'

I didn't say anything.

'I'm waiting,' she said.

I'd been lying to her since I met her, much like she said her father had been lying to her and her mother for years, and what she was asking me to tell her now lay dangerously close to the truth I could not speak. But if I was going to continue to insist upon inserting myself into her family's private affairs, it was inevitable that I offer her some explanation, however diluted, as to why I felt the need to do so.

'When we ran together, your father and I were young and not too smart. We did some things I'd be embarrassed to admit to. One of those things should have ended very badly for me, and the only reason it didn't is because R.J. intervened. If I told you I've been looking for a chance to repay him ever since, I'd be lying through my teeth – but now that that chance has presented itself, I intend to take full advantage of it.'

'You're talking in riddles. Daddy intervened how? In what?'

I shook my head. 'I'm afraid that's one of those "cans of worms" you were talking about that I've got no business opening.'

'I see. I'm supposed to answer all of your questions, but you're not supposed to answer any of mine.'

'Right now, I have no reason to believe the things you're asking me about are in any way relevant to the discussion at hand. But if that should change—'

'You'll tell me everything. Whatever I want to know, without exception.'

And there he was again, in the guise of his only child: my old friend R.J. Burrow, goading me into a corner from which he knew I could find no escape.

'All right,' I said.

She didn't know what she was asking. The promise I'd just made – that I would tell her all there was to know about the secret that had apparently haunted her father to his grave, should I decide it had indeed had some bearing on his murder – was one she did not want me to keep.

Because sometimes ignorance truly is bliss, and once it is gone, asking God to have it back is a wasted prayer.

TEN

There was a story people used to tell about Paris McDonald that none of us heard until it was too late to heed it as a warning.

McDonald was a boxer out of the Hoover Gym on Hoover and 78th Street who was hammering his way through the local dregs of the middleweight division while R.J., O' and I were in high school. A flat-faced black man with disproportionate eyes, he was a plodder with a solid jaw who could take whatever an opponent had to offer for nine rounds and still have a good right with which to counter in the tenth. Unfortunately, his right hand was the only one God had given him, his left barely up to the task of meekly tapping someone in the face two or three times a round, so by the mid-seventies, he had come as close to national attention as he was ever going to get.

No one could make McDonald believe it, however.

Even after Jimmy Ray Hill snapped the retina of his right eye loose in the sixth round of a 1976 fight Hill would eventually win on a TKO in the eighth, McDonald thought he was on the road to a shot at the title. An unranked pug had nearly blinded him, and still he soldiered on. No sooner had the doctors sewn his right eye back together than McDonald was back pounding the heavy bag in the gym, attached to a new trainer and manager who were far less vocal about his risk of re-injury than the two men they had replaced.

By the time the California State Athletic Commission declared him fit to re-enter the ring eight months later, his right hand had become nearly as useless as his left. Three bouts into his ill-conceived comeback, the referee had to step in to stop a nineteen-year-old southpaw from Corpus Christi, Texas, named Ricky Torres from beating McDonald to death in two rounds, and that put an official end to the unremarkable career of Paris 'the Tower' Mc-Donald.

It didn't, however, put an end to the Mc-

Donald legend.

The way I'd heard the story, McDonald tracked down Luis Corrales at his home in Montebello six days after his license to fight in California was permanently revoked and broke the left arm of the forty-four-year-old father of two so badly, his doctors nearly amputated it above the elbow to save his life. Corrales emerged from six hours of surgery having no clue who had attacked him on his front doorstep, and it only added to his confusion to have the police tell him later that it had been McDonald, whom he could barely remember. Corrales was a boxing referee by profession, and to the best of his recollection, he had only worked a single fight involving the man who had nearly killed him.

Had he known McDonald better, he would have understood that one fight was all McDonald ever needed to make a new enemy. Aside from being delusional about his limitations as a boxer, McDonald had a persecution complex second to none, and there was always someone he could hold responsible for his every failure and disappointment. In the case of his fight with Jimmy Ray Hill, that man was Luis Corrales. In McDonald's estimation, Hill may have caused the eye injury that would ultimately make him such an easy target for Ricky Torres sixteen months later, but it was Corrales who had given Hill the chance. McDonald had knocked Hill down with a rare combination two rounds prior to his getting hurt, and McDonald felt that should have been the end of the fight right there. But no – Corrales's count had been slow, any fool could see it, and Hill had made it back to his feet before the referee could reach a count of eight. The bell ending the round sounded shortly thereafter, Hill recouped, and McDonald's eventual destruction was assured.

As conspiracy theories went, it didn't make sense. It wasn't logical. But that was the way they say the man's mind worked. Paris McDonald went through life feeling cheated, and he never let a perceived slight pass without making somebody pay for it. No matter how tenuous their guilt, no matter how long he had to wait to exact payback.

As our last days together in Los Angeles were drawing to a close, three weeks before Christmas, 1979, R.J., O' and I knew nothing whatsoever about Paris McDonald. We'd never heard of him as a boxer, and were nearly as unaware of him as a bodyguard and limo driver, the two new careers he'd taken up upon doing his fifteen months for the Luis Corrales assault. And yet, when his paranoia inevitably struck again, turning him against the second cousin for whom he now worked, my friends and I were by some bizarre coincidence among the casualties of their ensuing blood feud.

The only thing the four of us had in common was a desire to hurt the same man. But because that man was Excel Rucker, it was connection enough to stain all our lives forever.

* * *

Unlike the last time I'd checked, there was a single phone message waiting for me when I returned to my motel room following my meeting with Toni Burrow. It was from a man who identified himself as Walt Fine.

'A friend in Bellwood asked me to give you a ring,' he said. 'I tried you on your cell, but something happened, I dunno, I couldn't leave a message. What a racket, cellphones, huh?' He left a call-back number and hung up.

I was calling him back on the landline phone in my room when my cellphone rang.

'What's going on, Quincy?' I asked without preamble. He was watching over my business in my absence, but the assignment involved so little, I was certain he was only calling to check up on me, his lunatic business partner running loose in California only days after I'd nearly clubbed a teenage boy to death for reasons I'd been unable to adequately explain.

'You just got a phone call, Handy. I thought you'd wanna know right away,' he said.

'From who?'

'Your daughter. She asked me where you were, but I acted like I didn't know. I hope that was the right thing to do.'

'Coral? What did she want?'

'She didn't say. Just said she needed to speak to you about somethin' important.'

I closed my eyes, digging deep to find the courage to ask my next question. The only one that really mattered.

'How did she sound, Quincy?'

He answered right away, but it felt to me as if he'd counted to ten first. 'She sounded good, Handy. Real good.'

I was sure that Quincy was smiling.

No matter how it comes upon you, no man is ever adequately prepared for fatherhood. It is too inexact a science.

I don't speak from any particular wealth of experience. I have only one child, and much to my regret, I have not always been the active parent to her I strive to be today. Still, I have played the role of teacher and care-giver to the little girl turned young woman named Coral White long and well enough to have learned that it is not a job for everyone. The amount of sacrifice and restraint it requires is beyond the powers of many. Those who look for shortcuts in its greatest demands – lectures in lieu of conversation, money instead of affection – would often be better suited abandoning a child altogether than attempting to care for it at all.

The damage I have done to Coral is something I am still attempting to fully assess. She never knew her mother, just as I barely knew the woman myself, so the burden of raising her to adulthood was all on me. To say that I wasn't ready to take on that kind of responsibility at the time it was thrust upon me would be an understatement; I was still learning the names of streets in St Paul and it was everything I could do to keep from running back to LA, a bigger coward then than when I'd left. In those early years, if Coral needed more than a nursemaid and disciplinarian, she didn't get it; that was all I knew how to be. It wasn't until she entered her teens that I evolved into something approaching a real parent – loving, committed, *connected* – and by then, the die of her unhappiness had been cast.

At some point in late adolescence, she discovered solace in self-destruction. From mindless suitors I despised to illegal substances I'd never heard of, she bounced from one poison pill to another, looking for something I had either failed to give her, or had been too slow to offer up. Whether these things were cries for help or simply shows of acting out, I reacted to all her antics with the same self-righteous condemnation, unable to fathom how all my years of nudging and prodding could result in such ingratitude. She had no idea how much I'd given up for her, all the excuses I could have made to go my own way and let her fend for herself.

Six weeks after her nineteenth birthday, she left home for good, and I only caught glimpses of her over the next three years. What I saw and heard during that time gave me no reason to think she would outlive me. She had taken the sorrow of a motherless child and made a funeral blanket out of it, a shroud she could curl up in to retreat from all the warmth and light of the world. I lived every minute waiting for the phone call that would officially mark the end to her suffering, but I never gave her up for dead. I continued to hope she could turn things around and return to the living, lured by the turn I had finally taken toward a more forgiving model of fatherhood. I had learned from my previous mistakes that it wasn't judgment she needed from me, but empathy, and I left my door open for her offering only that.

It took a long time, but one day she decided we had both suffered enough, and she came back home to St Paul.

Our relationship remains far from ideal. Her recovery is a fragile thing, and my fear of its ephemeral nature hangs over us like a cloud. But we love each other without apology now, and speak on the phone with reassuring regularity. Sometimes, we even go so far as to chat in the flesh, over lunch or dinner.

We are finally at peace with one another, save for one last, perhaps eternal point of contention.

'Handy, where are you?' Coral asked, using the only name for me she has ever felt comfortable with. 'I need to see you.'

Quincy had been right on two counts: She did in fact call me within minutes of talking to him, and she did sound good.

'I'm out in California. What's going on?'

'California? You mean LA? What are you doing out there?'

'An old friend died. I'm helping the family make arrangements. Are you OK?'

'I'm fine. In fact, I have great news.'

'You got a new job?'

Last I'd heard, she was working in tele-marketing and hating every minute of it.

'No. I mean, yes, but that's not why I need to talk to you.' For a long moment, she left me with nothing to listen to but the air passing in and out of her lungs. 'God, I don't like doing this over the phone. I wanted to tell you in person.'

'Tell me what, Coral?'

'Please don't get mad at me. But ... I think I found my mother.'

Now I was the one to fall silent. Both of my hands clenched up into fists without my conscious knowledge. 'No,' I said flatly. 'You didn't.'

'Yes. I did. I found her picture in an old newspaper at the library. Her name is Susan Yancy, she was a radio dispatcher for the MPD.'

She waited for me to say something.

'Hello? I'm right, aren't I?'

'No. Goddamnit, girl, how many times do we have to go through this?'

'You're shouting at me, Handy.'

'Your mother is dead. She died three weeks after you were born. You have to let this go.'

'No! Why do you keep telling me that? Her picture in the paper matches the one you gave me of her exactly. It's the same woman, Handy. It's my mother. I've finally found my mother.'

There was nothing I could say to dissuade her. She had heard all my pronouncements on the subject before, a thousand times, and in light of the hard evidence to the contrary she was convinced she had just discovered, she was more determined than ever to reject them.

'Coral, baby, listen to me. Don't do anything more until I come home. Please.'

'I want to meet her. I want to talk to her. She still lives here in the city, I've already found a listing for her.'

'Coral, please. Don't do this. Promise me.'

'I can't, Handy. She's my mother. I've waited all my life for this.'

'Yes, yes, I know, but—'

She was gone.

I called every number I had for her and never got an answer. I sat in total darkness, save for a single sliver of light seeping past the curtains of my motel room's only window, and worked the keypad on the phone until the futility of the effort sank in too deep to ignore.

I had to stop her. She didn't know what kind of heartache she was about to buy for herself. I had never involved Quincy in my personal affairs before, but now I had no choice. I was half a continent away, and I couldn't do what needed to be done over the phone.

'I'll do my best, Handy,' Quincy said when I'd called back to tell him what I wanted him to do. His voice was leaden with the burden I'd just placed upon him.

His best was all I could ask for. I prayed that would be good enough.

ELEVEN

I have a small leather tool bag I always carry. I would no more go somewhere without it than my right shoe.

Its contents aren't much – a soldering iron and some solder, a screwdriver with multiple tips, wire cutters, needle-nosed pliers, a tiny voltmeter and leads – but they get me by. They're usually just enough to let me peel a project's skin open and root around inside, maybe even nudge it into performing the function for which it was designed.

People not in the repair trade see a complexity to machines that is generally more imaginary than real. Pared down to their bare essence, objects as diverse as clothes dryers and computers, VCRs and grandfather clocks all operate as a consequence of one simple principle: movement. Electrons, gears, levers and cables – these are the things that shift position or change state to create a desired effect, allowing a telephone to transmit sound or a lawnmower to cut grass. When this movement does not occur, or does so too soon or too late or with the wrong degree of force, critical sequences break down and mechanical failures ensue. The end result may give the appearance that the entire machine is gone forever, when in fact it is merely the victim of a single, perhaps even easily corrected malfunction.

The reel-to-reel tape recorder I'd found in Culver City was but the latest example of this principle. On the surface, it was inoperative, a thing that just sat there staring at you when you turned it on and asked it to move tape. But once I'd set my modest little tool kit loose upon it, it soon became apparent that it was salvageable. A broken drive belt; a pulley with stripped teeth; tension rollers that needed a good cleaning. These were all things I could fix, given a part or two.

It would take a little time and accomplish almost nothing. One more ancient tape recorder on the shelf of whatever second-hand store I decided to donate it to was not going to change the world in any discernible fashion, for better or for worse. The only point in bringing such a relic back to life would be the exercise itself. The exercise was what defined me, as it probably always will. I take things apart and put them back together again, all for the sake of learning the answer to a single, unrelenting question:

Why?

'Somebody tried to kill you?'

'That's not exactly what I said. I said somebody almost did.'

I gave O' a rough sketch of my almost fatal

visit to Moody's bar the night before.

'Jesus. Sounds like you were lucky as hell.'

'Yeah. You could say that.'

'You don't think so?'

'I'm still trying to figure out what I think. He didn't just want my car, O'. He wanted me, too.'

'Either that, or your bank card. 'Jackers do that shit all the time. Make a driver take 'em to the nearest ATM just to make a withdrawal. You probably weren't in any real danger, Handy, till you started fucking with the man.'

There was a part of me that believed him. His explanation for what had happened to me was perfectly reasonable. But the part of me that was still shaken up, the part that couldn't stop seeing the nose of that brother's gun staring me in the face going on twelve hours later, was not so easily convinced. The mood I'd been in lately, the role of random victim did not seem to suit me.

'Maybe,' was all I said to O'.

'Did my friend Mr Fine call you?'

'Yeah, this morning, but I was out. I'm going to call him back as soon as I hang up with you.'

Walt Fine was O's contact with the Santa Monica PD, and his was the second call I'd missed while I was out having breakfast with Toni Burrow.

'So. Is that it? You just called to tell me you almost got whacked last night?'

'Actually, I was calling to ask another favor. Just in case.'

'Just in case what?'

'Just in case I see that boy from the bar again.'

The irksome chuckle I thought he'd respond with never came. 'Man, didn't I just tell you what that was?'

'Yeah, I know. I'm losing it. All the same, if you could hook me up with somebody with some hardware to sell, I'd rest a little easier.'

'You could rest easy now if you'd knock all this shit off and go home. God, man, can't you hear what you sound like?'

'Hey, you're right, this was stupid. Forget I called, huh?'

I started to hang up, but he called my name until I brought the receiver back to my ear.

'Handy, you still there?'

'I'm here.'

'Shit. I can't promise you anything about "hardware", all right? I'm the mayor of Bellwood, my street nigga suit ain't been out of the closet for a long time.' He sighed deeply. 'But if I can think of somebody who might know somebody, I'll see what I can do.'

'Thanks. I'd appreciate it.'

'A piece of advice, Handy? All those people you see in the rear-view mirror of your rental car? None of them is trying to kill you either.'

O'Neal Holden's friend Walt Fine was a sergeant for the Bellwood City Police Department. He was a pot-bellied, stoop-shouldered redhead who had the look of a long-time law enforce-

111

ment veteran, somebody who should have made detective somewhere ages ago, but he was wearing uniform blues when we met Tuesday afternoon in the covered picnic area of a public park out in Gardena, just as he'd requested.

'Let me just ask you, right off: You have a problem with people of the Jewish persuasion?'

It was the first thing he said to me upon my arrival, and it knocked me off stride before I'd ever said a word. I was already wondering what business I had to be here, and how big a mess I could make of things working so far outside the realm of my expertise, and now I had no doubt. Against a pro like Fine, I was bound to botch the job of interrogation.

'Me? No. Why would I?'

'Because our friend the mayor does, I think. We've always gotten along, don't get me wrong, but I sometimes get the feeling that, if it weren't for the occasional need, he wouldn't choose to deal with my kind at all.'

I looked Fine straight in the eye and said, 'I seriously doubt that's true.' Mildly surprised, because I would have thought O's senseless hard-on for Jews would have proven itself too embarrassingly ignorant, and politically inexpedient, to hold on to all these years.

Fine took a seat at one of the stone dining tables in the area, and I joined him on the opposite side. The day had turned slightly overcast, so the shade we were sitting in was no draw for the park's only other visible visitors, three toddlers and a pair of adults moving about a playground in the distance.

'I understand you and the mayor go back a ways.'

'Yes,' I said.

'And Burrow too?'

I hesitated before answering, unsure of what O' did or did not want this man to know. 'R.J. was a good friend of mine as well, yeah,' I said eventually.

'So what do you wanna know?'

'Whatever you can tell me about where Santa Monica PD's investigation stands at the moment. Mayor Holden tells me you used to work out there.'

'Four years. I left in '02 to come to Bell-wood.'

'But you still have friends in the department?'

'I still have friends everywhere. I'm that kind'a guy.' He grinned in a way that had me envisioning a burning cross on my own front lawn. 'Mind if I ask what your interest in the info is? This a professional matter to you, or a private one?'

'Strictly private. I'm just a friend of the family checking status.'

'The family can't do that themselves?'

'I think they're concerned that your friends in Santa Monica are a little hesitant to tell them everything there is to know.'

'Or that what they are telling them is total bullshit. That what you mean?'

'You want to know where I'm coming from before you talk to me. OK. I'm not a cop, and

I'm not an investigator, and nobody's hired me to do anything. I'm just an old friend of the deceased who's not going to sleep worth a damn if the police fuck this one up, accidentally or otherwise, so yeah, I'm sticking my nose in where it doesn't belong. Now, does that answer all your questions, or did I leave something out?'

Fine found a crumpled pack of cigarettes in a pocket of his uniform shirt, asked me if I had any objections to his lighting one up. I shook my head and watched him get one going, his first draw off it long and deep, as if it had been days since his last smoke.

'I don't have to tell you how disappointed I'd be, word got around I'd been talking to you,' he said.

'No. You don't.'

'Mayor Holden and I get along real well, his unfortunate anti-Semitism notwithstanding. He asked me to find out what I could about the Burrow investigation, and I was happy to do it. The man who signs all my checks, what am I gonna say, no?'

'But I'm not the mayor.'

'No. Not even close. So if somehow, some way, the wrong people find out about this—'

'You're going to take it up with me, and not His Honor. I get it. Anything else?'

He didn't like being pushed, because pushing was always his job, but he could see from the look on my face that this was one dog who had jumped through his last hoop.

'You've got fifteen minutes. First question.'

'Suspects. Do they have any?'

The man in the blue uniform nodded, blowing a cloud of smoke up over both our heads. 'One.' He produced a small notepad, fanned through its pages until he found the one he needed. 'Some user and abuser named Darrel Eastman, E-A-S-T-M-A-N. Black, twenty-five years of age, no distinguishing physical characteristics. They say he left a thumbprint on the dash of the car Burrow was found in.'

'"User and abuser." I take it that means he's a crackhead?'

'Crack, crank, heroin. You name the fruit of the tree, he's had a taste of it.'

'He ever do any dealing?'

'A couple ounces here or there. Nothing major.'

'Any history of violent crime prior to this?'

'Just the thirty-one flavors of assault all junkies dabble in, includin' a few involving a firearm. But no, no homicides, if that was gonna be your next question.'

'What about 'jacking cars?'

'He might've had an auto beef or two in his jacket. Why?'

'I understand the car R.J. died in was stolen, and the police say he's the one who stole it. But if this guy Eastman knew how to boost a ride, why couldn't he have done it?'

Fine showed me a little shrug to cast the idea off. 'Maybe 'cause he would've had to leave more than a thumbprint in the car if he had,' he said.

I could have disputed that, but I let it go. 'Speaking of which – your friends have anything besides the print to connect Eastman and R.J.?'

Fine checked his notes, shook his head. 'Not that my guy mentioned.'

'And the murder weapon?'

'What about it?'

'Have they found it yet?'

'No.'

'Then they can't tie that to Eastman either.'

Fine shrugged again, took another hard drag off his cigarette.

'Do they at least know what it was?'

'A nine-millimeter semi-auto, possibly a Glock.'

I finally started taking notes of my own on a legal pad I'd brought along for the purpose. 'Tell me about the car.'

He read from his notebook. 'Ninety-eight Buick LeSabre four door, dark blue, license number 5TNC641. Registered owner one Irene Duffy, D-U-F-F-Y, of Los Angeles. You want the address?'

I jotted it down. 'Where is that, exactly? Hollywood?'

'Hollywood or Los Feliz. Sounds more like Los Feliz.'

'And that's where the car was stolen?'

'According to the owner's statement, yeah. What's the problem?'

'He stole a car in Los Feliz to make a drug

connection twenty miles away in Santa Monica?'

Fine gave me a blank look, unmoved by the
discrepancy.

'Had Ms Duffy reported the car stolen prior to
it being found out at the pier?'

'No. She said she didn't even know it was
gone till the detectives called to question her
about it.'

'And did she know either R.J. or Eastman?'

'Uh-uh.' Fine shook his head, ground his
spent cigarette into the stone surface of the
picnic table, and expelled one last lungful of
smoke through the side of his mouth.

'Besides Eastman. Are they looking at anybody else?'

'Like who?'

'Like somebody with a motive other than the
coke in the car. R.J. must have had an enemy or
two somewhere. At work, at church...'

'My guy said, according to everybody he and
his partner talked to, your boy Burrow was a
very nice man who got along well with everybody. Bein' on the pipe was apparently the only
vice he had worth mentioning.'

Fine turned his head to watch a young blonde
in workout togs and running shoes do her pre-
jog stretching nearby. He would have recalled I
was still sitting there eventually, but I decided
not to wait. I capped my pen and stood up.

'You've been very helpful, Sergeant. I appreciate your time.'

He turned around to face me, gave me that

117

poker liar's grin I found so unsettling again. 'Hey, no problem. Any friend of the mayor's is a friend of mine.'

There were other questions I could have asked him, of course. Like how a uniformed cop could be in so good with the plain-clothes detectives of the Santa Monica PD, when the latter breed of policeman generally loathes having anything to do with the former. But I had a hunch I already knew the answer to that: Fine used to be one of the plain-clothes boys himself, before he'd either turned his detective's badge in voluntarily, or had it taken away.

Which of the two it had been wasn't all that hard to figure out, either.

TWELVE

Excel's people in Inglewood had a thing for Chinese.

They ordered take-out from a local restaurant called the Jade Inn at least once a week, and it was always the same lanky Asian teenager who made the delivery. R.J., O' and I saw him come and go on so many occasions, we eventually came to realize that only Excel Rucker himself came in contact with the safe house's four occupants with greater regularity.

'That's our in,' O' said one day, referring to

the delivery boy.

R.J. and I agreed immediately, and the three of us set about learning as much as we could about the kid and his place of employment. By following the little weather-beaten red Toyota he drove, we discovered that the Jade Inn was located on Manchester Boulevard, less than two miles from the home we intended to rob, and that he almost always took the same route there. A quiet, long-haired teenager with the stooped-back posture of an old woman, he never got beyond the apartment's front porch, but he was sometimes left standing before the cracked front door while whoever had answered it for him disappeared inside to find his money.

It wasn't much of an opening, but we knew it was more than any of us were likely to get. If we hijacked the kid on his next run to the apartment so that one of us could make the delivery in his place, nobody inside the house was going to buy it. In fact, we were reasonably certain that Excel's people would respond to a black man showing up at their door, claiming to be an employee of a Chinese owned and operated eatery, with a bullet between the eyes, no questions asked.

That meant the kid would have to go up there himself, just as he always did. And then ... what?

Our initial thought was that he'd go with the understanding that we had a man back at the restaurant who would kill every soul in the building, staff and customers alike, if he didn't do exactly as we said. We'd tell him to talk his way into the apartment somehow, maybe by asking to use the phone or the bathroom, then leave a window or back door open for us to slip through later that night, when we'd have at least an outside chance of catching most or all of the occupants sleeping. We'd go in, take what we wanted, and get out without ever having had to fire a shot.

Such a plan might have worked, with a lot of luck and flawless execution, but it wasn't fool-proof enough for our tastes. It involved too many variables that could get somebody killed, starting with our delivery boy patsy, and for O' and I, if not for R.J., this last was simply an unacceptable risk.

We needed another, less unpredictable way in, and so the three of us spent two days trying to devise one, tossing ideas back and forth at each other like bickering old women. When we eventually succeeded, we had pieced together a scheme that didn't hinge on the kid's ability to perform, and seemed to all but guarantee that we'd encounter no resistance upon entering the apartment.

It was a perfect plan that blew up in our faces, but not in a way that any of us could have possibly anticipated.

We were worried our first little trick hadn't worked until O' got a late night call from Frankie Chang, a classmate of his at UCLA, who said he'd just taken an order for some

Peking dumplings and sweet and sour spare ribs from a woman named Linda Dole.

Dole was the hot-tempered female resident of Excel Rucker's Inglewood safe house, and she'd called Frankie instead of the Jade Inn because we'd put a fake flyer in her mailbox the day before alerting her to the restaurant's 'new' phone number. In order to intercept the restaurant's delivery boy on his next trip to the apartment, we had to know exactly when that trip would be happening, so O' was paying Frankie $50 a day to answer his second house line with the proper greeting and inflection of a Jade Inn employee, and alert us to any calls intended for the restaurant he might receive.

It was money well spent.

Frankie tipped O' off just after nine on a Friday night, our third week of watching the Inglewood duplex, and as soon as O' thanked him and hung up the phone, he and I left O's apartment to tell R.J., who was out in Inglewood monitoring the place.

It was showtime.

How much thought either of my friends gave to calling the whole thing off, I will never know. It was the riskiest and most complicated job we had ever attempted, so they must have had their doubts. All I can say for certain is that, now that the moment had come to fish or cut bait, the idea of doing the latter crossed my own mind more than once. Suddenly I could see all the myriad ways this train could fly off its tracks and how high the body count could be if it did. Did I still need to hurt Excel Rucker that badly?

I did.

The three of us went over the game plan one last time, then O' drove me to the Jade Inn, where I went in alone to place a food order identical to the one Linda Dole had given to Frankie Chang. I left with the food fifteen minutes later and O' stayed behind in the car, where he waited for the kid in the red Toyota to attempt delivery of Dole's original order, which R.J. had just called in on Dole's behalf.

The route the kid always took to the safe house invariably led him south down a stretch of Tamarack Avenue that was as dark after ten p.m. as it was desolate, and when he arrived there, O's Camaro riding close enough behind him to peel a sticker off his bumper, I was waiting, strolling along the sidewalk with the sack of Chinese food under my arm like an elderly local out for his evening exercise.

The kid heeded the stop sign at Kelso and O' plowed right into him, hard enough to do some damage without causing injury. The kid got out of his car first, instinct taking over before common sense could kick in, and O' joined him, the two men meeting at the point of collision to shower insults and accusations upon each other.

O's size and theatrical outrage should have had the teenager paralyzed, but the kid was in his face right up until O' showed him the gun. At that, his hands fell limp at his sides and he froze, peering so intently down the barrel of O's

Smith & Wesson, I feared he might see all the way into the nine's empty magazine. But no – the gun had his attention and his respect, and when O' used the nose of it to order a 180 degree turn, the kid came around to show me his back like a trained seal.

It only took me a few seconds to slip over to the red Toyota and exchange bags through the driver's side door the kid had left open. He sensed something going on behind him, but O' put the gun to his nose the instant his head started to turn, and I was back on the sidewalk, leaving the scene with R.J.'s order of Chinese food, before he had a chance to register anything amiss.

I was three blocks away when O's Camaro burbled up to the curb alongside me, the man behind the wheel grinning like a crazed degenerate.

I jerked the door open and got in. 'You didn't hurt him, did you?'

'Naw.' He smoked his tires taking off again. 'He's gonna have to go home and change those pants, though.'

We laughed, slapping two open palms together loud enough to raise the dead.

'Just as long as he makes his delivery first. If you scared him too bad, he might run, and then we're fucked,' I said, voicing one of our greatest concerns about the plan we'd just set into motion.

'I don't think he will. He's a pretty tough little bastard.'

I began to rummage through the contents of the brown paper sack in my lap, looking for the container of spare ribs. 'You want some of this?'

'I do if that's the right bag.'

'Shit. You saw me make the switch.'

'Yeah, I saw you. But that doesn't mean you didn't fuck it up.'

I found the ribs, popped one into my mouth to gnaw eagerly on the bone. 'Satisfied?'

'Not yet. Ask me again in an hour.'

In one hour, if I *had* fucked up, I was going to be out on my ass. Only moments after picking it up, I'd spiked every course of the meal I'd ordered at the Jade Inn with a liberal dose of chloral hydrate, a liquid sedative we'd purchased from an intern of R.J.'s acquaintance who worked at a hospital in Culver City and dealt prescription meds on the side. He'd given us his assurance that a few ounces of chloral hydrate would render a large adult unconscious less than an hour after he'd ingested the drug, and the test we'd done using O' as a guinea pig had proven his sales pitch to be not only accurate, but somewhat understated. A chloral hydrate-spiked chocolate shake had knocked O' out in exactly forty-six minutes, and left him that way for several hours afterward.

'This all going to work, O'?' I asked him now.

He checked my face, saw that I'd grown serious.

'Guess we'll just have to wait and see,' he said.

124

THIRTEEN

The Coughlin Construction business complex was in Torrance. It took up most of a full city block, and consisted of one four-story office building and a half-dozen or so utility structures, all surrounded by a security fence crowned with razor wire any minimum-security prison would have been proud to own. Heavy machinery spread colors of gold and green in various lots all around, tractors and earth movers, forklifts and bulldozers. The guard at the gate didn't care for my looks, but I'd called ahead to arrange for a pass, so he had little choice but to instruct me where to park and wave me on through.

The man I'd come to see had been R.J.'s immediate supervisor. He was Coughlin's chief of security, a bullish, stone-jawed black man I remembered seeing at the funeral named Mike Owens, and getting him to agree to see me on such short notice, just before three on a Tuesday afternoon, had been the hardest work I'd ever done over the phone.

'I'm afraid I don't have much time for you, Mr White,' he told me the minute I'd taken my seat in his office. It had a window looking on to a vast spread of workers' cubicles, but the view it afforded him of life in the Coughlin lane was hardly worth the cost of the glass. 'Tell me again who you are?'

'Just a friend of the family. R.J. and I went way back.'

'And you're here because?'

'Because his wife and daughter would like to be sure the police don't miss anything significant in their investigation into his murder.'

'Anything significant. Like what?'

'I'm not really sure. Anything that could lead to the right people being held responsible, as opposed to the wrong ones, I suppose.'

'I see. You're a private investigator, then?'

'No.'

Something in the room was intermittently making a dry, buzzing noise that was wearing on my nerves, and the focus of my thinking kept shifting to the mystery of its origin. Between that, and answering the same questions about how R.J.'s murder was any of my business, I was becoming one impatient sonofabitch.

'No?'

'I'm just doing the ladies a favor, Mr Owens. They've asked me to talk to some of R.J.'s friends and co-workers to see if anybody might know what happened to him, and that's what I'm doing. If you don't feel comfortable talking to me because I lack a private investigator's license, I'm sure they'll understand.'

Which, of course, was my way of telling him

they wouldn't understand at all.

'I've got no problem talking to you,' Owens said, straightening a necktie that could have come off the rack at any drugstore in the world. 'Anything I can do to help Bobby's family, I'm only too happy to do. But there are matters of confidentiality to be considered here, Mr White, as well as the trouble I could conceivably get into with the police, who'd probably take my talking to you as some kind of sign that I'm as concerned about their competency as you are.'

'Of course. Except that nobody's saying the police are incompetent. Yet.'

He fell back in his chair and nodded, determined to be as difficult to move in person as he had been over the phone. The irritating buzz in the room erupted again; it was coming from somewhere on the computer workstation behind him. 'So what would you like to know?'

'Why don't we start with the most obvious question first: You have any idea who might have killed R.J., or why?'

'Absolutely none. The man was an extremely likeable person and a fine employee. We're going to miss him here at Coughlin a great deal.'

'How long had you worked together?'

'Nine years. He was here when I hired on.'

'Did you consider him a friend?'

'A friend?'

'As opposed to just a fellow employee.'

'We didn't socialize with each other outside

of the office, if that's what you're asking. I was his supervisor, and he was my subordinate. But we were friendly, sure.'

'Was he more than "friendly" with anyone else here?'

'Sorry, I don't follow.'

'I'm wondering if there was anyone here at Coughlin in particular he might have spent considerable time with *away* from the job.'

'You talking about a woman?'

The question caught me off guard. 'Not necessarily.'

'Good. Because if you were, I'd have no comment on the subject. We have rules against employee fraternization here, Mr White, but anything our people choose to do after hours that has no impact on their work performance is entirely their own business.'

He was telling me R.J. had been having an affair with a co-worker by way of not telling me. What I couldn't determine was whether this was intentional, or inadvertent.

'Assuming their relationship with R.J. was strictly platonic, if I wanted to speak to the people who were closest to him here at Coughlin, who would they be?'

'You thinking somebody here killed Bobby?'

'Not at all. I'm simply thinking it might be helpful to ask the people who knew him best how he'd been doing lately.'

We stared each other down. Owens, because all this was making him extremely uncomfortable, and me, because he was giving me nothing else to do. Meanwhile, the raspy, cough-like sound that kept drawing my attention rejoined our conversation, and this time I caught enough of it before it went away to recognize what it was.

'Sylvia Nuçnez and Doug Wilmore are the ones who first come to mind,' Owens said. 'Sylvia works in HR and Doug's one of our senior uniforms; he and Bobby came in together, I believe.'

I wrote the names down. 'Any chance either of them are here right now?'

'Doug's out in the field, but Sylvia should be around. I'll point the way to HR on your way out if you like.'

'I would, thanks.'

'We about done? Don't mean to rush you, but I'm a little pressed for time this afternoon, like I said.'

'I just have two or three more questions. I'll make them quick.'

'Please.'

'R.J. was a security consultant for Coughlin, is that right?'

Owens nodded.

'Could you explain what that means, exactly? What did he actually do?'

Owens had to give his answer some thought before offering it. 'Basically, he toured all our work sites to assess their potential for theft, and suggested ways to make them more secure.'

'That's it?'

Owens shrugged. 'Pretty much.'

'Sounds like a fairly simple gig.'

'It isn't rocket science. But it does require a certain amount of knowledge and expertise.'

'And R.J. had it.'

'After eighteen years in the field? Most certainly.'

'Would you consider the work stressful in any way?'

'Stressful? No. The police asked that question too, and I told them the same thing. Whatever pressures might have led Bobby to get himself killed that way, they didn't have anything to do with his work here at Coughlin. He had a good job, he did it well, and everybody here seemed to like him. End of story.' He stood up. 'Now, I'm sorry, Mr White, but that's really all the time I can give you today.'

'Of course. Many thanks for your help,' I said, getting to my own feet for fear he might carry me out otherwise, chair and all. I shook his hand, said, 'If I left you my number, would you have Doug Wilmore call me when he has a chance? Providing he'd be willing?'

When Owens grunted affirmatively, I wrote the number on the back of one of his business cards and left it on his desk. 'Now where would I find HR?'

He gave me directions and I started for the door, only to turn back at the last minute, as if I'd just remembered something I'd nearly for-gotten to ask. 'Oh, one last thing...'

He had his arms crossed now. 'Yes?'

'When I called today, I originally asked to

speak with Mr Allen, but the receptionist told me she couldn't find anybody by that name in her directory. That's how I ended up talking to you. Is Mr Allen no longer with the company?'

I thought I saw the man's eyes flicker slightly, but I could have been mistaken. 'I don't know anybody named Allen. Who's he?'

'R.J.'s daughter says he's the man at Coughlin who originally got R.J. hired on here. The name's not familiar?'

'I'm afraid not. Maybe he left before I came aboard.'

'How about Darrel Eastman? That name ring any bells?'

'Eastman? Sorry.' He shook his head.

'You've got a bad fan in that PC case,' I said by way of farewell, gesturing at the computer behind Owens as its cooling fan's death knell started up again. 'You might want to get it replaced before you cook your motherboard.'

My conversation with Sylvia Nuez was woefully brief. A full-bodied, almond-skinned woman with dark brown hair and flawless skin whom I took to be in her middle forties, she was seated at the first desk I saw when I walked into Coughlin's Human Resources office. She was warm and friendly for about five seconds, and then I told her who I was and what I wanted.

'Mr Owens told you to talk to me?' she asked, keeping her voice low out of obvious concern for the one other person in the room, an older white woman feeding documents into a copying machine behind her.

'He said you and R.J. were good friends. I was wondering—'

'R.J.? You mean Bobby?'

'Bobby, right. R.J.'s what we called him in high school. Listen, if you'd rather we don't talk about this here—'

'There isn't anything to talk about,' she said, cutting me off for the second straight time. 'Bobby and I were friends, sure, but I'm friends with a lot of people here. I can't tell you anything about him that anyone else who worked with him couldn't.'

She wasn't going to change her mind, no matter what I cared to offer in the way of encouragement. Some people braced themselves for a fight in such a way that their body language alone made the futility of pushing them abundantly clear, and Sylvia Nuez was one of them. Perhaps this was why R.J. had been drawn to her, as I could sense myself being drawn to her now.

I apologized for bothering her and left.

Out in the parking lot, just as I was unlocking the door to my rental car, I saw a white Ford Explorer with the Coughlin insignia emblazoned upon its doors pull into a marked space along a row lined with similar vehicles. The middle-aged white man who got out from behind the wheel happened to be someone else I remembered seeing at R.J.'s funeral seven days before. The surly, firmly set expression on his face was the same, but today he was wearing a dark blue blazer with the Coughlin logo stitched on to its breast pocket, and as he approached the administration building's main entrance, he walked with the authority of someone who knew the place backwards and forward.

'Pardon me,' I said, closing my car door to approach him carefully. 'You wouldn't be Doug Wilmore, by any chance?'

He stopped and regarded me with some suspicion, eyes like a bird of prey's taking me in from head to foot. 'That's me. How can I help you?'

I told him who I was and what I wanted, deviating little from the story I'd fed Mike Owens and Sylvia Nuez moments earlier. Wilmore softened a little upon hearing it all, but not much; twenty seconds in his company, and I could already tell the only time he let his guard down was when he was asleep.

'Bobby was a good guy. Naturally, I'd be happy to help you any way I can,' he said. 'Except, I don't know what I could possibly tell you that the police don't already know. Bobby and I just worked together, that's all.'

'Mike Owens says you were his closest friend here, that the two of you may have even started with the company at around the same time.'

'That's right, we did. I started back in March, '87 and Bobby came aboard that same July. We worked together for a long time, so we were buds, sure. But it wasn't like we were brothers or anything.'

'Then you wouldn't know what he might have been doing, on or off the job, that could have led to his murder?'

'No. I wouldn't. I wish I did.'

I ran Darrel Eastman's name past him, just on the off chance it would mean something to him, but that was something else he couldn't help me with. When I asked him about a Coughlin employee named Allen, however, his eyes took on a different light.

'You mean Cleveland Allen?'

'Is that his name?'

'He's the only Coughlin employee named Allen I ever heard of. What's he got to do with Bobby?'

'His daughter believes it was Allen who got him hired on here. She said they met while R.J. was still in prison and Allen was there running a job training program of some kind. You did know R.J. had been to prison?'

Wilmore nodded. 'I knew.'

'Then it's possible he and Allen met the way I just described?'

'I don't know. I suppose so. Look, Mr White, I'd like to be of help, like I said, but I've just told you about all I know. What happened to Bobby was a dirty shame, and I hope they catch the asshole who killed him real quick.'

'That makes two of us. But—'

'Sorry, gotta go. Best of luck to you.'

He walked off and disappeared into the building. Something about bringing Cleveland Allen

134

into our conversation had sent him ducking for cover.

On my way out of the Coughlin Construction complex, the same guard who had barely let me in stopped my car at the gate.

'You Mr White?' he asked.

'That's right. Something wrong?'

He handed me a note with a phone number scrawled across it. 'Sly says you should call her at that number in an hour.'

'Sly?' I caught on before he could answer, said, 'Oh, right. Sylvia.'

He raised the gate for me, his face as blank as a fresh sheet of cardboard. 'Have a good day.'

Sylvia Nuez had me meet her after work at a little coffee house out in Westchester, a full eight miles away from the Coughlin Construction offices. It seemed like a long way to drive just to talk, but I suspected she had put that much distance between the two sites for a reason.

We sat at a back table with my black coffee and her foam-capped latte, and at her urging, I told her all over again who I was, and why Mike Owens had suggested I share my questions about R.J. with her.

'What kind of "friends" did he say we were? I'll bet I can guess,' she said. She was a handsome woman, but there was a snake spitting venom beneath all the sexy good looks, and she didn't appear to care who knew it.

'He said you were "good friends".'

'He didn't say we were lovers?'

'He gave me the impression R.J. was involved with somebody at Coughlin, but he didn't say it was you, specifically.'

'Well, I guess it depends on your definition of "involved".'

'And yours is?'

'We got together every now and then to talk and unwind. If that's your idea of being involved, then I guess that's what we were.'

She smiled, moved by nothing even remotely akin to amusement.

'And sex wasn't part of the deal?'

'Of course it was. But only when I could get him to think about it, which I'm sad to say, wasn't very often.'

'You were in love with him?'

'Love? No. I couldn't afford to be in love with him. Bobby was a really fine man, and something you don't see every day: a married man who didn't really care for fooling around.'

'Then he was happy at home.'

'Have you tried asking his wife that question?'

'In my experience, it isn't usually the wife who knows the answer.'

She nodded her head. 'Bobby wasn't happy anywhere. Home, work, made no difference.'

'Any idea why?'

Sylvia Nuez took a small sip of her latte, giving herself one last chance to walk away before telling me more about 'Bobby' Burrow than I had any right to know.

'Because of what you did,' she said.

The earth braked slowly to a stop beneath the legs of my chair. 'Say again?'

'You and him and the mayor. O'Neal Holden. Before the three of you promised never to see each other again.'

I could have acted like I didn't understand, just to buy myself some time to think. But time to think wouldn't have changed a thing about the spot I suddenly found myself in.

'What did he say we did?'

'You saying you don't remember?'

'I'm asking you what he told you.'

'He told me you made a big mistake. That the three of you crossed somebody you never should have crossed and a lot of people got hurt because of it.'

I reached for my coffee cup, got it an inch off the table before putting it down again.

'If you're worrying somebody other than me might know about this, you can relax. I haven't told anybody and I don't think Bobby did, either. He said he couldn't, that he was betraying a solemn vow just telling me what little he did.'

And so he had been. Just as we had all sworn that night in O's mother's garage never to see or speak to each other again, so too had we promised never to reveal our reasons for disbanding to anyone. That R.J. had apparently gone more than twenty years without breaking that promise, and then had only done so in the most vague and non-specific manner, was a testament to his having had more strength of conviction than either O' or I had ever given him credit for.

'What about the police?' I asked. 'You didn't tell them?'

'I had no reason to. Bobby said the guy you had all the trouble with has been dead for years, and all the police wanted to know was whether anybody at Coughlin ever saw him do drugs.'

'And you said?'

'I said I never saw him do any drugs, no.'

She gave me a look that insisted I try again.

'But that was a lie.'

She fell silent, having come full circle back to that place where getting up and walking out without saying another word might be her smartest move.

'You want an answer to that? We'd better get something straight first. I've been taking a big chance talking to you like this, Mr White. I'm a single mother with two kids in college who can't afford to lose her job because she ran her mouth off to the wrong stranger. You want your business to be safe with me, I need to know mine and Bobby's will be safe with you.'

'I understand.'

'Do you?'

'Yes. I do. Did you ever see R.J. do drugs?'

She gave herself one last chance to back out, decided not to take it. 'Yes. But there was no way I could tell the police that. What was I supposed to say, "I watched him get high from time to time, but I never partied with him"?

138

They would've laughed in my face.'

'So what kind of drugs was he using?'

'Grass, mostly.'

'And?'

She looked away to hide her embarrassment. 'A little rock. But only lately.'

'What do you mean, "lately"?'

'I mean all we ever did was weed until about five or six weeks ago. Then one day, he pulls out this pipe. I wasn't down with it at first, at my age it seemed ridiculous, but' – she shrugged – 'it was Bobby, so...'

'Why the switch?'

'I don't know. I asked him that myself, but he couldn't say. I figured he was just looking for a different reaction. Something that would make him less depressed, not more.'

'Exactly how depressed was he?'

'It would depend. Some days, he was fine, but on others, he was miserable. All he could talk about was dying. Whatever you guys did, the guilt was killing him.'

She let her gaze, hard and unflinching, prompt me for a response.

'You already know more about it than you should,' I said. 'You'll have to trust me when I tell you you're better off just leaving it at that.'

'I deserve to know.'

'No, you don't. Nobody does. Knowing would only make you care for him less.'

I watched the tears I thought I'd see much sooner finally pool in her eyes.

'Do you know who his connection was for the

drugs?'

'The grass was mostly mine. I don't know where he got the rock.'

'Any chance it could have come from a man named Darrel Eastman?'

'Darrel Eastman? He knew somebody named Darrel, but I don't know if his last name was Eastman.'

'Who was that?'

'Some kid he'd been trying to help for a while. He was mentoring him, I think.'

'Mentoring him?'

'Yeah, you know – spending time with him on his off hours. Trying to keep him out of trouble.'

'Drug trouble?'

Nuez shook her head. 'Bobby never said what kind. We never talked about him. I only know about him at all because Bobby used him as an excuse a few times not to see me. Who's Darrel Eastman?'

I told her. Walt Fine wouldn't like it, but I was fairly confident that if the Santa Monica PD found out I knew the identity of their prime suspect, it wouldn't be because Sylvia Nuez had called to tell them about it.

'Oh, my God,' she said.

'You have any idea how I might find this Darrel R.J. was mentoring? Or where he and R.J. may have gone when they got together?'

'No. I'm sorry.'

'You're sure?'

'I'm positive.'

'He never visited R.J. at work?'

'Not that I'm aware of. I mean, I've never seen him before, so I wouldn't have known it if he had.'

I described the young brother I'd wrestled with in Moody's parking lot the night before.

'I don't know anybody like that,' she said.

'OK.' I didn't want to let it go, but I couldn't see the point in asking any more questions she didn't have the answers to. 'Tell me what you can about a Coughlin employee named Cleveland Allen.'

Again, as I had with Doug Wilmore earlier, I'd struck a nerve by dropping Allen's name. 'Mr Allen? He used to be a company VP. So?'

'What do you mean, "used to be"?'

'I mean the company fired him about a year ago. He liked to sexually harass female employees and we finally had to call him on it one too many times.'

'A year ago?' Mike Owens had said he'd been with Coughlin for nine years, and had never heard of anybody there named Allen.

'Well, it might not have been a full year yet. It might be more like ten months. But what's your interest in Mr Allen? You don't think he had something to do with Bobby's murder?'

'I don't have any reason to think so, yet. But Mike Owens denied any knowledge of him and when I talked to Doug Wilmore on my way out of the Coughlin parking lot a few minutes ago, he treated Allen's name like a four-alarm fire.'

'You talked to Doug? Why?'

141

'For the same reason I'm talking to you. Owens said he was one of R.J.'s closest friends at Coughlin.' Off Nuez's silence, I asked, 'Are you saying he wasn't?'

'No, they were friends, all right. I'm just surprised to hear that Doug agreed to talk to you. He can be a pretty surly character.'

'Sounds like you could elaborate on that for a while if you wanted to.'

She shrugged. 'Let's just say Doug can sometimes have the same problem with a girl saying "no" as Mr Allen did. Only difference is, Doug knows how to go away after a while.'

'And Allen didn't?'

She shook her head. 'He was a pig, and an expensive one at that. Before he was fired, Coughlin had to pay two female employees six figures each not to file suit against him and the company both. Which is probably why Mike and Doug acted the way you say they did when you mentioned his name. Nobody's ever told us we can't talk about Mr Allen, but they don't exactly encourage it, either, especially on company grounds.'

'Did Allen and R.J. work together?'

'Sure. Mr Allen was head of sales and Bobby was the sales division's chief of security for a while.'

'Say that again?'

'I know. It sounds weird, doesn't it? Chief of security for sales. But those are the people who need watching the most sometimes. The ones who know where all the business is.'

'Watching for what?'

'Fraud, industrial espionage, vulnerability to terrorism – you name it.'

I mulled it over. 'And that's what R.J. was doing when Allen got fired? Looking for signs of impropriety on the part of the sales department?'

'That was part of his job, yes.'

'Then he could have been the one who blew the whistle on Allen.'

She thought about it. 'I suppose so.'

'Any idea where Allen is now? I'd like to talk to him.'

'For what?'

'If he blamed R.J. for what happened to him at Coughlin, he might have had a motive for murder. It does seem odd that he would have waited almost a year to do it, but—'

'Mr Allen couldn't have possibly murdered Bobby,' Nuez said flatly. 'He's dead. He killed himself just weeks after we let him go.'

Having just learned that R.J. may have in fact known Darrel Eastman – the man the SMPD believed to be his murderer – pursuing Cleveland Allen as an alternate suspect in his killing would have been a questionable use of my time, at best. Still, I was disappointed to hear he was dead. Whether he'd had anything to do with R.J.'s murder or not, I'd been looking forward to asking Allen about the role he'd allegedly played in getting an ex-con hired on at Coughlin as a security guard. How could he and R.J. have hit it off at Lancaster that fabulously?

'How are you for time?' I asked Nuez, checking my watch.

She shrugged. 'I'm OK. I'm an old divorcee living in an empty nest these days, like I said, so there isn't much point in rushing back home.'

She smiled, but all it did for either one of us was make our hearts a little heavier. She was smart and resilient, obviously, and pleasing to the eye, but loneliness was the cold, dark center beneath the sultry exterior. I wondered how much R.J. could have done to relieve that loneliness, and how much worse it had become now that he was gone.

'Did R.J. ever mention a man named Excel Rucker?' I asked.

It was the first time I'd dropped the dealer's name to anyone since I'd returned to Los Angeles. I'd been determined not to bring Rucker into any conversation until someone gave me a reason to do so, but by admitting she was at least partially aware of our history with the dealer, Nuez finally had.

'X-L?' Nuez asked.

'Ex-cel. Rucker.'

'No.' She shook her head. 'Is that the man you robbed?'

'No. What about Paris McDonald?'

'No.'

'Linda Dole?'

'No. Wait.'

'Linda Dole?'

She shook her head again. 'McDonald. You

said his first name was Paris? Like the city?'

I nodded.

'Well, Bobby never talked about him, at least not with me, but he did do a lot of reading about a Paris McDonald.'

I felt my mouth go dry. 'What kind of reading?'

'Newspaper articles, mostly. And magazines, too. You're talking about the ex-boxer who just became a minister in prison, right? They used to call him "the Tower"?'

I nodded again. 'Why was R.J. reading about him?'

'He said they'd met each other once out at Lancaster, when Bobby was doing time up there and McDonald was waiting for a transfer to Pelican Bay. Bobby saw a TV news report about him and was so amazed by the story – you know, convicted killer turns Jesus freak – he said he just had to know if it was for real or not. So—'

'They met in prison?'

'That's what Bobby said.'

I couldn't imagine it. If the two men had crossed paths for so much as an instant at Lancaster, one or both of them would surely have died there. The only thing I could think was that their meeting was a lie, something R.J. had to tell Nuez to explain his interest in someone he otherwise had no business giving a damn about.

'How long ago was this? When R.J. saw the news report and started doing all the reading?'

She thought it over, produced a little shrug. 'I

don't know. A couple of months ago, maybe.'

In other words, not long before R.J. was murdered.

'What is it? What's wrong?'

I told her it was nothing, but she didn't believe me. I didn't care. I'd heard all I needed to hear and was ready to call it a day.

FOURTEEN

I had a visitor waiting for me when I returned to my motel room. He'd been sitting in his parked car in the lot, watching my door, and the minute I had my key card in the lock, he got out to approach me.

'You Errol White?'

I spun like a weathervane, the face of my friend from Moody's bar immediately coming to mind. But this wasn't him. This was a twenty-something, clean-shaven white man wearing a blue dress shirt, tie, and black slacks. He could have been the top man in a mailroom somewhere, and maybe he was, but his buzz-cut hair and thick neck were suggestive of something slightly more sinister.

'Package from Bellwood,' he said, handing me a large, padded envelope that bore no mark of any kind.

Had his meaning been unclear, I would have had to seek understanding elsewhere, because he didn't stick around to field any questions. He was back in his Saturn sedan, driving off the motel lot, in the time it took me to get all five fingers of one hand wrapped around the parcel he'd just delivered.

Inside my room, using a metal nail file for lack of a knife, I sawed through layers of packing tape to free the envelope's contents, a thick cocoon of bubble-pack and cheesecloth with something black and heavy at its core: a Taurus PT-92. It was an old soldier of the streets, egregiously scarred and shorn of all identifying serial numbers, and its magazine was loaded with the maximum number of ten silver-tipped, 9 mm rounds.

Understandably, O' had declined to send a card along with it.

What do you tell a motherless child about the woman who abandoned her? Do you speak the truth to protect yourself, or concoct a lie to protect the child?

As her father, you are doomed either way. No matter how you couch it, the truth will always leave you with blood on your hands, and a lie will inevitably expose you as a fraud. The day will come when you will have to answer all of her questions, and whether you defer that day for twenty-five minutes or twenty-five years, both her pain and your guilt will be just as unbearable.

My decision to tell Coral as little as possible about her mother was made from the moment I first brought her into my home. I was barely able to cope with the truth myself, so I naturally lacked the stomach to share the burden of it with her. I told her her mother was dead, thinking I was closing the door on any hope she might dare cultivate for an eventual reunion. For most of Coral's life, she was willing to believe it, satisfied merely to be given more and more details about the woman I'd led her to believe was her mother. Ultimately, however, as she grew older and I was forced to add layer upon layer to the lie I had told her, she began to suspect her mother was not dead at all, and took to studying all the physical evidence of the woman's existence I'd provided her over the years for clues to her mother's whereabouts: a few pieces of cheap jewelry, a handwritten letter addressed to me, and finally, most damning of all, an old photograph.

In it, a tall, lovely black woman with fair skin and a heart-stopping smile, dressed in white linen blouse and skirt, kneels beside a chocolate Labrador retriever, laughing because the animal won't keep still for the camera.

'You kept that photograph?' the woman asked me now, talking on the telephone from wherever it was in Minnesota Quincy had somehow managed to track her down.

'Yes. I'm not sure why.'

'You'll forgive me if I'm stunned. You never showed that kind of sentimentality while we were together.'

'No, I don't suppose I did.'

'What is it that you want, Handy? Your friend said you're in serious trouble, and you need my help.'

I told her what I'd done. It helped that I couldn't see her face, and that she couldn't see mine, but only marginally. If I live another fifty years, I'll never make a more shameful and deflating confession.

It took her a long time to respond.

'My God. And now, what am *I* supposed to do?'

'If she finds you? The only thing you can do. Tell her the truth. Just please, God, break it to her gently.'

'Why don't *you* tell her the truth?'

'If I thought she'd believe it, I would,' I said, 'but nothing I tell her now means anything to her. She thinks everything I say is a lie.'

'And isn't it?'

I let that pass. She was giving me all the grief I had expected she would and I was in no position to deny her the privilege.

'Susan, please. Listen to me. This isn't about what you owe me. The mess I made of what we had together, you'd have every right to hate my sorry ass until the day I die. But what I'm asking for is for the girl. She's OK now, but she wasn't for a long time. If she comes to you and you say the wrong thing, or aren't careful about how you say the right one, I could lose her all over again. Maybe for good this time.'

I was putting her in a box from which there was no noble escape. She would either agree to help me, or risk doing damage to a young woman she didn't even know. Still, Susan Yancy didn't have to believe the situation was as dire as I described. I had lied to her about much lesser things before.

'Goddamn you, Handy,' she said.

I had been lying on my back in the dark of my motel room, listening to the moonlit world outside murmur and moan for a full two hours, when I finally sat up and called Sylvia Nuez. I'd asked for her home number before leaving her at the cafe in Westchester, using the excuse that I might have some reason to talk to her about R.J. again later, but I think we both knew what my real interest was. The only surprise was how quickly I'd found the need to call.

I talked my way into an invitation to her apartment in Culver City and that's where I spent the night. My motel room was an echo chamber for the voices of Susan Yancy and my daughter Coral, and I simply lacked the courage to endure them without company until morning. As for Sylvia Nuez, whatever reasons she had for taking me into her bed were left unsaid, though I had the sense they were no more complicated than mine. She was a smart and handsome woman without a partner, undeserving of the loneliness that fate had resigned her to, and I was someone she'd stumbled across and found oddly compelling. The space that

R.J. had once occupied in her life was now empty, and for one night, at least, she could make do with me as his replacement.

Our lovemaking was a model of gentle efficiency. What it lacked in physical heat was more than made up for by its slow, meandering purity. Neither of us was a kid anymore, and sexual performance had long ago become a non-issue in the face of things like honesty and reciprocation.

When we were done, we lay in each other's arms and took turns drifting in and out of sleep, filling the gaps with small talk that was less about ourselves than the only thing we really had in common: R.J. Burrow.

'Do you ever miss him?' she asked me eventually.

'No.'

'But you loved him.'

I tried to picture him as I remembered him, peeling the years back one by one until I could see the flash of his grin and feel the sting of his laughter, especially after he'd just made me the butt of a cruel joke.

'Yes,' I said.

'What about O'Neal Holden?'

'What about him?'

'Do you think *he* loved Bobby?'

It should have been an easy question to answer. O' had been R.J.'s friend longer than I by several years, and there had always been a special bond between them that I could only envy. But the love O' appeared to have for R.J.,

151

like everything else about Bellwood's future mayor, could not be taken at face value. O' was a man who believed that life was an endless series of trade-offs, and if he had thought affection was the price he had to pay to keep R.J. on the leash, he would have gladly paid it.

'I don't know,' I said.

FIFTEEN

O' had been right about the Jade Inn's delivery boy: He delivered Linda Dole's order to Excel Rucker's safe house just like the fender bender he'd had with O' had never occurred.

From a safe distance, my friends and I watched him arrive at Dole's duplex and leave, all of us sitting in the reefer cloud that was forever trapped inside R.J.'s old Dodge Monaco.

'I thought I told you to lay off the smoke,' O' grumbled.

'I been sittin' in this car all damn day. What else was I gonna do to occupy myself?'

The obvious answer was, anything less likely to impede his ability to watch Rucker's house or draw the attention of the police, but O' was wise enough to know how little good it would have done to say as much.

152

'Everybody home?' he asked instead.

'Yep. Three niggas, one woman. The fat boy went out for a while, but he came back 'bout fifteen minutes ago.'

We sat in R.J.'s car for well over an hour after the Jade Inn delivery boy departed before making any move to approach the house, committed to giving the chloral hydrate all the time it needed to render everyone inside unconscious. It was a long wait, and an unnerving one. R.J., especially, had a hard time dealing with the certainty that somebody somewhere was going to eventually notice us – three brothers sitting out on the street in a strange car reeking of Mary Jane – and call the cops. But a long wait was part of the plan, and we forced ourselves to endure it. O' wasn't going to fuck this thing up playing too close to the margins, and neither was I.

'What do you think?' O' asked finally.

It was eleven thirty. All but a few houses on the block were fully dark, an ostensible indicator of sleeping occupants within, but yellow light still shone behind the blinds in the front windows of the dealer's duplex apartment. This could have been a bad sign, except that our weeks of surveillance had established a consistent routine for the people who lived there, and it invariably involved their shifting the lights from the front to the back of the apartment by eleven o'clock each night. Their failure to do so by now was a strong suggestion, if not actual proof, that Linda Dole and her companions had

153

fallen out in the living and dining rooms where they'd eaten the spiked Chinese food, before they could make their usual exodus to the bedrooms at the rear of the residence.

'I think it's time to make the call,' I said, climbing out of the Dodge.

Dole had given O's friend Frankie Chang her phone number when she'd called what she thought was the Jade Inn to place her food order, and I sprinted around the block now to dial the number from a payphone. It was a risky thing to do. We were taking a chance that the ringing phone wouldn't rouse somebody who might have otherwise remained unconscious, but this was the only way we could think of to determine if someone in the house was still capable of meeting our impending invasion with force. I took a deep breath, dropped some coins into the phone, and made the call.

'Well?' R.J. asked when I got back to the car and jumped in.

'We're good to go.'

'Nobody picked up?'

I shook my head. O' asked how many times I'd let it ring, and I told him – ten – then asked, 'Any movement inside?'

'Nothing.'

Which gave us one more reason to believe the chloral hydrate had done its job. In evenings past, we'd always been able to catch an occasional flash of movement behind the apartment blinds when Dole and her friends were awake and ambulatory.

'Let's do this thing, then,' I said.

We all got out of the car together, R.J. and I to start for the house, and O' to go play lookout from inside his less conspicuous Camaro, which was parked on the other side of the street nearby.

'You fools have got fifteen minutes, starting now,' he said. 'You're not outta there in fifteen, I'm coming to get your asses.'

R.J.'s active role in the robbery was non-negotiable, because our plan had already called for him to spend hours in the Dodge alone and there was no way O' and I could ask him to go on doing so. But who would enter the apartment with him had not been so easily decided. O' and I were equally determined to be right on top of R.J. when the deal went down, close enough to prevent any high drama he might get it in his head to cause, and neither of us would settle for the position of a mere street observer without a fight.

'You don't know him like I do. You can't control him like I can,' O' had said, outside of R.J.'s presence.

'Maybe not. But I'm the one who wanted to do this thing, and I'm the one who'll have to live with it if anything goes wrong.'

'Ain't nothin' gonna go wrong if you let me go in with him.'

In the end, unable to reach an agreement any other way, we drew straws to settle the matter, and I won out. Still, even now, O' was hoping I'd change my mind.

'You sure you wanna do this?' he asked me one last time.

We both knew I wasn't sure. I was scared and beleaguered by doubt, envisioning every possible misstep any one of us could take that could bring this night to a terrible end. But this was my show, a monster of my own creation, and I wasn't going to stand off to one side while O' and R.J. took the brunt of its considerable risks.

'Doesn't matter whether I'm sure or not,' I said. 'I'm going either way.'

With that, I walked off, not bothering to tell R.J. to follow. The clock was running now and I couldn't put the next ten minutes behind me fast enough.

'Yo, hold up!' R.J. whispered.

He caught up to me quickly and the two of us marched in lockstep to the duplex's driveway, time beginning to move with breakneck speed. Under a half-moon fighting to be seen past an endless parade of cloud cover, the entire street was deathly silent, save for two dogs barking in response to a bleating car alarm many blocks away. R.J. and I eased up the side of the house toward the backyard, barely glancing at the apartment's windows as we went by. All was quiet and still within, but that hardly mattered at this point; nothing could stop the machine we had set into motion now.

We reached the apartment's back door and I immediately went to work trying to breach it. Without asking for it, the job of opening locked doors for our crew had somewhere along the way fallen to me, and I'd learned to do it fairly well. A lock was just another mechanical device, after all, and finessing mechanical devices was my specialty, even back then. While my picking tools scratched away at the deadbolt's tumblers like a mouse gnawing a hole in a wall, R.J. watched and listened intently for any sound of discovery on the other side of the wrought iron portal, his black .45 already in hand.

I popped the lock in just over a minute and eased the door open, its hinges issuing a tiny, unnerving squeak of complaint. R.J. pulled a nylon stocking over his head, and I did the same, then he nodded impatiently at the Beretta still jammed in the back pocket of my Levi's: *Take it.* I shook the order off, entertaining the childish notion that I could guarantee not having to use it simply by leaving the weapon where it was, but R.J. wasn't having it. He yanked the gun from my pocket himself and shoved it into my right hand.

This time, I didn't complain.

It had been agreed that I would lead the way into the house, but R.J. started in without me. I put a hand out to grab him and turn him around, and even in the darkness of the porch, behind the nylon mesh of his mask, I could see the wild grin on his face.

In the five years I'd known him, I'd seen R.J. Burrow do damage to a lot of people. I'd seen him uproot teeth and break bones, snap limbs from their sockets and pound a man's skull with his fists like a safe he was trying to crack bare-handed. But I had never seen R.J. kill anyone, and I had always been of the belief that he couldn't, that his capacity for violence flirted with that limit only to stop just short of it. Now I realized how little reason I had to believe such a thing. The man on that back porch with me seemed not only capable of murder, but braced for it, as if it were something he'd been waiting his whole life to experience.

Not for the first time over the last several days, I wondered if seeing Excel Rucker pay for his disrespect of Olivia Gardner could really be worth all this – and coming to the same, un-relenting conclusion, I pushed past R.J. into the dealer's safe house to exact my revenge.

The utility pantry we stepped into was dark and tomb-like, as was the small, filthy kitchen beyond, but from somewhere in one of the lighted rooms past them both, the murmur of a television could be heard. We entered the kitchen and paused to listen for live voices, R.J. hovering close behind me; I turned to look at him, and he shook his head in reply: *Nothing*.

I crept to the open door leading to the dimly lit dining room and peered in. A man I recognized as one of Excel's soldiers-in-residence sat at a garish, glass-topped table cluttered with newspaper, slumped over at the waist, his head turned sideways on the plate of Chinese food he'd been eating when he had apparently collapsed.

R.J. nudged my arm and nodded, confidence soaring, and moved past me and the dozing soldier to push farther into the apartment alone. He curled around the edge of the living room archway and, without warning, threw his gun hand up, as if about to fire into the room...

But he was only making ready for something that wasn't there. Coming up behind him, I spied the figures of two more, seemingly unconscious people: Linda Dole, lying to one side on an old, tattered couch, her eyes closed and her mouth open, feet still grazing the floor; and the second soldier, the larger of the two, down on the living room carpet, drooling spit, limbs all akimbo. A small TV chattered and blinked from a faux-wood stand situated between them, and several open Jade Inn cartons littered their surroundings with noodles and fried rice.

R.J. showed me three fingers, satisfied, and the two of us turned simultaneously toward the hallway behind us, where the fourth and final member of Excel Rucker's worker bees had to be waiting. Tired of taking R.J.'s lead, I moved first this time and, gesturing for him to stay put, edged into the black hallway toward the three doorways it opened on to. Two of the doors were closed and dark, but the first was standing open, leaking a pale, shimmering light into the hall. I slipped up to the door frame, the Beretta a heavy stone in my hand, and in the muted glow of an old table lamp, saw a disheveled bedroom in which Linda Dole's overweight partner lay asleep on a single bed against one wall. He was on his back atop the unmade bed, fully clothed and snoring soundly. One leg was hanging over the side of the mattress, his left arm thrown over his eyes.

I looked back over my shoulder at R.J. and nodded an all-clear.

He came up beside me, took a brief look at the man in the bedroom himself, then whispered, 'OK. You stay out here and keep an eye on everybody, and I'll go find the goods.'

That hadn't been the plan, and he knew it, but I didn't argue with him. I could see it was an improvisation worth trying. R.J. couldn't do much damage looking for the drugs and money, but left in charge of watching Excel's people, there was no telling how he might react – or overreact – to one of them showing signs of life.

I watched him gingerly open the next door down the hall and quickly close it again, no doubt finding a bathroom on the other side. He moved on to the door at the end of the hall, threw this one open like a DEA agent making a bust and, when nothing happened, reached in to turn on the lights. I couldn't see much of the room from where I was standing, but it looked like a second bedroom, larger than the first. R.J. disappeared inside for several seconds, then stepped out again to report his findings.

'We got it,' he said, too excited now to bother

with keeping his voice down.

He went back into the room to secure the take and, resisting the temptation to follow, I returned to my business as guard dog. I gave Linda Dole's partner one more glance, saw he hadn't moved an inch since the last time I'd seen him, and went back out to the front of the apartment to check on the others. All three seemed just as frozen in time as their friend in the bedroom.

I took a position in the living room, just outside the hallway, where I could see Linda Dole and the two soldiers, and the doorway to the front bedroom. It was the closest I could come to having a clear view of all four of Excel's people at once. I checked my watch and saw that R.J. and I had been in the apartment for fourteen minutes now. O' would be crashing the party any second if we didn't get the hell out.

I was about to go move R.J. along when the man in the dining room let out a small groan. The sound brought my heart to a stop. I forced myself to approach the table where he sat to get a closer look, gathering my nerve for what I might have to do should he begin to stir in earnest ... but he didn't. He never moved, and he never made another sound. He just continued to sit there, slumped over the table, breathing with the ragged rhythm of a man far closer to death than consciousness.

As I stood there watching him, fear abating, my gaze drifted aimlessly across the layers of newspaper scattered across the tabletop around his head. I hadn't seen a newspaper in days. The only news I'd had any interest in had been relative to this apartment and the people in it, and all the curiosity I normally had about the world had been shoved to one side. Without thinking, I lifted the stocking up over my eyes and stuck a hand out to sift through several sections of the *Los Angeles Times*, perusing headlines and photographs, skimming over the details of the previous night's Lakers game and the latest incredible performance by the team's rookie point guard, a kid named Earvin 'Magic' Johnson. In moving things around, I unearthed something on the table I hadn't noticed before: a half-eaten hamburger and an empty French fries bag, the latter bearing the unmistakable double-arches of the McDonald's logo.

I understood the implications of my discovery immediately.

I opened my mouth to call out to R.J., body poised to turn and go get him, and felt something hard and cold nose into the back of my neck. I didn't have to see him to know the man standing behind me was the fat one I'd last seen asleep in the front bedroom, or that the object he had pointed at the top of my spine was a gun.

'Put it down, motherfucka,' R.J. said.

I dared a sideways glance, even as Linda Dole's lover did the same. Standing in the living room, R.J. had the Colt pointed directly at the fat man's head.

'I ain't gonna say it twice, all right?'

Sweat was sluicing off my back like rainwater down a drainpipe, but Excel Rucker's man had it even worse; the stench he was giving off was overpowering. Still, he kept the gun pressed against my neck. Not because he wasn't terrified, but because he hadn't yet decided which was the lesser of two evils: having R.J. kill him now, or waiting for Rucker to do it later.

I thought about what I would do in his place, and lost all hope.

He finally made up his mind, and the revolver dropped first to his side, then out of his hand and down to the floor.

'Shit,' he said, his voice breaking.

I started to pick up his gun, but R.J. stopped me cold. 'Cover your face, nigga!'

He was right. I'd forgotten the nylon stocking I'd lifted up and away from my eyes in order to scan the newspaper, and I'd almost made the unforgivable mistake of showing the other man my face. I jerked the stocking back down over my chin, burning with embarrassment, and snatched his gun up off the floor before shoving it into the front of my pants.

The fat man started to weep. Tears slid down both sides of his face, and his body shook like a wind-up toy. 'We can make a deal,' he said to me. 'You ain't gotta do this.'

'Shut up,' I told him.

He caught the finality in my voice and set himself to scream, but I slammed a fist across his jaw before R.J. could move in to save me the trouble. The big man fell like a stone, eyes rolling up in his head, and for a while I stood over his unconscious form, unappeased, face warm with rage and vision blurred.

'He's out,' R.J. said, putting a vise-grip on my shoulder. 'Leave 'im be and let's get the fuck outta here.'

Only now did I see the heavy bundle in his hand, a baby blue bed sheet tied into a make-shift, bulging sack.

'Is that—?'

'Yeah. Let's go!'

We ran out the same way we'd come in, both of us laughing like idiots, and almost didn't see O' in the driveway, coming the other way with his own head sheathed in nylon, until we'd trampled him underfoot.

'Hey, what—'

We didn't stop. We just sped right past, saying nothing, taking it for granted the man we thought of as our leader would show the good sense to follow soon enough.

SIXTEEN

What I had told O' about my dietary limitations at R.J.'s funeral a week ago had been true. I couldn't eat the way I used to. High blood pressure had trimmed all the fat and most of the flavor from my daily menu years ago, so that things like sausages and buttered bread were former delicacies of choice I could now only look upon from afar. I've learned to live with the constant deprivation, but there are times I want to break a chair over a waiter's head just to feel a little better about it.

'Are you sure you won't join us?' Frances Burrow asked me again.

I had made the mistake of coming around the house Wednesday morning just as R.J.'s widow and daughter were sitting down to breakfast, and Frances Burrow seemed intent upon sharing their aromatic wealth of bacon, fried eggs and toast with me.

'I'm quite sure, thank you.'

She looked considerably better today than she had two days earlier. Her face was still clouded by grief and you could barely hear her when she spoke, but the robe she'd been wearing into the noon hour on Monday had already been

165

exchanged for real clothes and she was no longer moving like every step could be her last.

We were all sitting at the dining room table. Frances was at one end, with Toni and I on opposing sides of her. Toni was silent and uneasy, watching me warily. All I could do was guess, but I imagined she was fearful of the news I might have come here to deliver, and resentful of the fact I had not shared it with her first, outside her mother's presence.

'You found out something,' Frances Burrow said.

It wasn't so much a question as an expression of thanks for an answered prayer.

'I've learned a thing or two that could be important, but I can't say how much until you and your daughter answer a few questions for me.'

'Of course. Anything.'

She and I both waited for Toni to offer a similar note of encouragement, but all she said was, 'What kind of questions?'

In truth, I was anxious to ask only one, the one I'd been carrying around in my head ever since my meeting the day before with Sylvia Nuez. But rather than ask this question now, looking to satisfy nothing as much as my own gnawing curiosity, I put it off to broach another, more germane subject.

'It's my understanding the police have identified a suspect in R.J.'s murder. Were either of you aware of that?'

Both women said they weren't, Frances

Burrow with some degree of outrage.

'Who is it?' she demanded. 'Has he been arrested yet?'

'Not as of yesterday afternoon. And I can give you his name, but only if you ladies can promise me this conversation will remain strictly between the three of us, at least for the time being. The person who gave me the information made it quite clear that he didn't want the police to find out he'd been talking to me.'

'We understand.'

'No, wait. We don't understand anything,' Toni said. 'How—'

'That's enough,' Frances Burrow said, cutting her daughter a look that carried more force than a slap in the face. 'If he says we have to keep quiet about it, then we'll just have to keep quiet about it.' She turned to me again. 'You have our word, Mr White. Please go on.'

I looked at Toni, hoping she'd give me some small sign that her mother did indeed speak for both of them – but there was nothing on her face to see but embarrassment.

'His name is Darrel Eastman.' I found the notebook I'd been making notes in and opened it up. I'd decided to start mapping out all my questions for people beforehand, rather than try to remember them as I went along. 'He's supposed to be an habitual drug abuser with a long arrest record that R.J. was mentoring somehow. Have either of you ever heard of him?'

Toni Burrow shook her head, but R.J.'s widow hesitated.

'Did you say "Darrel"?'

'That's right. Last name Eastman. You know him?'

'No.' She paused to think, mind reaching backward in time to draw a piece of memory closer to view. 'But I remember Bobby got a call from somebody named Darrel once. He told me it was somebody from work.'

'At Coughlin?'

She nodded. Like me, her daughter was watching her intently now, all interest in being sullen forgotten.

'How long ago was this?'

'Two, three weeks ago, maybe. I was the one who answered the phone. It was just after dinner. Is he a young man?'

'I was told he's twenty-five.'

'Then it must have been him. He asked to speak with Bobby and told me his name was Darrel. Before I could ask what his call was regarding, Bobby walked in, took the phone from my hand, and asked to be left alone.'

'Then you don't know what they talked about.'

'No. I only know the call made my husband very angry. He never got calls from work here at home and he didn't care for the imposition.'

'Hold on a minute,' Toni Burrow said, addressing me. 'Are you saying somebody at Coughlin *did* murder Daddy?'

'No. At least, I don't think so. I was out at Coughlin yesterday, and nobody I spoke to

168

could connect Eastman to Coughlin in any way.'

'Then someone had to be lying to you,' Frances said. Meaning, of course, that R.J.'s word that Eastman's call had been work-related was unassailable in her eyes.

I glanced at Toni, saw a small, wry smile cross her face: Go ahead, it said. Challenge her delusions and see how far you get.

'Did you ask R.J. about the call afterward?'

'Yes, but he wouldn't talk about it. He just said he had to go into the office, and left.'

'Did that happen often? His having to go in after hours?'

'Up until recently, almost never. But in the last year or so, it was happening three or four times a month. That was why he was so angry that night. It was the third time in a week he'd had to work late.'

I hadn't asked Mike Owens or Sylvia Nuez about R.J.'s general work schedule, so I didn't know if overtime was unusual for him or not.

'But you say he didn't usually receive calls at home from work.'

'He didn't. Usually, he either already knew he had to go in and left right after dinner, or worked straight through without ever coming home.'

I paused for a moment, on the threshold of taking R.J.'s widow somewhere I knew she would not care to go. 'Is there any chance he was somewhere other than at Coughlin on any of those occasions?'

169

She looked at me like I was crazy, and her daughter did likewise, but I'd put this line of questioning off long enough. There were things I had to know if I wanted an accurate picture of R.J.'s life just before he died, and I'd never come to know them if I continued to tiptoe around his widow like a dozing bear I was afraid to stir.

'Of course not,' Frances Burrow said, smiling at the absurdity of my question. 'Where else would he have been?'

'Well, like I said, I was told Eastman was somebody R.J. was working with outside of Coughlin. That he was a troubled young man R.J. was trying to help stay straight in some way.'

'I don't understand.'

'Neither do I,' Toni added.

'What I'm suggesting is that R.J. was acting as some sort of surrogate father to Eastman. Perhaps as part of a volunteer program he was involved in or something, I don't know. Would that have been possible?'

'Not without my knowledge,' Frances said.

'But if he was spending more and more time away from home—'

'Who have you been talking to, Mr White, that believes they knew my husband better than I did?'

I chose to answer the question directly. 'One of his co-workers. A woman named Sylvia Nuez.'

'Oh, yes. I know all about Sylvia.'

'You do?'

'Certainly. She's harmless. She was a distraction for Bobby and nothing more.'

I waited for her to explain.

'Their relationship was casual at best. Perhaps even sexual on occasion. But my husband loved me and I loved him, and that's all there is to it. Anything Sylvia Nuez has to say about Bobby is strictly conjecture.'

'Mother, what are you saying?' Toni asked, apparently hearing all this for the first time.

Her mother turned to her, said, 'I'm saying that being with your father all these years involved all kinds of compromises you know nothing about, and leaving him be to spend a few meaningless nights with women like Sylvia Nuez was one of them.' She looked back at me. 'He had only one wife, Mr White, and that was me. I'm the one who knows what he was and wasn't doing, not Sylvia Nuez.'

'Yes, ma'am. But regarding what she said about Darrel Eastman—'

'Bobby wasn't acting as a surrogate father to anyone. He had no interest in that sort of thing, and even if he had, he certainly wouldn't have started with someone like Darrel Eastman, if he's half the criminal you say he is.'

'Mother...' Toni said, seeing the corner R.J.'s widow was painting herself into.

'What? Your father couldn't be near people like that and he knew it. Troubled young drug addicts and street thugs. Even if he thought he could help them, he would have never taken the chance.'

'Then do you understand what you're saying? If Daddy didn't know Eastman from Coughlin, and he didn't know him from some kind of volunteer work he was doing – what else does that leave?'

Frances Burrow surprised me. I was expecting outrage and drama; utensils clashing with china, a harried dash from the room. But all my hostess did was turn to stone.

'No,' she said simply.

I cut Toni off before she could answer. 'All right. Why don't we forget about Eastman for a moment and talk about Cleveland Allen instead.'

Both women looked at me expectantly.

'I understand he was the director of sales at Coughlin when R.J. was the chief of security for that division. R.J.'s supervisor didn't want to talk about him, but Nuez told me Allen was fired ten months ago for violating the company's sexual harassment policy.'

'That isn't true. He was fired for stealing,' Frances said.

'Stealing?'

She nodded her head. 'They told everyone that sexual harassment story just so he could avoid prosecution, but they fired him for embezzlement. He was skimming money off the top of some of his biggest accounts.'

'R.J. told you that?'

'Yes. He felt horrible about it. Mr Allen was the one who got him his first job at Coughlin. If

172

it hadn't been for him, Bobby might never have gotten work after ... after he went away,' she said, almost forgetting for a moment that I wasn't supposed to know about R.J.'s more recent criminal history.

'Did R.J. have anything to do with his termination?'

'No, but Mr Allen thought so. He came to the house once in tears. Drunk. Bobby wouldn't let him in, but they talked out on the porch for almost an hour. Even from the bedroom upstairs, I could hear him begging Bobby to fix it. "You can fix it," he kept saying, over and over. "You can fix it." But there was nothing Bobby could do. He didn't have the power to "fix" anything at Coughlin.'

'Why all these questions about Allen?' Toni asked.

'Yes. I was wondering the same thing,' her mother said.

'Allen committed suicide shortly after his firing. I admit it's a bit of a stretch, but if he blamed R.J. for losing his job – and it sounds like he did – someone he left behind might have held R.J. equally responsible for his death.' I turned to face Frances again. 'What do we know about Allen's family? Did he have adult children?'

'I really couldn't say. Bobby almost never talked about him, and the only time I ever saw Mr Allen was that one time here at the house.'

'I'm sorry, but I still don't understand,' Toni said. 'If this Darrel Eastman killed Daddy, why

173

should we care if Allen's family blamed him for Allen's suicide?'

'If Eastman did kill R.J. and nobody put him up to it? You probably shouldn't care,' I said. 'But until he's in custody and we know those things for certain, we might be wise to consider the possibility that Allen hired him to kill your father.'

Only marginally convinced, R.J.'s daughter nodded in assent.

'I'm not a professional investigator like yourself, so I'm probably paying more attention to some things than they deserve,' I said. 'I just don't want to overlook anything. Or anybody. Take Paris McDonald, for example.'

'Who?' Frances asked.

'Paris McDonald. He's a former boxer doing life up at Pelican Bay who's apparently just become an ordained minister. Sylvia Nuez says R.J. was following the press on him fairly closely just before he died.'

'Why?'

'That's what I was hoping either you or your daughter could tell me this morning. What could R.J.'s interest have been in a man like McDonald?'

'They were friends,' Toni said, matter-of-factly.

I'd heard her perfectly well, but I needed to hear it again to be sure. 'Friends?'

'They were corresponding with each other. I found a letter from McDonald among Daddy's papers the other day, responding to one Daddy

174

had apparently sent to him. It was an invitation to come visit McDonald up at the prison, and I think Daddy may have actually gone. I assumed he was just someone Daddy met and befriended during his time away.'

Her mother shot her a look, seeking to end her loose talk then and there, but Toni said, 'He knows Daddy was once incarcerated, Mother. I told him yesterday.'

Frances Burrow seemed poised to make good on all the fiery histrionics I'd been expecting from her earlier when the doorbell rang. It stopped R.J.'s widow cold, but I barely heard it. The thought of R.J. and Paris McDonald meeting up at Pelican Bay, for any reason whatsoever, would not allow me to focus on anything else.

On the bell's second ring, Toni said, 'I'll go get it,' and rose to leave the room. Frances glowered in my direction for a brief second – I, the overly curious snoop who had somehow weaseled his way into the darkest corners of the Burrow family closet – then hurried off to follow her daughter.

By the time I joined the pair in the living room, Toni was closing the front door behind two men she had just let in: one of them black, one Hispanic, both sporting the weary vigilance and off-the-rack dress-uniform of all plain-clothes detectives everywhere.

Seeing me, the black man, older and larger than his partner, said to Frances Burrow, 'You've got company. Perhaps we should come back later.'

'Nonsense.' She turned to me. 'Handy, these are the policemen working on Bobby's case for us. Detective Saunders' – she nodded toward the black man – 'and Detective Rodriguez. Did I get that right?'

'Yes, ma'am,' both cops murmured in unison.

'This is Handy White, detectives. He's an old family friend of Bobby's from Minnesota who's been trying to help Toni and me get through this very difficult time.'

Saunders just nodded his head, but Rodriguez showed more initiative. 'Trying to help how?' he asked.

'Any way I can,' I said.

'So we hear. You were out trying to help at Coughlin Construction yesterday, weren't you?'

I didn't have to ask how they knew; it would have turned my opinion of Mike Owens upside down if he hadn't ratted me out by week's end.

'That's right. I thought somebody there might remember something useful.'

Saunders, whose refusal to accept the onset of baldness had left his head divided into four separate, feuding islands of gray-speckled hair, decided he didn't want Rodriguez playing cop alone. 'Useful? How do you mean?'

'He means useful to *us*,' Toni said, moving around the room to set herself squarely between the detectives and me. 'Those of us who'd like to see the person or persons who murdered my father put away for good.'

'And you don't think we're trying hard enough to make that happen. Is that it?' Rodriguez asked.

'Not at all,' I said. 'All the lady's trying to say is that we all want the same thing here.'

'I'm sure we do, sir,' Saunders said. 'The thing is, my partner and I are the only ones whose job it is to get it done.'

If he'd been trying to nail the door on the subject shut, he couldn't have done a better job. I had no counter for his argument, and for a long moment, at least, neither did either of the Burrows.

'My daughter and I didn't ask for Mr White's help so he could make your job more difficult, detectives,' Frances said in time. 'But we were concerned that some of the conclusions you seem to have reached about my husband might cause you to take too narrow a view of his murder.'

The two detectives exchanged a glance. Saunders spoke before Rodriguez could: 'We base our views in every case on the evidence at hand, Mrs Burrow. Nothing more.' He directed his attention to me. 'We would appreciate it, Mr White – most especially since you have no legal license to do so – if you would put off any future efforts to play policeman until my partner and I have officially closed our investigation into Mr Burrow's death. That way, it won't be necessary for us to arrest you on the charge of interfering in police business which, I'm sure, would only make these fine ladies feel worse than they already do.'

'The only thing that could make us feel

worse, detective, is another day going by without knowing who killed my husband,' R.J.'s widow said.

'It just so happens, ma'am, that we've come here this morning to tell you that we think we may have found that individual,' Rodriguez said, mustache twitching. 'But I'm afraid that's something we'll have to insist upon discussing with you in private.'

He trained a disdainful gaze upon me, but that wasn't the reason for my sudden unease, nor Toni Burrow's. Out of the corner of my eye, I could see that she, too, was waiting to hear what her mother would say next, and whether it would seal my fate by including some mention of Darrel Eastman's name.

'Don't be ridiculous,' Frances said. 'I've told you, Mr White is a very dear friend. Anything you have to say to me or my daughter about Bobby's murder you can say to him, as well.'

'Mrs Burrow...' Saunders started to protest.

'The detectives are right, Frances,' I said. 'This is a private matter between you and them, and in any case, I was just on my way out.' I turned to Saunders and Rodriguez. 'I'd like to thank you two gentlemen for showing me so much patience. You can rest assured I'll be doing everything I can from here on out to make this meeting our last.'

Rodriguez looked as if he wanted to respond, but he let me go without bothering.

SEVENTEEN

For all the things I'd found different about Los Angeles since I'd left it for St Paul, one thing, at least, had apparently not changed: You still couldn't get to LAX without a fight.

Maybe this wasn't the case back in 1929 when the city fathers turned a wheat field in Westchester into Los Angeles International Airport. Housing in the area had yet to boom and the 405 freeway was over thirty years in the future. But at some point in time, after the airport had become 'freeway close', it also became unreachable, a far island surrounded by motor vehicles that you could neither quickly nor easily approach, day or night. It was that way during all my years as an LA resident, it had been that way two Mondays ago when I'd dropped in for R.J.'s funeral, and that's how it was today, twenty-six years and millions of dollars in obvious attempts to rush traffic along later.

I would not have been making the trip at all had O' not insisted. I would have preferred to be doing almost anything else. But when you called the mayor of Bellwood to insist upon an unscheduled meeting, you had to go wherever his itinerary made it convenient for him to see you. O' had said he was attending a business conference at a hotel outside the airport, and he could give me ten minutes if I could show up in fifteen, so I headed west down Slauson Avenue only minutes after I'd left Frances and Toni Burrow in the hands of the SMPD to see how fast my rented econobox could make the trip.

As I drove, I was struck again by how foreign some parts of the city were to me now. Fox Hills, in particular, had shape-shifted in my absence from little more than a shopping mall to a sprawling mass of industrial and residential complexes. Land nobody used to want had at some point in the last twenty-plus years turned to gold, and seemingly uncontained development had ensued.

I turned south on Sepulveda Boulevard and kept right on rubbernecking, taking in this brave new world with all the slack-jawed wonder of a farm boy who'd never seen a Burger King before. Somewhere just past Centinela, I got careless and drifted out of my lane; I awoke in time to avoid sideswiping a black pickup truck twice my rental car's size, but too late, I was sure, to satisfy one observer: the driver of a distant patrol car reflected in my rear-view mirror.

The car was hanging too far back for me to make out its markings, but the telltale halftone paint job and rooftop light bar were unmistakable.

Men of color like myself, children of urban

180

environments in which the police do not always put justice ahead of the compulsion to mete it out, learn early on to be afraid at moments like this. Our fear is almost never a rational one, but we feel it just the same. We have seen too many men and women in uniform abuse the power they have been given by turning a simple traffic violation into cause for search, seizure and public humiliation – or worse. One minute you're handing over your license and registration, and the next you're lying nose-down in the street, in the rain, waiting for the cops who pulled you over to become convinced they've mistaken you for someone who actually deserves their interest, let alone their contempt. Thus, we see a car with white doors and colored fenders coming and grow stock still, and hope against hope it will reveal itself to be not a police car at all, but a mere imitation, just a squad car lookalike driven by a rent-a-cop from one private security firm or another.

I couldn't yet tell what this one was.

The 9 mm Taurus O's delivery boy had given me the night before was in the rental's glove box. It was a foolish place to keep it, but then, I hadn't asked for a gun just to regret not having it if the need arose to use it. If I got pulled over and the car was searched, I'd spend the night in jail and be sent home, at best. At worst, I'd do some serious time and give R.J.'s widow and daughter one more thing to lose sleep over. In either case, my days as the great defender of R.J.'s memory would be over here and now.

The blue-and-white patrol car, still a half-dozen car lengths back, finally edged out of my lane into the next. I waited for the single occupant – a nebulous uniform shielded behind the glare of the windshield – to hit the lights or the siren, but he did neither. He just kept coming, seemingly content to keep pace with me and nothing more.

If I'd been holding out any last hope to this point that the cop and I would never meet, getting rear-ended at the next major intersection relieved me of this notion entirely. The collision wasn't much more than a tap, but it had been just hard and noisy enough to make ignoring it unrealistic. I looked up into my rear-view and saw a middle-aged Asian in a loud checkered shirt cursing his own stupidity as he got out of his car to check the damage. I didn't want to, but I pushed my own door open to join him.

He was chattering something about spilling a drink as we came together at the point of impact. He was apologizing profusely, seeking both my mercy and full attention, but I gave him neither. I was too busy watching the blue-and-white cruiser behind him complete an abrupt U-turn in the middle of the street and race off into the distance.

It wasn't something I'd never seen a cop do before; uniforms in patrol cars often changed direction without warning, lights and siren off, like a kid on a new tricycle. Still, I had to wonder.

Was it the hassle of taking an accident report that had sent this policeman running, or me?

'You don't have that thing on you right now, do you?'

O' was looking me over carefully.

'What thing?'

'That thing you asked me to find for you yesterday.'

We were less than a mile from LAX, walking around the block along Century Boulevard after I'd drawn him away from the conference he was attending at the Crowne Plaza Hotel, and he wanted to make sure he wasn't running the risk of being caught fraternizing with a man who had a 9 mm semi-automatic in his pocket.

'No,' I said, shaking my head.

'I'd give you hell about being late, except for the fact you're doing me a favor, getting me away from that bore-fest back in there. Forty-five public servants sitting around a banquet room talking about "Controlling the IT Costs of the Modern Municipal Infrastructure". Can you believe that shit?'

I told him about the small fender-bender that had held me up.

'You OK? Nobody got hurt?'

'Everybody's fine. The cars, too.'

'This shit must be pretty important. You call my private number less than twenty-four hours after I give it to you, then damn near kill your-self trying to make a meeting. What's going on?'

I stopped walking so he'd be forced to deal with the news head-on.

'He was talking to Paris McDonald, O',' I said.

'R.J.?'

'His daughter said they were exchanging letters. He might have even visited McDonald in prison.'

'Bullshit. Why the hell would he do that?'

'Because McDonald invited him up.'

'McDonald didn't even know him.'

'He wasn't supposed to. But maybe something happened to change that.'

We were standing directly under the airport's incoming flight patterns, and monstrous jets were scraping the sky just over our heads every few minutes, howling loud enough to unseat teeth. O' waited for the latest one to go by, then said, 'Let's keep moving,' and started walking again.

'Have you seen these letters they allegedly wrote to each other?'

'There's only supposed to be one. But no, not yet.'

'Then we don't know who contacted who first.'

'Does it matter?'

'Of course it matters. If R.J. made first contact, it's possible he never told McDonald anything. But if McDonald found *him* first, that can only mean McDonald knows the works. About R.J., about us – everything.'

'Except R.J.'s the only one dead,' I said, and

then quickly added, 'so far.'

'Which is all the more reason to believe we've got nothing to worry about. You seen any more of your boy from the bar?'

I shook my head.

'Well, there you go.'

'Assuming he's the one I need to be looking out for, and I'm not so sure that he is. Unless his name is Darrel Eastman.'

'Darrel Eastman?'

I told him who Eastman was, and of the call Frances Burrow had said R.J. might have taken from him at the house one night, pausing every two dozen words or so to let a jet aircraft roar past.

'How come I'm not surprised?' O' said.

'What's that supposed to mean?'

'It means this Eastman fits the cops' theory and mine of R.J.'s murder to a T, and R.J. knew him. Brother drove out to the beach with a lowlife acquaintance to get high and got jacked. Damn, Handy, how much more evidence of that do you need?'

'It's a nice theory, O', but it doesn't explain everything. Like how it is he got himself killed within weeks of hooking up with the last man any of us should have ever wanted to see. You telling me that was just a coincidence?'

'It's not a very likely one, I'll admit, but it's possible. Is Eastman in custody yet?'

'Not as of yesterday, but things could be different today. I was by to see the Burrow women this morning and the detectives working R.J.'s case came around just as I was leaving.'

'Do we know what this Eastman looks like, at least?'

'No.'

'Then he and your friend from the bar could be one and the same.'

'Could be. But how would Eastman have latched on to me, and why? Why target me before you?'

'Maybe because I've been keeping my nose out of R.J.'s murder, and you haven't?'

It was a small dig, but a deep one.

'You still think I should be back home, waiting for them to come to me?'

'What "them"? Right now, as far as we know, Eastman was a lone gunman, and even that hasn't been proven yet.'

'And McDonald?'

'When you can tell me what was in this letter you say he wrote R.J., or connect him with either Eastman or whoever it was that spooked you so bad the other night, we can talk about McDonald. Until then, I don't see any point in either of us losing sleep over the poor bastard.' He checked his watch, just as he had the last time we'd seen each other and he'd grown tired of my company. 'I've gotta be getting back. Anything else I should know about?'

If for no other reason than to be thorough, I told him about Cleveland Allen. He didn't find much to get excited about in that line of discussion, either.

'This guy Arlen blames R.J. for getting

canned, so when he offs himself, his wife or somebody has R.J. whacked in retaliation?' O' shook his head. 'That's pretty damn weak, Handy.'

'I never said it wasn't. But you asked what I've been hearing and thinking, so I told you. And the man's name was "Allen", by the way.'

We hurried through what remained of our tour of the block and parted ways at the hotel entrance where we'd started.

'Tell me something, O',' I said. 'What color are the cruisers for the Bellwood PD?'

He looked at me quizzically. 'Say what?'

'Would they happen to be blue and white?'

'They're blue and white, yeah. But what about it?'

'Your friend Walt Fine would not have any reason to be following me around, now would he?'

'Fine? Hell, no. Jesus, now you think Fine's been following you?'

'Just asking the question, O'. No need to get excited about it.'

He wanted to pursue the matter further, but he could see I would have left him to do so alone if he had.

'Try to get hold of that letter, Handy,' he said. 'Whether it had anything to do with R.J.'s murder or not, you and I need to know what he and McDonald could have been writing to each other about. Don't you think?'

Without waiting for an answer, he turned, the automatic lobby doors moving aside for him like servants before their master, and disappeared inside the hotel.

I hadn't slept well Tuesday night. I'd been too worried about Coral. She still wasn't answering her cellphone and, since yesterday morning, had not attempted to call my own. The only reason I wasn't completely panic-stricken was that I hadn't heard from Susan Yancy either, who had promised me she'd let me know if my daughter managed to contact her.

I had led Coral to believe that Susan was her mother, and that had been a lie. I had used Susan's photograph as a prop, something to lend physical credence to the elaborate fable I had invented to slake my daughter's thirst for knowledge of her past, never guessing that someday, Coral might prove resourceful enough to connect that photograph to the woman who'd posed for it almost thirty years before.

Now the bill for this foolish deceit was coming due, and 1,900 miles away from home, my only hope of controlling the damage was by proxy. It wasn't a fair burden to keep placing on my friend Quincy, but there was no one else to ask.

He was having lunch at the shop when I called immediately after my meeting with O'. I could hear the big man chewing throughout our conversation.

'Pizza from Captain Jack's?' I asked.

'Turkey burger. No cheese. Doc says I've

188

gotta lose ten pounds by the end of February.'
He paused to take a swallow of some kind of
drink. 'That lady call you yet? Ms Yancy?'

'Yesterday.'

'Good. To tell you the truth, I didn't think she
would. She really don't like you, brother.'

'No. That's true enough. Was she hard to
find?'

'A little. She wasn't at that address you gave
me, and the people who were never heard of
her. Information didn't have nothin' on her,
either. But I got a friend works at the Post
Office, you remember Dante Daniels? The one
comes in here wearing all that silver?'

I told him I did. Daniels had more rings on his
fingers than most people had teeth in their
mouth.

'Well, he got me another address for her, up in
Linden Hills, and he gave me her married name
too: It's Pilgrim now. That's how I finally found
her number in the book.'

I was encouraged to hear all this, but unsure
of how much I should be. It sounded as if
finding Susan Pilgrim might prove too difficult a task for Coral herself to accomplish
before I could get home to stop her, which was
just the way I wanted it. But this was only a fair
assumption to make if she had no greater
informational resources at her disposal than
Quincy, and that seemed highly doubtful. Coral
had already found an old photograph of 'Susan
Yancy' at the library, probably by using a computer to search the Internet, and for all I knew,

another hour or two of similar computer work could link that photograph to 'Susan Pilgrim' a dozen different ways.

'I can't let Coral find her, Quincy,' I said. 'And I can't come home until my business here is finished.'

'What do you need me to do, Handy?'

I told him he had to go find Coral and get her to call me, even if he had to dial my number and put the phone up to her ear himself.

'No problem. Where do you want me to look for her?'

I gave him all the contact info for Coral I had, and told him to try her first at work. The last time we spoke, she'd told me she had just started a new job without offering any details, but I figured someone at her old place of employment might have an idea where she'd gone.

'They probably won't want to talk to you, for security reasons and all that, but—'

'Hold on, Handy,' Quincy said abruptly.

'What?'

'You ain't gonna believe this, but she just walked in.'

'Coral?'

He didn't answer. He wasn't there. I called his name several times, pulse building, but all there was at the other end of the line was silence. Then I heard muffled voices and another long stretch of nothing. Too long.

'Hello?'

It was Coral. Sounding angry and distraught.

'Coral! Girl, where the hell have you been?'

'I didn't come here to talk to you, Handy. I came here to talk to him.'

'Quincy? What for?'

'I want him to tell me where she is. I know he knows.'

'No, he doesn't. Leave Quincy out of this.'

'You're not going to stop me, Handy. You don't have to help me if you don't want to, but you're not going to stop me.'

'OK. OK,' I said, convinced that to do anything else but give in to her at this point would just send her running off again. 'You want the truth about your mother, I'll tell you the truth. But not now. Not like this. When I get back home, we'll sit down and talk, and anything you want to know, I'll tell you.'

'Is Susan Yancy my mother? You can at least tell me that much now.'

'No. If I answer that question, I'll end up answering fifty, and I don't want to have this conversation over the phone.'

She mulled over my offer.

'So when will you be back?'

'Two, three days at the most. I'll call you the minute I get back, I promise.'

There was another long pause as she decided how much this latest of all my promises to her was worth.

'All right,' she said. 'I'll give you three days. If I don't hear from you by Sunday—'

'Monday,' I cut in.

'Monday. Fine. If I don't hear from you by

then, I'm not ever going to ask you about this again. I'm just going to find out what I need to know on my own, no matter how long it takes. I'm serious, Handy.'

'And in the meantime, you're going to leave this thing alone. You aren't going anywhere near Susan Yancy or anybody else to talk about this.'

'Agreed,' she said, if only after a while.

It was a bargain I regretted immediately. But it bought me four days.

Four days to focus on R.J.'s murder without the distraction of fearing for my daughter's sobriety, if not her life, throughout, and four days to figure out what I was going to tell her when I got home. That I would have to tell her the truth was finally a given.

What wasn't was how I could possibly speak it so that it didn't leave her with a heart that would never heal.

EIGHTEEN

Being Excel Rucker's second cousin, Paris McDonald knew a few things about him that O', R.J. and I never figured out on our own, for all the time we followed the dealer around prior to ripping him off. Most of these things were of little import, but one proved to be anything but: Excel was a devoted family man.

Over the four weeks in which we had him under surveillance, we had seen him interact with women and children, of course, some of whom he'd even shown some serious affection for. But he was a player who lived alone, and he shared his bed with more than a few female partners, so the idea that he had a wife and children somewhere never really occurred to us.

Paris McDonald knew that Excel had both. Though the woman was his wife by common law alone, she was the mother of his only acknowledged offspring, two sons and a daughter, and she lived with all three in a tiny two-bedroom house out in Hollywood. The boys were in early adolescence but the girl was just a little thing, not even old enough for kindergarten.

I myself had seen them all at least once. I had trailed Excel to their home one night and watched from a distance as he came and went in the space of three hours. The woman – tall, busty and seriously Afroed – had come to the door alone upon his arrival, but all the kids had poured out of the house with her to send him off when he left, just before midnight. He gave each of the boys a long, soulful handshake, kissed the woman full on the mouth, and took the little girl up in his arms to bury his face in her throat, sending her into hysterics.

Her beauty took my breath away.

The scene was perfectly befitting a man bidding his family goodnight, yet I failed to make the connection that evening, and only made it days later after circumstances forced me to view everything I had seen the dealer say or do in a different light. Despite the puerile nature of his trade, Excel Rucker was a man with many lovers and friends, and few people he called upon while I or my friends were watching ever treated him with much more affection than the four he visited that night – and that night alone – in Hollywood.

Knowing who and what they were to Rucker would not have changed a thing for my friends and me, in any case. With family or without, he would have been the same target to us. The trouble we planned to cause him was not supposed to affect anyone but the man himself, and right up until the moment – two days after the Inglewood robbery – we discovered that someone else had chosen that same week to bring Excel Rucker to his knees, there was no way we could foresee how it could.

Our take from the Inglewood safe house heist was just over 140,000 dollars, and that was only the cash. We counted it four times to be certain. Going in, we had thought we might get sixty, maybe seventy grand at best, plus another twenty or thirty in coke. We were wrong on both counts.

O' bought a second-hand scale at a flea market and we weighed the stolen blow at a kilo and a half. We figured that to be worth about seventy-five Gs on the street. To my surprise, none of us touched an ounce of it, nor suggested that we do so; our resolve to flush every gram, as near as I could tell, remained resolute.

For two days, while the money and coke sat hidden away in a locked storage bin in the back of O's mother's garage, the three of us vacillated between laugh-out-loud giddiness and abject terror, proud of ourselves one minute, frozen stiff with fear the next. We had put a serious hurt on Excel Rucker, to be sure, and it was both exhilarating and terrifying to try and predict how he would react to the insult.

The vengeance I'd been seeking on Olivia Gardner's behalf had been exacted, and it felt good to know it, to warm my heart by the fire of the ridiculous notion that I had somehow made the world a more just place because of what I'd done. But I wasn't satisfied. Satisfaction would only come later, after I had seen some concrete evidence of Excel's suffering, and could rest assured that the scars we had left him with would not soon fade away.

That he would come looking for us had always been a given, so we had planned ahead to be ready. There was a club he liked to frequent on Century Boulevard called the Lazy Duck, where everyone knew his name and he was catered to like a visiting dignitary. Talk flowed freely in the joint, so we staked it out, thinking it was as good a place as any to listen out for word of the robbery and Excel's response to it. O' spent a few hours in there the night immediately following the Inglewood heist, and I went in the night after that.

O's report held few surprises. The club that first night had been buzzing with exaggerated stories of 'four' niggas ripping Excel off to the tune of 'a half-million' even before the dealer himself stormed in to offer a 10,000 dollar reward to anyone who could tell him where to find the motherfuckas who'd jacked over his people and stolen his money. Both the reward and his level of outrage – which O' later described as profound, if not particularly electric – were right in line with our expectations.

The following night, however, I saw a somewhat different Lazy Duck.

'Something's not right,' I said when we all hooked up down in R.J.'s basement the next morning. We were determined to do everything

196

in secret now, even to the point of taking all physical contact with each other underground.

'Not right?' R.J. asked, immediately agitated.

'He didn't come in the whole night, and nobody's talking about the robbery anymore. At least, not so I could hear.'

'So?'

'So I should've been hearing *more* talk about it, not less. It was like something else was on everyone's mind.'

'Something like what? Spell it out, Handy,' O' said.

I told them what I'd seen: a house full of people in a mood as black as death, not shouting to be heard over toned-down music but whispering conspiratorially beneath it, and then only in brief, isolated exchanges.

'You think they were on to you?' O' asked.

I shook my head. 'It wasn't about me. It was about fear. I think they were all afraid.'

After a beat, R.J. said, 'Maybe Excel's been goin' off. Talkin' about killin' niggas at random or somethin' crazy like that if he don't find the ones who ripped him off.'

'If that were the case, he would've been in there saying so. Him, or one of his people.'

'He's right,' O' said. 'Man comes in to raise hell one night, then doesn't even send somebody around to do the same the next? It don't add up. Till he finds us or his money, or both, he should be kicking down a hundred doors a day, personally.'

'So what are we supposed to do?' R.J. asked.

'We don't do anything. We just stick to the plan. Minimize all contact and stay away from anyplace Excel's people might see us. Especially you two. In the meantime, I'll do some checking around, see if I can't find out what the fuck is going on.'

Neither R.J. nor I asked him how he intended to go about it. O' knew a lot of people we didn't, and he was as protective of their names and occupations as a narc of his prize snitches.

'You better be careful who you talk to,' R.J. told him, in a rare instance of his playing advisor to his old friend, rather than the other way around. 'Wrong people find out you been askin' questions 'bout Excel, it could get back to 'im.'

'I think we all better be careful,' I said. I hadn't really given much thought to being afraid up to now, but the vibe at the Lazy Duck the night before had shaken me up, like a bad dream overrun by the living dead.

Something just wasn't right.

'What was it?' Toni Burrow asked.

'The letter first,' I said.

It was the deal we had made over the phone: She'd let me see the letter Paris McDonald had written her father if I told her why I needed to read it. It was the second time in as many hours I'd been forced to grin and bear the short end of a woman's hard bargain. First Coral, now Toni. Some days are just like that for a man, I guess.

We were sitting on a bench at Leimert Village

198

Park, not far from her mother's house, taking in the shade of a sycamore tree that was ringed by a handful of people sprawled out on the grass, dozing or chatting or sipping from a container sheathed in brown paper. I didn't tell Toni, but the little park – really no more than a wedge-shaped island of grass stuck in the heart of a small but resilient patch of retail shops in the Crenshaw district – was the place where her father, O' and I had said our final goodbyes more than twenty-five years before. At a few minutes after one on a Wednesday afternoon, the park and its environs looked completely different from the way I remembered them, and yet exactly the same. It was as if the names on all the signage had changed, but the buildings they were attached to had not. Unlike Fox Hills, developers had seen no need to change the face of the earth here, and their neglect was both a blessing and a curse that had left the area just as quaint, and economically anemic, as ever.

I did not want to tell Toni Burrow the rest of my story. I was certain I had told her too much already. But O's suggestion that I find out what was in the letter Paris McDonald had written to R.J. – if in fact such a letter did exist – had served no purpose other than to reinforce my own thinking in the matter. I would have liked to have learned more about Darrel Eastman first, but since I couldn't imagine how I might go about it without involving the police, gaining access to McDonald's letter was my next most logical move.

Naturally, I had initially balked at Toni Burrow's terms for showing me the letter; I had kept the secret she was demanding I share with her for more years than she'd been alive, for her father's sake almost as much as my own. But I had also promised her the day before that I would not ask for her help again without explaining my reasons for needing it, and I knew she would hold me to my word.

Up until now, as I had described her father's complicity in a twenty-six-year-old armed robbery, she had reacted with little surprise or wringing of hands. She had allowed me to tell the tale my way, without interruption, as if she were listening to a man speak of things she had always understood to be true. But she had not heard the worst of it yet, not by a long shot, and even this far in, more than halfway into the telling, I was searching for some way to skirt around my story's end to spare her the knowledge of it.

She haggled over the letter for a while, hesitant to trust that I would go on talking once she'd given up the one thing she had to bargain with, but eventually, she reached into her purse and produced it.

It was sheathed in a white, business-size envelope addressed to 'Mr Robert Burrow'. The envelope was weathered and worn and folded vertically down the middle, like something R.J. might have been carrying around in a pocket or inside his wallet, and it bore the postmark – dated that September 11th – of

Pelican Bay Penitentiary in Crescent City, California.

Inside was a single sheet of lined, yellow paper, one side blank, the other scrawled upon in the small, delicate handwriting of a monk. The date at the top preceded the one on the postmark by three days, and this is how the letter read:

Dear Brother Burrow:

I thank you for your letter of Sept. 3. It was good to hear how much my story has encouraged you to make your own peace with God. Though your sins may be great, He will forgive them all, as He has forgiven mine, if you will only ask. But you are afraid, and that is understandable. Perhaps you would like to visit me here at the penitentiary sometime soon so that we can pray for you together? Let me know, and I will try to arrange it. No man is beyond redemption. If someone like me can be saved, so can you.

Your Friend in Christ,
Paris McDonald

Toni Burrow let me read the letter several times without interruption before she found my silence unbearable.

'Well?'

I wasn't sure what to make of it. It was reassuring on some fronts, ominous on others. It did seem to confirm that R.J. had reached out to McDonald first, voiding O's concern that the reverse had been true because McDonald knew us all. But the letter also served to prove that my old friend had written McDonald out of some desperate need to seek forgiveness – forgiveness for something McDonald may have consequently heard R.J. confess to in person, up at Pelican Bay.

'This was all you could find? There was no copy of R.J.'s letter to him?'

'No. I've looked everywhere. What does it mean, Handy? What does that letter, or Paris McDonald, have to do with my father's murder?'

'If this was as far as their contact ever went, probably nothing.'

'But it wasn't. I've already told you, Daddy went up there to see him.'

Much to my dismay, she'd found a credit card statement that indicated R.J. had bought a round-trip airline ticket to Crescent City for the twenty-seventh, twelve days after the date of McDonald's letter and only three days before R.J.'s murder. The statement alone didn't prove Toni's father had actually made the trip, and neither the airlines nor the authorities at Pelican Bay would ever confirm such a thing without a court order, even to a private investigator, but Mike Owens at Coughlin had told her R.J. had called in sick that day and her mother had no memory of him being at home.

'McDonald was this "Excel Rucker's" cousin, you said. The dealer you all robbed. Daddy visited him for a reason, and that reason got him killed.'

'No.'

'We had a deal, Handy. You promised to tell me everything.'

'There's no relevance to the rest of it. At least, not yet.'

'We had a deal,' she said again.

And we did. That was the inescapable fact of the matter. She had held up her end of our bargain, and now it was my turn to hold up mine. It was either that, or prove myself a liar she could never trust again.

'Do you remember what you told me yesterday about your mother? That she only *thinks* she wants to know the truth about your father, because she can't believe the truth could be all that terrible?'

'I remember.'

'Well, you were right. She really doesn't want to know.' I shook my head, issuing a final warning. 'And neither do you.'

I was trying to frighten her, and I did. I could see it in the way her gaze upon me softened up, and the little breath she had to take before she could speak. But it didn't matter. She wasn't the kind to let something go just because it scared the hell out of her.

'Tell me,' she said.

So I did.

I'd come back to Los Angeles following R.J.'s funeral in pursuit of a pipe dream, the preposterous belief that I could involve myself in the fallout from my old friend's murder just enough to keep the past in the past. But it couldn't be done. I could see that now. Wheels had been set in motion that would eventually, inexorably bring what R.J., O' and I had done twenty-six years ago to light, and I no longer had the hubris nor the energy to fight it.

I could maybe reduce the damage the revelation would do, but that was all.

I knew the news was bad the moment I heard O's voice. Even over the phone, he always sounded as unflappable as a stone – but not today. Today, less than twenty-four hours after I'd last seen him down in R.J.'s basement, he sounded like somebody who'd just watched a mushroom cloud paint the far horizon red.

'We've got real trouble, Handy,' he said.

'What kind of trouble?'

'You were right about all those people at the club the other night being afraid. That's exactly what they were. But not for reasons that have anything to do with us. At least, not directly.'

I waited for the hammer to drop.

'Somebody snatched his little girl,' O' said.

'What?'

'His daughter. He's got a daughter somewhere and somebody grabbed her, late Saturday night. They think it might've been his cousin Paris, that big motherfucka he uses as a bodyguard sometimes.'

'You talking about Excel?'

'Man, who the fuck else would I be talking

about? You're goddamn right, Excel.'

All the rest of it spilled out of him then, like bile he could no longer keep down. The little girl was four years old, her name was Sienna Jackson, and somebody who'd cut the screen off her bedroom window and stolen her from her mother's house three nights ago was demanding a half-million dollars from Excel for her safe return. It would have been a difficult amount of scratch for the dealer to raise under the best of circumstances, but only days after a pair of thieves had taken him for over 200 grand, it had to be all but unattainable.

'We have to give it back,' I said. A stone was growing hard and cold at the pit of my stomach and my throat was as dry as dust.

'The money?'

'Everything. The money, the drugs...'

'It's too late for that. He had a deadline of midnight last night to pay up. The girl's probably already dead.'

'Fuck that. Man ain't gonna kill his own niece,' I said.

'If this fool Paris is the one who did it, they say he could do that and a lot worse. Nigga's crazy on his best day, and Excel put a bonfire under his ass, slapped him around last week in front of a house full'a women for giving him some attitude. He ain't been seen or heard from since.'

'That doesn't mean he snatched the girl.'

'Let me ask you something, Handy: Did you know Excel had a daughter? I didn't, and I bet

R.J. doesn't, either. Only the people closest to him know about it, most likely, and whoever took the girl not only knew who she was, they knew where she lived. It *had* to be the cousin.'

'OK, so maybe it was. That doesn't change anything. We still have to get that money and blow back to Excel.'

'How? Go back to his crib in Inglewood and leave the shit on the porch? Ain't nobody left alive back there, Handy. Excel's killed everybody in the whole goddamn house.'

'Say what?'

'The man's lost his mind. He can't pay the ransom, and he's jackin' up anybody and everybody he thinks is responsible. That's why it was so damn quiet at the club the other night – he's going off in all directions, and nobody knows what the nigga's gonna do next.'

I told him it didn't matter. We had to return Excel's money, and fast. There was nothing we could do to help the people we had robbed in Inglewood, but God willing, we might still have time to save the girl.

O' and I hashed out a rough plan for dropping the drugs and money where Excel could retrieve them in a way that involved little risk of exposure, then tried to reach R.J. by phone to bring him into the discussion for the first time. O' had waited until now to alert him to the situation, knowing how badly the news of the child's kidnapping was going to mess with his head; already having some idea how we might reverse our tragic error when we talked to him would help diminish R.J.'s immediate impulse to do something reckless or self-destructive – or both.

But R.J. was nowhere to be found.

He was supposed to be sitting tight just like O' and I had been, straying from his phone at home only to do those things that would most mimic his regular routine, but in the course of two hours, we called him four times without reaching him. We left two messages with his mother, who claimed total ignorance of his whereabouts, and hung up twice when his mumbling, black-hearted father answered the phone instead.

'Goddamn that fool,' O' said, livid.

We decided to make the drop without him. Time was too precious to waste, and in truth, neither of us believed R.J.'s opinion or approval was required for us to do what needed to be done.

But when we arrived at O's mother's place, R.J. was there waiting for us, pacing the front porch like a junky in a bad way. He knew. His face was hard set in a scowl laced with fear and when he came down the walk to greet us, I had to wonder just how far over the edge his mind had slipped.

'Man, where the fuck have you been?' O' snapped, before R.J. could get his mouth open to speak.

'To hell with that. Have you—'

'I asked you a question, nigga!'

It never ceased to amaze me how O' and O'

alone could use this tone with R.J. and make him snap to attention, rather than throw a punch that could break the cap off a fire hydrant. 'I went out to get somethin' to eat. Ain't shit back home in the fridge. You fools heard what's goin' down? About Excel's kid?'

'We heard,' I said.

'Shit, what're we gonna do? They say—'

O' raised his hand, said, 'We can't talk about it out here. Let's get in the garage.'

The garage facing a back alley was O's exclusive sanctuary here. His older sister Marion had taken over his old bedroom when he'd moved out of the house five months before, so to maintain a place to chill at his mother's, he'd taken over the garage. It was too cluttered with junk and storage boxes to actually accommodate a car, so his mother had never found much use for it. O' had put padlocks on all the doors and furnished the interior with an old convertible couch, small-screen black-and-white TV, and a component stereo system notable only for its laughably mismatched speakers.

'I wanna know what the hell we're gonna do,' R.J. said, the minute we all made it inside. He wasn't crying now, but his eyes were ringed with fire, a sure sign that he'd been doing so earlier.

'The only thing we can do,' O' said. 'Give Excel his shit back and hope it ain't too late.'

'But it *is* too late!'

'Says who? You know something we don't?'

I asked.

'I know the man had till last night to pay up, and he didn't. He couldn't. And the nigga who took the girl don't play.'

'His cousin?'

'Word's all over the street, I couldn't go no-where without hearin' how crazy this mother-fucka is.'

'They know it was him for sure?' O' asked.

R.J. nodded. 'They say he came right out and admitted it the last call he made askin' for the ransom.' He shook his head from side to side, trying to find the sense in it. 'That little girl's dead, and we're the ones who killed her. Am I right? We all clear on that? We're the ones killed her.'

He was looking directly at me.

'Fuck that,' O' said angrily. 'We haven't killed anybody. Till somebody tells us other-wise, we've gotta assume the child's still alive and operate accordingly. And that means stop all this fuckin' around and get Excel's shit back to him as fast as we can.'

'Yeah? How?'

O' ran the plan he and I had come up with down for him: drop the money and drugs in a dumpster somewhere, then let Excel know where to find them as soon as we could get him on the phone personally.

R.J. was shaking his head again before O' could even finish, said, 'There ain't time for all that. We could be waitin' hours just to get Excel on the phone!'

'You have a better idea?'

'No, but that shit ain't gonna work. We gotta come up with somethin' else.'

'He's right,' I said. O' turned, surprised. 'The deadline's come and gone and Excel knows now this man Paris is the kidnapper. With half the world out looking for him, Paris isn't going to fuck around. He's going to do whatever he's going to do with the girl and jet.'

'If he ain't already,' R.J. said.

'The only prayer we have of saving the girl, if she's still alive, is finding Paris ourselves and paying him off directly.'

'What? That's crazy,' O' said.

'Maybe so. But I don't see what else we can do. And we sure as hell can't just sit around here and do nothing.'

'Damn straight,' R.J. said.

'You're both trippin',' O' said. 'Every nigga in the city's out lookin' for this fool Paris, you just said so yourself, Handy. Even if he was willing to deal with us, we'd never find him before Excel does.'

'You're the man with all the connections,' I said. 'Maybe the same people who tipped you to the kidnapping could tell you where Paris is hiding.'

'Ain't no need for that. I think I know,' R.J. said.

O' shot him a skeptical look. 'Say what?'

'This Paris – he's the big brother with the beard and tiny eyes, right?'

'The man Excel was always leaving outside

the door everywhere they went, yeah. So?'

'So I followed him once. One night when I was watchin' Excel. I was thinkin' about boostin' his ride.'

'His ride?' I asked.

'Yeah, you know – he's the one drives that '69 Riv with the gold wire rims. Emerald green, cherried to the max. I was thinkin' about liftin' it, so I followed him to the crib. Only, he didn't go to the crib, 'less the nigga lives way the hell out in Simi Valley.'

'Simi Valley?' O' repeated incredulously. In those days, over a decade before a jury there would set the cops who beat Rodney King free and, consequently, the heart of Los Angeles on fire, the Ventura County city R.J. was referring to was little more than a suburb in the making, all arid hills and model homes for housing tracts years away from completion. A place, in short, where black people like Paris McDonald were as scarce as thirty-story high-rises.

'I couldn't believe it, either,' R.J. said. 'I damn near turned around before he stopped. But after a while, I got curious – like, where the hell was homeboy goin'?'

He didn't bother to explain why O' and I had never heard any of this before, and neither of us asked the question, because the answer was so painfully obvious: How could he tell us about a joyride he'd taken out to Simi Valley on a night he was supposed to have been watching Excel Rucker?

'So where *did* he go?' O' asked, growing

impatient now.

'Some white girl's house out there. Funky little place with a wagon wheel by the door and shit all over the yard. She was sittin' out on the porch, smokin' and waitin' for him, when he showed up.'

'And?'

'And what? They went inside and I left, soon as the lights went out.'

'That's it?'

'That's it. I looked the Riv over a little first, to see what kind'a alarm he had on it, then I raised up. I bet he's out there now, with Excel's little girl.'

The garage fell still as O' thought it over. Eventually, he turned to me and asked, 'What do you think?'

'I think if I was a brother looking for somewhere to hide, and a place to hold somebody hostage where she'd be hard as hell to find, a crib that far out in the boonies wouldn't be a bad choice,' I said. 'It's for damn sure the last place I would've thought to look for him.'

O' nodded in agreement. 'Yeah. That's what I'm thinking, too.' He looked over at R.J. 'Can you find this place again?'

'Absolutely,' R.J. said.

We were all going to ride out to Simi together, until R.J.'s Dodge took four tries to start. With its engine idling like somebody had poured sand down the carburetor, O' looked back at me from the front seat and said, 'I don't like it.'

He was right. If we went all the way out there to that white girl's house and needed to leave in a hurry, and R.J.'s Monaco refused to turn over...

'You want me to drive?'

'Yeah. Hell, yes.'

He opened his door to get out and then I remembered. 'Wait up.'

'What?'

'I'm low on gas. We'd have to stop first.'

'Fuck!'

'Hell, man! I wasn't counting on driving to Simi goddamn Valley tonight.'

O' blew out a deep sigh. The fools he had to put up with...

'All right. If we could trust this piece of shit to get us there and back, we'd all go together, but we can't. And we can't wait around for you to gas up, neither, so me and R.J. are gonna go on ahead while you get gas, then follow us out.' He looked to R.J. 'Can you tell him how to get where we're goin'?'

For a man who'd probably only seen the names of the streets and freeway exits involved one time in his life, R.J. did an admirable job of giving me directions. My chances of getting lost were better than I would have preferred but there was nothing to be done about it; we needed my car for backup, just as O' had said, and we didn't have time to waste pumping gas.

I climbed out of the Monaco without another word and my two friends took off. I crossed the street and started back down the block to where my Fairmont sedan was parked. It wasn't until I was inside the car, about to pull the driver's side door closed behind me, that I saw another living soul. A hand reached out of nowhere to grab my shoulder and the long barrel of a revolver met my gaze when I spun around.

'I'm lookin' for a nigga named O'Neal Holden,' Excel Rucker said.

NINETEEN

If in fact, only three days before his death, R.J. had flown out to Pelican Bay Penitentiary to make his peace with Paris McDonald, he was not alone in wanting to do so. I had been playing with the idea myself for years.

There was no one else left to seek forgiveness from, and seeing McDonald to make a full confession promised the only form of closure I could ever hope to find. But how would such a meeting play out? What would it accomplish? These were questions I couldn't answer, no more than R.J. could have, and it was the not knowing that kept me away, day after day, year after year, as shackled to my oath of silence as ever.

And then R.J. died. From the moment Frances Burrow called to inform me of his passing, I had taken the news as a sign that my own end was near, and that God or the devil – one or the other – had finally given me the excuse I'd been waiting for to unburden my soul before the one person who could save it, consequences be damned.

Thus I had opened a desk drawer in my home two days before R.J.'s funeral, withdrawn the letter from Pelican Bay Penitentiary I'd received and set aside months prior, and submitted my official request to visit an inmate there named Paris McDonald.

I didn't give too much thought to what I would do if my request was granted. Maybe I'd go, and maybe I wouldn't. I was only interested in having the option. I had a feeling my life was about to move in highly abrupt and unpredictable ways, and if I were somehow called to take a meeting with McDonald – if fate and circumstance left me no other alternative – I wanted to be capable.

Now, eleven days after I'd placed my visitation papers in the mail back in St Paul, I no longer had to wonder if there'd been any point. I had reason to believe that R.J. had already met with Paris McDonald himself, and I couldn't help but suspect that the nature of their conversation held the key to R.J.'s murder. I could go on with my amateurish attempts at homicide investigation pretending otherwise, but I would only be fooling myself, seeking to avoid something as certain and inescapable as gravity.

What terrors might be waiting for me in the

prison town of Crescent City, California, I couldn't say. I only knew that, when and if I received clearance to visit Paris McDonald at Pelican Bay Penitentiary, it was a journey I would have little choice but to make.

I had no right to expect it, but Toni Burrow agreed to go on helping me in whatever ways she could. Knowing now what she did, she could not have been faulted for cutting me off without another word; I had taken what she had always believed about her father and turned it upside down, enlarging all the bad and reconstituting the good, so that the man she was left to remember must have felt like something she had only imagined. She was angry and hurt, as victims of great deceptions always are, and she made little effort to conceal how much of her rage was reserved for me.

But I was not the one she hated most.

Before we parted ways at Leimert Village Park, I asked her to get me a current address for Cleveland Allen's survivors. Something her mother had said that morning was bothering me, and I couldn't shake it loose.

Frances Burrow said the night Allen had come by the house to see R.J., he had seemed to believe her husband could get him his job back at Coughlin. 'You can fix it', she had quoted Allen as saying, over and over again. But Allen had been a VP and R.J.'s superior at Coughlin. What could have made him think R.J. had the power to reverse his termination?

It took Toni Burrow less than an hour to call me back with the information I had asked for. She had returned to her mother's home immediately after our meeting and, apparently making better use of a laptop computer and Internet connection than I could have, found a Los Angeles-area phone number and address for one Estelle Allen, whom she assured me was Cleveland Allen's widow.

I eschewed the phone number to drop in on her unannounced. She lived in a converted condominium complex out in Torrance that was clean and freshly painted, its two-story facade a picture postcard of green grass and geraniums. Its origins as a low-rent apartment building, however, were hard to miss, as was the security intercom out front. I had been hoping to take Estelle Allen by surprise, but it seemed that wasn't to be.

'Yes?'

The voice crackling over the intercom handset was shrill but vibrant, incongruent with the image of a bitter, middle-aged woman still trying to come to terms with the death of her husband.

'Mrs Allen?' I asked.

'Yes? Who is it?'

'My name is Errol White. I was friends with a man named R.J. Burrow, who worked for your late husband at Coughlin Construction. Would it be possible for me to come in for a moment to ask you a few questions?'

'R.J. Burrow?' She hadn't been happy to hear

217

the name. In the time it took her to find her voice again, I was able to watch a teenage boy across the street parallel park a green Honda like he was wearing a blindfold. 'Are you with the police?'

'No ma'am. But—'

'Then I have nothing to say to you. Please go.'

The line went dead.

I started to redial her unit, then set the intercom handset back on its hook.

It would have been easy to leave. She didn't want to see me, and I wasn't likely to change her mind by harassing her over the intercom. But something about the way she had dismissed me wouldn't let me walk away. It wasn't indignation I had heard in her voice, as I'd been expecting, but trepidation. She was afraid of something.

I stood around the building's entrance with the intercom's receiver back in my hand, waiting to do an act for someone either going in or coming out. I wasn't sure how long I could loiter this way without drawing unwanted attention to myself, and I felt like an idiot, but it was either this or go home. I hung the receiver up, went through the motions of double-checking an entry in my cellphone, then picked the receiver up again and pretended to call a unit. Right on time, a heavy-set black woman with three small children – one in her arms, and the other two at her feet – labored to herd them out the door. I pulled the door open for her, did some play-acting with the intercom handset before hanging it up – 'Hey, never mind, somebody's coming out' – and then squeezed in behind her.

She barely nodded thanks.

I found the door to Estelle Allen's condo and paused a moment before knocking, having come this far without actually formulating a plan as to how I would proceed. In short order, I realized the only way to go was to play it by ear, and rapped on the door. Once, twice. And then:

'Who is it?'

Angry now.

'It's Errol White, Mrs Allen. I just need a moment of your time, please.'

'I told you I don't want to talk to you. How did you get in here? Go away before I call the police!'

I took a shot in the dark: 'Do you really want to do that?'

Silence.

'R.J. was a close friend, Mrs Allen. If you want to call the police, go ahead, but I'm not going anywhere until I've spoken with you.'

I waited through another lengthy silence, imagining her standing there on the other side of the door's peephole, trying to measure my resolve. Finally, there was the sound of the locks being thrown back, heatedly and in some haste, and the door was jerked open to reveal a white woman in her late fifties, early sixties; unnaturally slender, dressed for a non-existent party, thick eyelashes winking beneath a massive blond wig crawling with curls.

'I don't know anything,' she said.

'About what?'

'Whatever it is you're here to talk about. R.J. Burrow, Cleveland, Coughlin Construction – whatever.'

'May I come in?'

'No. Ask your questions and leave.'

She still had her left hand on the door, so anxious was she to get our business over with and send me on my way.

'I've been told your husband's death was a suicide. Is that so?'

'That's right. Last February. What of it?'

'The people I've talked to say he was distraught over Coughlin's letting him go, but they tell conflicting stories as to why that happened. Depending on who you ask, he was either defrauding the company or sexually harassing employees.'

She just stared at me.

'Which was it, exactly?'

'The sex thing. I thought you wanted to talk about your friend?'

'R.J., right. I was also told your husband held him responsible.'

'Responsible?'

'For his firing. R.J.'s widow says, shortly before his death, your husband went out to their home one night to ask R.J. to get him his job back.'

She shook her head emphatically. 'I wouldn't

know anything about that.'

Either telling her first lie, or her least convincing one.

'Did you happen to know R.J. yourself, Mrs Allen?'

'No. I mean, of course. Cleveland would mention his name from time to time. They worked together, why wouldn't he?'

'They only worked together? I thought they might be friends.'

'Friends?' She almost laughed out loud. 'Why would they be friends? The only reason Cleveland ever hired that man was because—'

She stopped short, a hair's breadth from finally betraying an unguarded thought.

'Was because of what?'

Turning ashen as I watched, she swung the door toward my face, said, 'I'm not answering any more questions!'

I put a hand out to block the door and took a step toward her. 'Why did your husband think R.J. could undo his firing, Mrs Allen? What did R.J. know that could have given him that kind of power at Coughlin?'

'Nothing! Leave me alone!'

She was leaning on the door with all her might now, struggling to force it closed, but for all she had to put behind it, she may as well have been trying to push a bulldozer up a steep embankment. I just let her go, wondering if she might scream.

'What did he know?' I asked again.

Breathless and livid, she gave the door one

last, meaningless shove, then snapped, 'It wasn't *what* he knew. It was *who* he knew!'

My surprise must have been comical to see. '"Who?"'

'He had another friend. Just like you. He was the one with the power and the connections. And he's the reason Cleveland's dead.'

'Who are you talking about?'

'I can't give you his name. If he finds out I've been talking to you, he'll cut me off. Go away!'

She took hold of the door again.

'Just tell me yes or no: Are you talking about O'Neal Holden?'

A spark of recognition flickered in her eyes, then was gone.

'You never heard that from me,' she said, before finally closing the door.

My brother's friend Jessie Scott, the reporter who worked for the local paper out in Bellwood, had called me Tuesday afternoon, but I'd only spoken to her long enough to get her number and promise to call her back. Though I was curious to hear what she might have to say about Bellwood's mayor and the quality of his work for the city, I couldn't find a reason to make talking to her at length a priority.

Until now.

I was lucky enough to find her at her desk when I placed the call, and we agreed to meet in an hour at the offices of her employer, the *Bellwood Carrier*, only blocks from Bellwood City Hall. Jessie Scott was a lovely young

Vietnamese woman with a ready smile who came down to greet me in the building's lobby, then escorted me up to the company cafeteria on the second floor, where we talked for the twenty minutes she said she had to spare.

'You're wondering where the name comes from,' she said after some small talk was out of the way.

'Excuse me?'

'Scott. Doesn't sound like something my family brought with them from Vietnam, does it?'

'I assumed it was your married name,' I said, though I hadn't really given it much thought.

'Actually, my adopted parents gave it to me. I'd give you the whole story of how they found my brother and me in a shelter down in Long Beach when I was six and he was only four, except that isn't what you came here to ask me about, is it?'

'Maybe I could hear about it some other time.'

'Chance said Mayor Holden is a friend of yours.'

'Since high school. It's been years since I've seen him, though.'

'Oh?'

'I live in St Paul now. I only came back for a funeral.'

'I'm sorry.'

'Yeah. Anyway, I was thinking about looking O' up before I go back, but my brother tells me I may not like the man I find if I do. He says O' might have his hands in some things down here I'd be better off not knowing about.'

Jessie Scott didn't say anything.

I twirled a fork around in the fingers of both hands, said, 'He tells me if anyone would know for sure, it's you.'

She shrugged. 'I might know a thing or two. Have you read my stories on the mayor?'

'I can't say that I have. What do they say?'

'They say your old friend is an extremely popular servant of the people here who has a way of getting things done that sometimes borders on the unreal.'

'You think he's dirty?'

'I think the numbers and his accomplishments don't always add up. He's a charming man, but charm alone can't explain some of the deals he's been able to broker.'

'What kind of deals?'

'Service agreements. Property acquisitions. Construction contracts.'

'Construction contracts?'

I'd tried to make it sound like an innocent question.

'Since the mayor's been in office, Bellwood's been experiencing quite a building boom. A new high school, two new industrial parks, and three blocks down the street—'

'City Hall,' I said.

'Yes. You've seen it. Beautiful, right? It came in on time and on budget at twenty-two million – or at least, that was the advertised price.'

'I don't understand.'

'Neither do I, really. On the surface, everything looks legit. But like I said, the numbers just don't add up. The building should have cost the city a million more, at least.'

'*More?*'

'We had an audit done. By our estimates, Bellwood – and, by extension, Mayor Holden – was billed twenty-two million for a complex that could have easily cost as much as twenty-six.'

She smiled. 'Of course, we might have just gotten a great deal. There's nothing to indicate any corners were cut in getting the building to come in at that price. But we think there might be another explanation.'

'Which is?'

'The builders are making up their losses on other projects for the city. They've done two for us since, with another one on the drawing board, and oddly enough, all the cost overruns they were able to avoid building City Hall have proven unavoidable for each. Again, we haven't found any evidence of malfeasance yet, but we're still looking.'

I nodded, my worst fears about O' slowly taking shape.

Jessie Scott studied me closely, not sure what to make of me yet. 'Does any of this tell you what you wanted to know?'

'It might. Was Coughlin Construction one of the builders you've been talking about?'

'Actually, they're *the* builder I've been talking about. How did you guess?'

'I heard a rumor that the mayor might have once had connections there.'

'What kind of connections?'

'Off the record?'

I wasn't ready to throw O' to the wolves just yet.

'If that's the way you want it,' Jessie Scott said, making a concession that clearly ran against the grain.

'A former employee named Cleveland Allen. He was a VP in sales there until they let him go late last year, either for embezzlement or sexual harassment, no one seems to know for sure.'

'And?'

'And he's dead. They say he committed suicide shortly after they let him go.'

'They "say"?'

'I'll put it to you the way you've been putting it to me, Ms Scott: "There's no evidence to indicate" it wasn't a suicide. The timing and neatness of his passing just run counter to my ideas of random happenstance, that's all.'

'As a good reporter, I'm obliged to ask what you mean by that.'

'What I mean is that I don't believe O' is capable of murder. The man I knew a long time ago didn't have it in him. But a lot of years have passed, and people change. The game he's in is as cut-throat as they come. You want to know what I came here to find out? I came here to find out if you think twenty-six years could have changed him that much.'

She gave the question a fair amount of

thought, murmured voices mixing with the clatter of dishes and silverware to provide us with the usual cafeteria ambiance.

'I don't really believe the mayor's capable of murder, no,' she said at last. 'To tell you the truth, I'm not even sure he's capable of the things I suspect him of. But you said it best yourself: Politics is a rough trade, and O'Neal Holden is only in it to win. If the stakes were high enough, and he felt this Cleveland Allen was a threat to him in some way ... Who knows?'

It wasn't the definitive 'no' I'd been hoping she'd answer the question with, but it wasn't an unqualified 'yes' either. Pared down to its bare essence, her opinion on the subject pretty much mirrored my own: O' was a decent, if ambitious man who was willing to do any number of things to get ahead short of taking another man's life – unless that man put him in a position where no other alternative seemed possible.

'I want to thank you for your time, Ms Scott,' I said.

'Wait. That's it?'

My cellphone began to ring.

'How about answering a few of *my* questions? *On* the record this time?'

I gently waved her off to take the call, seeing it was from my brother. 'What's up, Chance?'

'I need to see you, Handy. Right now,' he said.

'What's wrong?'

'I'll explain it all when you get here. Get a pencil and write down this address.'

I fumbled around in my pockets for the pen I'd been carrying and took down the address he gave me in my notebook. 'I've got it. What's—'

'Make it fast, brother.'

The line went dead.

I tried to remember the last time I'd heard him sound so uneasy, and couldn't. Even when he'd been under the wheels of addiction, it had always been near impossible to sense any anxiety in him.

'I'm sorry, I have to go,' I told Jessie Scott, standing up.

'Something wrong?'

'I'm not sure.' I shook her hand to discourage any more questions, thanked her again for her help, and left.

The address my brother had given me did not strike me as familiar. It led me to a tiny little house in Harbor City that looked like the people who owned it had long ago left this earth. Even in the fading light of dusk its dilapidation was unsettling: tattered roof, unkempt lawn, a gap-toothed porch railing that dangled from its moorings as if from a single nail. A small SUV I had seen in Chancellor's driveway two nights ago was now parked at the curb here, turned at an angle that was only noticeably askew if you viewed it with a paranoid's eye.

The ride over from Bellwood had taken

twenty minutes, and I'd spent every one compiling a list of possible reasons for my brother's unsettling call. They were all bad. He wasn't answering his cellphone but I tried it one more time just to make sure I really had no choice but to get out of the car. I got his voice-mail again and hung up.

I went to the door and rang the bell. The windows were dark to either side of me, gray drapes pulled closed to hide anything that may have been stirring behind them. I listened for the sound of voices and heard nothing. I rang the bell again and opened my mouth to call out, the greatest part of my fear settling now around the idea that Chancellor was already dead and I was walking into a trap to no purpose.

'Come on in!' somebody inside ordered. I didn't recognize the voice.

I drew the Taurus from the waistband of my pants behind me and tried the door; the knob turned easily in my hand. I entered the house and stopped just inside the door, peering into an interior as dark and bleak as the exterior. My heart sank, having seen homes like this before: dusty mausoleums reeking with the smell of bacon grease, every room too small for all the cheap and broken furniture packed into it. This was how the poor often lived, in dark, confining spaces overcrowded with the meager posses-sions that were as close to 'wealth' as they would ever come.

Off to my right, in the home's tiny living room, Chancellor sat at one end of a tattered, faux-leather couch, bound and gagged with duct tape. The young brother who'd come close to killing me at Moody's bar stood behind him, holding the blade of a knife tight against his throat.

I was too far away to be sure, but it looked as if Chance was blinking at me frantically, offering an apology the only way he could.

TWENTY

''bout fuckin' time,' the man looming above my brother said.

The forty-plus hours since I'd last seen him had not been good to him. He was covered from head to foot in soot and grime, like a vagrant who hadn't seen a shelter in weeks, and he looked as if he hadn't slept in days.

'Let my brother go. You wanted me, you've got me, you don't need him anymore.'

'Shut the fuck up and get in here! You ain't runnin' this show, *I* am!'

He took hold of Chance's hair and yanked his head back, hard, to better expose his throat to the threat of the knife.

I did as I was told and came into the room.

'Now throw me the gun. Easy.'

I tossed the Taurus on to the couch and

watched him reach down to pick it up with his free hand.

'Your name Darrel Eastman?'

'That's right.' He put the knife away in a back pocket. 'But I told you to shut the fuck up.'

I ignored him. He didn't want to kill anyone yet. If he had, Chancellor and I would have already been dead. 'Why'd you try to kill me the other night?'

'I didn't try to kill nobody. I only wanted to talk to you.'

'About what?'

'About my moms. Get down on your knees. Hands behind your head, now, or this motherfucka's dead. I mean it.'

This time I followed orders. He had the Taurus pointed at Chancellor's head now and could fire a round into his skull just by accident if I aggravated him enough.

'Your moms?' He'd said the word as if I should know exactly what it meant.

'You heard me. That's her over there.' He nodded his head to direct my attention to a black woman I hadn't even noticed before, so lifelessly had she occupied the room behind him. She was sitting in a wheelchair at the dining room table, hunched over a bowl, spooning something into her mouth with the slow, unsteady motions of someone who was barely capable of the act. 'What, you don't recognize her? Maybe you need a closer look.'

He eased his way back to the table, keeping the gun trained on the back of Chance's head all the while. As my brother used his eyes to ask me the obvious question – *What the hell is going on?* – Eastman wheeled the white-haired woman into the room to join us, parking her alongside the couch where I could easily see her face.

It was sad and misshapen, one side crushed in like a broken eggshell, and her body was all folded in on itself. Her left arm sat in her lap at an unnatural angle and her gaze was as black and empty as that of a grazing cow. It was clear that she no more knew what was going on around her than did the chair she was sitting in.

'Dear Jesus,' I heard myself say.

It was Linda Dole.

We had never seen her with children, but that proved nothing. If she'd had a child somewhere, it was unlikely she would have attempted to raise it in the safe house of a crack dealer.

'Don't worry,' Eastman said. 'She ain't gonna hurt you. She can't hurt nobody no more.'

'I don't understand. We thought—'

'She was dead. Yeah, I know. That's what R.J. said he used to think, too.'

'R.J.? You don't think *he* did this to her?'

'R.J.? Hell, no! But he's the reason it happened to her, and so are you. You and some other nigga. Ain't that right?'

I didn't say anything.

'R.J. said there was three of you. That you were the ones the man was after when he put momma in that wheelchair.'

'Excel Rucker.'

'Damn right, Excel Rucker. He wasn't already dead, I'd'a killed the motherfucka a long time ago.'

'Like you killed R.J.?'

'I didn't kill nobody. He *wanted* me to kill 'im, but I didn't. I just ran off. When I left, he was still alive.'

'What do you mean, he wanted you to kill him?'

'I mean he drove me out to the beach and told me what you niggas did, then put a gun in my hand and begged me to shoot. I didn't even know who he was till that night. I thought...' He stopped, a look of childlike melancholy drifting over his face.

'What?'

'That he was my *friend*. Just some kind'a Big Brother who only wanted to help me get straight. But that was bullshit. He was just usin' me to make himself feel better 'bout what you all did to moms.'

He was starting to get worked up, his voice taking on a serrated edge that promised only worse things to come. My brother noticed it too; his eyes were full of fear and he was becoming more animated on the couch. Down on my knees with both hands clasped behind my head, however, my only weapon gone, there was nothing I could do to help either of us but keep Eastman talking, pray he'd give me an opening sooner or later I could use to make a move on him.

'How did he find you?' I asked.

'Find me? How you mean, find me?'

'You say R.J. knew who you were. How did he know?'

He shrugged to say he didn't know. 'He used to hang at this liquor store near my crib, and one day we just started talkin'. He was all right. I liked him.' The admission stuck in his throat like a sharp bone. 'Next thing you know, we was friends. Least, that's what I thought.'

'Where's your crib?'

'You know where it is. It's my mom's old crib in Inglewood, same one you niggas jacked.'

It figured. Had R.J.'s nagging guilt ever moved him to revisit the place, and he'd seen Eastman and his mother there together, he would have quickly understood the nature of their relationship and how much of their joint suffering was a result of our doing.

'What are you going to do now?' I asked.

'What do you think I'm gonna do? I'm gonna do to you what I should'a done to R.J.' He shoved Chancellor's head to one side with the nose of the Taurus, just to remind me he was still holding it. 'Soon as you give me that other nigga's name.'

Now I was confused. Why would R.J. give me up and not O'? 'Don't you have his name?'

'R.J. never mentioned no names. All he said was there was three of you jacked Excel.'

'Then—'

'I started watchin' his house to see who showed up, and one day, there you were. I could tell just by lookin' at you that you was one of his 'boys. You were the right age and you had the same, sad look on your face as him. Like somebody'd just run over your dog, or somethin'.'

He came around the couch to stand in front of me and pressed the nose of the Taurus against my forehead. ''Cept it wasn't no dog that got run over, was it?'

His tone made it clear that he was all done talking, his need for O's name notwithstanding. I closed my eyes and waited for the sound of the shot, but I never heard it. What I heard instead was a dry cackle, as deep and ragged as a fat man's cough. I opened my eyes and saw Linda Dole shaking with laughter from the wheelchair, her left cheek streaked with tears.

The cold metal kiss of the gun slid away from my forehead and I looked up to see Eastman staring at his mother, mouth hanging open in amazement. It must have been the first time he'd heard her make a sound in years.

I came up off my knees like a stumbling bull and took hold of the Taurus with both hands. Eastman and I crashed to the floor as one, a mass of flailing arms and legs, and I made a point of being on top, looking to use every last ounce of my weight to crush the air out of him. He was stunned just enough to lose his grip on the gun and I wrestled it from his grasp. I'd danced this dance with him before and I knew I'd only get this one chance to end it before he did, so I turned the business end of the Taurus toward his face without thinking twice and pulled the trigger.

Nothing happened.

Like a fool I let Eastman get over our mutual surprise first and he was on me in an instant, raining hammer-like blows down upon my face in a flurry I could barely see. One right hand hit me flush above my left eye like a steel-toed boot and the lights in the room started to fade, a blur of color and motion dimming to a solid black.

I don't remember how I got his knife in my hand. By now I was operating on the only self-defensive mechanism I had left – desperation – and conscious thought played no part in my actions. One minute Eastman's blows were continuing unabated, and the next they had stopped, like an electrical current I'd abruptly thrown a switch to kill. I blinked through a field of sparks to see the man above me frozen in time, a balled fist suspended in the air beside his head, eyes agape with shock. I felt my left hand grow warm and damp and followed Eastman's gaze down to his right side just below the armpit, where I'd plunged the knife he'd lost in our scuffle into his flesh to the hilt.

I pushed him off me and he rolled to one side without complaint. Fighting for breath, I struggled to my feet and went to my brother, who had listed sideways on the couch in a brave but hopeless attempt to join in the fray. I eased the tape from his mouth and used Eastman's knife to cut the tape from his wrists and ankles, then asked if he was OK.

'Yeah. Is he dead?'

I looked back at Eastman and shook my head. 'I don't think so.'

'He was waiting for me at my car in the parking lot at work. He said he'd taken one of the boys and would kill him if I didn't come with him. But—'

'That was a lie. I get the picture. And you can apologize to me later. After you find a phone and call nine-one-one.'

Chance stood up from the couch and glanced over at Linda Dole, who from all appearances had gone back to being the disengaged catatonic she'd been when Eastman first rolled her into the room.

'Errol—'

'I can't explain anything to you now. Just do what I say. Eastman needs an ambulance and I've got a few more questions for him before it gets here.'

He was far from convinced it was the right thing to do, but Chance did as I asked anyway. As soon as he was gone, I moved in close to see if Eastman was still breathing. He was, but it was clear from the amount of blood he had already lost that neither of us had much time. His eyes held as much life in them as his mother's and his mouth was blowing crimson bubbles, lips trembling.

'Who killed R.J.?' I asked.

It took a while for the question to register. He shook his head with what little power he had left, but I couldn't tell what the gesture meant. Was he answering the question or telling me to go fuck myself?

'The police think you killed him and they aren't interested in alternate theories. Nobody cares what you have to say but me. If you're straight with me I might be able to keep you from taking the blame for a murder you didn't commit.'

It took him a long time to respond, drawing short breaths into his flooded lungs and then coughing them up on the exhale. His eyes filled with tears as I watched. 'He was always tellin' me to do the right thing. Like the pops I never had. But ... I kept fuckin' up, so...' He paused, losing focus, then started in again. ' ... so he quit on me. Drove me out to the beach and said fuck it, let's just get high together.'

'And that's when he told you what we did to your mother.'

He tried to nod with only limited success. 'He gave me the gun and said he wanted to die. But I couldn't...' A smile formed on his lips, as small and sad as his entire life had no doubt been up until now. 'I just ran away. Like a little ... bitch.'

He took one more long, labored breath and then grew still. His gaze turned black and cold and I finally had to look away. I could feel my brother watching us, having silently returned to the room. I knelt down in front of Linda Dole and peered deep into her blank and twisted face, vaguely aware of a siren building strength

238

somewhere in the distance.

'I'm sorry,' I said.

Eastman's mother only sat there, oblivious, waiting for her own turn to die.

TWENTY-ONE

My paternal grandfather, Lionel White, used to say that there were many paths a man could take during his time on earth, but sooner or later, they all brought him down the same one: cemetery road. There was no running from it, there was no hiding from it.

Driving out to Simi Valley late one Tuesday night in 1979, Excel Rucker in the back seat behind me, gun in hand, I knew that my turn on that fateful road had come. The only thing yet to be determined was whose death, exactly, awaited me at journey's end.

In his over-anxiousness to find out what had happened to Excel's daughter, O' had asked too many people too many questions, and word of his interest had inevitably gotten back to the dealer. Looking for O' at his mother's place, Rucker had missed him and R.J. by mere seconds, but had arrived just in time to latch on to me before I could follow them out to Simi.

Now I was taking Excel to them, and the little girl we were all hoping to find alive in Paris

McDonald's custody. I didn't know what else to do. Saving Excel's daughter had become my only concern in life, and getting myself killed by refusing to talk to her father would only have been counter-productive to that objective.

'You and this motherfucka O'Neal workin' for Paris?' Rucker asked me shortly after we started out in pursuit of my friends. Drifting in and out of the shadows in the back of the car, he was a mess, a sodden shambles of the sharply dressed, imperturbable ladies' man O', R.J. and I had come to know. If I hadn't believed his daughter's kidnapping could bring him this far to his knees before, I believed it now.

'No.'

'Don't lie to me, bitch! Why else would the fool be askin' all them questions about Sienna?'

I told him who we were. O' and R.J. had his coke and his money, and if we had to offer it as ransom to McDonald later, he'd find out the truth in any case.

'You the niggas jacked my house?' Rucker asked in disbelief. I eyed him in my rear-view mirror, watched as surprise gave way to crazed fury.

We had just eased on to the Harbor Freeway, heading north toward the 5. I'd broached the subject of gas but he wasn't having any; we were going to make it to Simi on what I had in the tank or stall somewhere en route, where I would die shortly thereafter. Traffic was relatively light just a few minutes shy of ten p.m., but I had the Fairmont doing a steady sixty-five, more than fast enough to kill us both if Rucker forgot where we were and caused me to lose control of the vehicle.

He jumped forward on his seat and pressed the nose of the gun into the side of my head, thumbing the trigger back so that I couldn't miss the heavy click it made. 'I ought'a blow your ass away right now,' he said. 'Wasn't for you, I would'a paid that motherfucka and got Sienna back a long time ago!'

'We know that. That's why we're taking what we boosted to McDonald now, to see if he'll take it in trade for your daughter. Assuming...'

I thought better of completing the thought.

'You're full'a shit,' Rucker said, pushing the revolver's muzzle deeper into my scalp.

'It's the truth. We know where he's hiding, we were on our way out there when you found me.'

He had far more reasons to doubt such a ridiculous claim than to believe it, but he opted to do the latter if only because it offered him something the alternative didn't: an excuse to go on hoping for a miracle. His little girl was still alive, and there was still a chance he could find her and bring her home safe to her mother. To think otherwise, even for a minute, was to surrender completely to the madness that was already overtaking him.

He asked me where we were going and I told him. Naturally, he wanted to know everything else: our names, where we lived and – most especially – how we'd worked the Inglewood safe house job. I kept my answers as short and

241

uninformative as possible, and lied where I dared. Looking ahead to a future that at the moment seemed dubious at best, if my friends and I were lucky enough to survive the night, the less Excel Rucker knew about us, the better off we'd be.

We rode in silence for a long time, my passenger's ragged breathing the only reminder of his company. Eyes wild, body motionless, he looked straight ahead through the windshield of the car like a wax figure that could do nothing else.

'You look familiar,' he said suddenly.

I pretended not to hear.

'Where I know you from?'

'Nowhere,' I said.

'Bullshit. I seen you somewhere before.' He thought about it. 'You hang at the Silver Fox?'

'No.'

'You ain't never been to the Silver Fox?'

'No.' I'd heard of the club, but I'd never been there.

Rucker grew quiet again.

'It was a party, then.' A pause. 'Over at Charlene Litton's place, or Little Joe's.'

I turned my eyes away from the mirror, seeking to hide them from his view.

'That's it. Little Joe's.'

Little Joe Brown was a well-known business manager for a number of local music acts who threw parties at his home in Ladera Heights that rivaled anything Hollywood could come up with. I never came as an invited guest, but

242

vouched for by one musician acquaintance or another I'd managed to squeeze through the door of a Little Joe house party more than a few times over the years.

'You know Little Joe?' Excel asked me.

'Yeah, I know him.'

'So why you wanna lie to me, nigga?'

'You asked where you know me from. Not where you might've seen me before.'

'That right?' He edged up on the seat again, poked the barrel of the gun into my chin beneath my right ear. 'You wanna say that again?'

'You're gonna shoot me, shoot me,' I said, wanting to put an end to all his questions about Little Joe Brown at any cost. 'This is your show. But if you want me to take you to your little girl, leave me the fuck alone and let me drive, all right?'

It was a bluff, and a weak one, but he knew I was right: If he killed me now, whatever chance he had of finding his daughter alive in Simi Valley would be gone. And yet he was conflicted; he wanted to kill me desperately. He didn't move for a long minute, breathing fumes and fire into my ear, until reason finally washed over him and he found the willpower to withdraw, kicking the back of my seat with a foot as he did so, just to let me know how close I'd come.

That was the end of all conversation for the duration of our trip, my gas gauge flirting with empty but, by the endless grace of God, never actually finding it. The Simi Valley Freeway, years away from serving a greater purpose than connecting Los Angeles county to a burgeoning cow-town, was as lonely as an abandoned child at this hour. Little in the way of light disturbed the black landscape to either side of the car, and in our stifling isolation my mind filled with jumbled thoughts about how things were likely to play out upon our arrival. If O' and R.J. hadn't already grown tired of waiting for me and had barged into the house alone, how would they react to the sight of my escort, herding me out of my own car at gunpoint? O' at least could be counted on to maintain some level of cool, but R.J. could not; it would not have been unlike him to start an all-out firefight right there on the street, Sienna Jackson be damned.

The directions R.J. had given me led us six blocks north of the freeway at the Tapo Canyon off-ramp to a little strip of asphalt labeled Adams Road. Denied the extravagances of sidewalks or street lamps, it was lightly sprinkled with single-story ranch homes that all seemed to be cut from the same sad and dilapidated cloth. Redwood siding rotted away while red brick crumbled and tiles leapt from rooftops like rats from a capsized ship. Everywhere, grass had turned brown and died, leaving the surrounding earth to return to its natural state of sagebrush and dust.

And this was what some white folks were fleeing the city to buy, just to put some distance between themselves and people like me.

The house we were looking for was pretty much as R.J. had described it. The ragged smile of a wagon wheel full of broken spokes stood against the dark front facade, and the path to the porch was littered with junk: an old manual lawnmower with rusted blades, an overturned wheelbarrow on a flat tire, a shopping cart that would never find its proper home again. A single wooden chair stood watch on the covered porch, a throw pillow spewing white stuffing on to its seat. There were no lights in any of its windows visible from the street.

As we approached, we passed R.J.'s Dodge, parked in the center of the large space between this house and its nearest neighbor.

The car was empty.

'Fuck,' I said, pulling over.

Alert and focused now, Excel asked, 'This it?'

'Yeah.'

'So where the fuck are your two bitches?'

'I don't know. That's their ride behind us. They might've gone in without me.'

And thinking about it, I could almost follow their reasoning. The last time I'd entered a stranger's house with R.J., I'd nearly gotten the both of us killed.

'Then I guess we better go in too,' Rucker said, opening his door.

We stepped out into the street together, the dealer taking great care to keep me aware of the revolver in his hand. 'You only alive right now 'cause I need you,' he said as we eased toward the house together. 'But you fuck up just once, your ass is wasted. You understand that, nigga?'

I nodded my head.

It was cold as hell and neither of us was dressed for it, adding to the misery of the long walk up the side of the house. I couldn't think straight. My mind kept skipping from one fear to the next, each more terrifying than the one preceding it. The house was empty. The child was dead. O' and R.J. had blundered into an ambush and gotten themselves killed along with the girl. No matter what scenario I envisioned, they all amounted to the same thing.

Cemetery road.

We inched up the driveway to the back of the house and on the way spotted an open window, its screen removed and braced against the wall below it. Neither of my friends was as good with locks as I, so this would have been their chosen way of gaining entry. O' would have been smart enough not to risk the racket of both of them climbing through a window, however; one of them would have gone in first and then unlocked a door for the other. This was proven out when I led Rucker around to the backyard and found a patio door someone had slid wide open and left that way.

Excel and I passed through the door into the house's living room, still looking for our first glimpse of light. Even in the dark, we could see that the place was a mess. Clothes and scraps of old meals were scattered everywhere, and what furniture there was was scarred and tattered, like remnants of a house fire that had fallen off a garbage truck on its way to the city dump. The room smelled of liquor and crack cocaine, and evidence of both sat upon the cracked-mirror top of a low coffee table.

Rucker put a hand in my back, ordering me to push further into the house.

We reached a hallway beyond the kitchen and stopped cold at its mouth: there was a light on in an open doorway at the end and we could hear voices coming from that direction, too faint to follow but impossible to miss. The man with the gun behind me gave me another nudge and I started forward again, my legs heavy, my throat dry. It took an eternity to travel all of twenty feet, O's voice becoming more distinct with my every step.

'Where is she?' I heard him ask with some impatience.

When Excel and I finally made it to the open door, we found ourselves peering into the master bedroom, where by the meager illumination of a night table lamp, O' and R.J. stood talking to a heavy-set blonde woman in pastel sweats whom they had obviously just rousted from bed.

My friends spun on their heels at the sight of us, startled, but Rucker put his gun up under my chin before either could fire his own and snapped, 'Do it and this motherfucka loses his goddamn head! Go on!'

O' and R.J. froze.

'Drop the pieces and kick 'em over here to

me. Hurry the fuck up!'

They both obeyed, first O', then with somewhat greater reluctance, R.J. He was trembling with rage, but his withering gaze was
directed solely at me. 'What the hell's *he* doin'
here?'

'Shut the fuck up,' Rucker told him. 'Ain't
nobody askin' the questions around here but
me.'

He shoved me into the room to give himself
space to operate and hunkered down to retrieve
the two handguns on the floor, shoving them
both into the waistband of his pants without
ever taking his eyes off of any of the four
people in front of him.

'Now,' he said. 'Where the hell's my little
girl?'

'We were just asking *her* that question,' O'
said, gesturing toward the blonde.

Clearly as confused as she was terrified, she
had the face of a wide-mouth bass and the body
of a dancer who'd forgotten how to put down
her fork. Her yellow hair ran down to her
shoulders, stringy and lifeless, and her eyes
were two tired, watery slugs of blue swimming
in shadow.

'Who're you?' Rucker asked, taking a step
closer to get a better look at her.

'Please don't hurt me,' she said, whimpering.

'I asked who the fuck you are!'

'She's McDonald's woman,' O' said. 'This is
her place.'

'So where's Sienna? Where the fuck is Paris?'

'I don't know,' the woman said, desperate to convince him, 'they were here when I came to bed! I've been asleep—'

Excel closed on her in an instant and struck her across the jaw with the weapon in his hand, hard. She stumbled backward, slammed off an oak wood dresser behind her and, with an inadvertent swipe of one hand, took most of the knick-knacks and toiletries sitting atop it with her on her way down to the floor.

'Where is she?' the dealer asked her again, livid now.

'She was in the back bedroom!' the blonde cried, spitting blood. 'Please don't hit me any-more!'

Rucker turned to me, hissed, 'Go get her.'

But before I could take a step, O' said, 'She isn't there. I've already looked, she's not in the house.'

And now the woman's sobs overpowered her. She scurried backward into a corner, cowering like a frightened child, and buried her face deep in both hands. 'It wasn't me. I never touched her, I swear!'

Rucker towered over her. 'What?'

'She wouldn't stop crying. I told him to leave her alone, but ... He wouldn't listen. He just kept hitting her and hitting her!'

Time ground to a sudden halt in the room. I felt my heart constrict and my stomach grow hard and cold.

'Aw, Jesus,' R.J. said.

Excel reached down with his free hand to

grab a handful of the woman's hair, snatching her back to her feet. *'What the fuck you tryin' to say?'*

She threw her arms up to defend her face, body convulsing with hysteria, cried, 'I think he killed her!'

Incredibly, Excel had no immediate response to this. As the blonde peered at him through the space between her arms, waiting for him to begin raining blows down upon her head, he just glowered back at her, stunning us all with a restraint no man in his position should have had any earthly right to possess.

Relieved, McDonald's woman began to cry uncontrollably again. 'He said if she died, he was gonna take her out and bury her some-where where nobody'd ever find her. That must be where—'

She never got the next word out. Excel shot her in the left eye without warning, then shot her again in the throat after her body had collapsed at his feet. The expression on his face – like that of a psychotic little boy twisting the head off a thrashing hen – is something I will remember until the day I die.

Had my life at that moment depended solely upon my own capacity for self-preservation, I would have surely lost it in the next. My legs were dead, my feet rooted to the floor, and my mind was a blank and ineffectual slate. Fear was my only functioning process. Even O' seemed powerless to move.

But R.J. was a different animal.

While O' and I stood there like lambs waiting for the slaughter, all of our smarts and superior wisdom as useless to us now as matches in a firestorm, R.J. did what he was wired to do, throwing himself at Excel Rucker before the dealer could turn his wrath, now fully blown, upon the three of us.

He had acted in the one split second Rucker gave him to do so, and still, he was almost too late. Distracted though he was, Excel saw him coming and whirled around to meet him, firing off a shot that caught R.J. in the side and damn near dropped him to his knees. In close quarters, R.J. could out-muscle any man, but now he was hurt; if he tried to disarm Excel by force, he would fail. When this realization dawned upon him, he did something O' and I had almost never seen him do in the middle of a fight: he improvised.

Fending off Rucker's revolver with his left hand, he reached into the waistband of the dealer's pants with his right, got his finger on the trigger of one of the two semi-automatic handguns wedged there, and fired. The explosion blew a hole in Excel's groin and bored through part of his right thigh, moving him to scream like something inhuman, his body stiffening, his eyes flying open in horror. He snatched hold of R.J.'s shirt, mouth agape but abruptly silent, and R.J. drew the nine all the way out of his pants to fire again, putting a merciful end to his misery.

Rucker's body tumbled sideways to the floor

to join the other one already waiting there, and R.J. soon threatened to follow, the left side of his shirt soaked with blood. O' caught him on his way down and the two of us helped him over to the bed, where I pulled the shirt away from his skin to inspect his injury.

'How bad is it?' O' asked.

'It's fuckin' bad,' R.J. said, grimacing with pain.

'No,' I said, tearing a long strip off the bed sheet to use as a tourniquet. 'Maybe not. Looks like a hole in the front and back. Bullet went right through.' I wrapped the tourniquet around R.J.'s torso and cinched it tight. 'Long as it didn't hit anything vital and we can stop this bleeding, he should be OK.'

O' nodded.

'We gotta get the fuck outta here,' R.J. said, eyeing the two bodies on the floor. He tried to sit up on his own.

'He's right. McDonald or the cops'll be here any minute,' O' agreed. 'But we've gotta clean this place up first.'

'Clean it up? Clean it up how?' I asked.

'So everything in here doesn't lead right back to us, that's how. Here—' He peeled the key to his apartment in Playa del Rey off his keychain and forced it into my palm. 'You and R.J. go on back to my crib and I'll hook up with you later.'

'What? Hell, no!'

'We ain't ... goin' nowhere without you,' R.J. managed to say.

'Both'a you fools shut the hell up and just do

it. The longer we stand here arguing, the better our chances of getting hemmed up, or worse.'

'And the girl?' I asked.

He nodded in the direction of the woman on the floor, a shadow passing over his eyes. 'You heard what the lady said. McDonald's out hidin' her body. Ain't nothin' we can do for her now.'

It wasn't something I was ready to accept, but I knew it had to be true. The house suddenly felt ice cold to me, and I got out of there as soon as I could lift R.J. to his feet.

Early in the drive back into the city, laying across the back seat of the car behind me, R.J. asked between shallow breaths, 'What's he gonna do?'

I'd been wondering the very same thing, and I gave him the only answer I could come up with.

'Start a fire,' I said.

TWENTY-TWO

The homicide detectives from the LA County Sheriff's Department who questioned me about the death of Darrel Eastman let me go on my own recognizance. They would have liked to have held me on suspicion of manslaughter, but they had no way to support such a charge. Both Chancellor and I claimed it was self-defense, Linda Dole was incapable of saying otherwise, and all the physical evidence at the scene seemed to corroborate our version of events.

Still, I was lucky. There were holes in the stories my brother and I told the detectives that bothered them, holes they could only imagine were created to make Eastman's death look less like murder than it really was. In truth, the omissions we made were only intended to reduce all of his talk about something R.J. and I had done years ago to put his mother in a wheelchair down to the incoherent ramblings of a crazy man. I knew better, of course, but Chancellor did not. To him, Eastman's accusations had made little or no sense, and so he was hardpressed to clearly articulate them in his statements to the authorities.

In the end, and without colluding to do so, the

two of us told the same essential story: Eastman had kidnapped my brother so that I might be forced to hear him plead innocent to the murder of my friend R.J. Burrow. He'd been following me around since the dead man's funeral and arrived at the conclusion that mine might be a sympathetic ear to his assertion that R.J. had still been alive when he'd last seen him, seventeen days ago down at the Santa Monica Pier. He'd had no interest in killing me until I'd made a play for his knife and forced his hand.

It was a fabrication that clung just close enough to the truth to win my freedom, temporary though it might be. Still, they only let me go after I'd been asked to go over the circumstances surrounding Eastman's death again and again for detectives Saunders and Rodriguez of the SMPD, who'd been notified of Eastman's killing and requested I be held at the Sheriff's station in Harbor City until they could talk to me themselves. My inability to leave R.J.'s murder alone, as I'd promised them I would only hours before, had somehow led me to kill their primary suspect, and neither man was terribly happy about it.

'You've just made a very bad mistake, Mr White,' Rodriguez said.

Much to his and his partner's chagrin, however, it wasn't a mistake they could easily put me behind bars for making. Eventually, like their peers with the Sheriff's Department, they had to concede that Eastman was only dead because he had come looking for me, not the other way around. My meddling in their open homicide investigation had drawn Eastman's interest, to be sure, and maybe if it hadn't he would still be alive. But nobody could say that for sure, and trying to prove as much to the District Attorney's office would have only served to extend a case Rodriguez and his partner now considered closed, despite my best efforts to convince them otherwise.

'He said R.J. was alive when he left him,' I told them more than once, referring to Eastman. 'He didn't do it.'

But Saunders wasn't listening, and Rodriguez didn't give a damn. 'Get this guy, Harry,' he said. 'Even now, he's playing detective.'

'I'm only telling you what the man said with his last breath. Why would he lie with nothing more to gain?'

'We would've loved to have been able to ask him that very question,' Saunders said. 'But it kind of looks like we missed our chance, doesn't it?'

'If you wanted all the answers to why he did what he did, you should've thought twice before sticking that knife in him,' Rodriguez said.

'Burrow tried to befriend the kid and got burned. Eastman was a bad egg he couldn't reform and that disillusioned him all to hell, so he fell off the wagon and took the kid out for a party. They had words in the car and Eastman lost his temper. What's so hard to understand?'

And so it went between us, around and around

and around again, until two hours had passed and we'd all had enough of the ride. By the time they shoved me out the door, I was halfway convinced they were right and I was wrong. Everything I knew about Eastman and R.J. that I'd made sure the two cops didn't only reinforced *their* opinion of his murder, not mine. R.J. had given Eastman every reason in the world to kill him – he'd gotten him high, told him he was an addict beyond redemption and then confessed to the crime that had pushed Excel Rucker to make a paraplegic of his mother – and the only excuse I had for believing Eastman hadn't taken the bait was his word.

So why was I still unsure?

It was going on nine p.m. when Chancellor drove me back to Linda Dole's place from the Sheriff's office to retrieve my rental car. It was a longer ride than the miles involved would have indicated. He had as many questions for me as the four detectives who'd just finished grilling me combined, and his were by far the ones I feared the most.

'What was he talking about, Errol? What did you have to do with Excel Rucker crippling Eastman's mother?'

Lacking the will to evade, I told him everything I'd told Toni Burrow that afternoon, with the single exception that I left Olivia Gardner out of it. It was a story he thought he already knew, but not like this.

The sordid tale my brother was familiar with

involved a vengeful cousin who had kidnapped Rucker's daughter for ransom and, with the help of a female accomplice, held her out in a house in Simi. Rucker went on a killing spree when he couldn't raise the ransom money, then tracked the cousin down to the Simi residence and tried to rescue the girl by force. The cousin – an ex-boxer who used to work for Rucker named Paris McDonald – killed Rucker and his female accomplice both, then set the house on fire in an effort to hide his tracks. It didn't work; he was arrested two days later at a Sunland motel and charged with three counts of murder. Despite the arson, blood evidence in a back bedroom of the house that had served as her prison strongly suggested that Rucker's little girl Sienna had been badly beaten, and prosecutors had had little trouble convincing a jury that McDonald had killed her before disposing of her body, which was never found.

As I turned this version of events inside out for my brother's benefit, rearranging the pieces in a way that only someone with personal knowledge of their true configuration possibly could, he let me speak without interruption, his eyes only leaving the road every now and then to check my face, trying to convince himself it was really me talking and not some stranger he'd never met and didn't want to know. When I was done, he pulled the car over to the curb and killed the engine, leaving us to sit there in the dark, each of us searching for the right words to say.

'I knew it,' he finally said.

'What?'

'I always knew you fools were into some kind of ignorant shit. You were never extravagant enough to draw attention to yourselves, but money for the little things was always too readily at hand, and a brother like R.J., at least, should have been broke every other month.'

'So why didn't you ask me what I was doing?'

'Because I didn't want to know. I was afraid you might be dealing drugs, and if you were...'

'It was all just a game, Chance. We were thieves, not thugs. Until the Excel job happened, we never hurt a soul.'

'So why fuck with Excel at all? What the hell made you target the one man who could make the game blow up in your faces?'

I had no answer for him. He studied me for several seconds, waiting, then suddenly understood.

'Olivia,' he said.

'I didn't plan for him to die, Chance. I just wanted him to hurt. She deserved that much from the sonofabitch at least.'

My brother was shaking his head from side to side, unable to speak.

'And after what he did to you – laughed in your face when you went begging for his help – I couldn't stand by and do nothing. I tried, so help me, but I couldn't.'

'She wasn't your woman,' Chancellor said, angry now.

'No. But that didn't stop me from loving her.'

259

And there it was, after more than a quarter of a century: the truth he had always suspected but had never challenged me to deny.

'So that's what this was all about? Six people and a little girl dead, and one woman crippled for life, because you were in love with Olivia Gardner?'

I couldn't even bring myself to nod.

'You stupid bastard. It was none of your business. She didn't need you to defend her honor, and neither did I.'

'I know that.'

'The hell you do. What happened to Olivia was her own fault, not Excel Rucker's or anyone else's. She went to that party and snorted his coke of her own free will, and she knew the risks involved. It took me a long time to understand that, but I finally got wise and moved on.'

'I'm happy for you. And I'm envious. Moving on is something I've been trying to do for over half my life now.'

Silence took over the car, flooding every inch of its interior like a noxious gas. When it became too much to bear, I said, 'So what happens now?'

'Excuse me?'

'You're a newspaper man, aren't you? I just gave you the biggest story you'll ever live to write. Are you going to write it?'

'Are you asking me to?'

'No. I just want to know where we stand after this.'

'We stand where we always have, Errol. I'm

your brother, not your judge. You and your friends tried to play God and got a lot of innocent people hurt. Somewhere along the way, either in this life or the next one, you're going to have to answer to somebody for that.' He shook his head. 'But not to me. I've got your back now, same as always.'

His loyalty deserved something more heartfelt than a small nod of thanks, but that was all I could muster without falling apart.

'I'm not the one you should be worried about in any case,' Chance said. 'Seems to me the person with the most to lose in all this is O'. If any of what you've just told me became a matter of public record, his career in politics would be finished. Have you thought about that?'

'Of course.'

'And?'

'And I'm not so sure anymore that he'd draw the line at killing R.J. to keep him quiet. Or me, for that matter.'

'You?'

'I take it the gun I asked you to hide before the ambulance came is here in the car somewhere? The one that failed to fire when I tried to stop Eastman with it?'

'It's in the trunk under the spare. Why?'

'O's the one who gave it to me. And I'd be willing to bet that if I broke it down later, I'd find out the firing pin's either been filed down or is missing altogether.'

'Jesus.'

'It's like you said: He had a lot to lose if R.J.

261

ran his mouth off to the wrong people. And it seems obvious now that in the last few months of his life, R.J. was on the verge of doing exactly that. He went to see McDonald in prison, perhaps to make a full confession. He sought out Linda Dole and made a reclamation project out of her son. Clearly, whatever guilt he'd been living with since I left for Minnesota had taken on a whole new dimension recently. The thing I don't understand yet is, why? Why after all these years did he suddenly feel the need to do penance?'

My brother shrugged. 'Maybe he'd just lived with it long enough. It was either do penance, or put a gun to his head.'

Which was essentially what R.J. had ended up doing if what Eastman had claimed happened out at the Santa Monica Pier two-and-a-half weeks ago could be believed. He'd just gone about suicide in a more creative manner than some. Stealing the car would have been his idea of irony – once a thief, always a thief – and goading Eastman into pulling the trigger for him would have killed two birds with one stone: his punishment and Eastman's right to revenge.

The punishment, R.J. had indeed received, in spades – but whether Eastman had taken his revenge or refused it, leaving the job of killing R.J. that night to someone else who had come along after he had fled, was still an open – and increasingly distressing – question.

Chance tried to talk me into spending the

night at his place, convinced now that O'Neal Holden had essentially tried to kill me once and would eventually try again, but I refused the invitation. There was a part of me that still wanted to give O' the benefit of the doubt for one thing, and I felt I had caused my brother enough grief for one day, for another. For the latter reason alone, I jumped into my rental car the minute we arrived at Linda Dole's residence and quickly drove off.

As there had been the day before, someone was waiting for me at my motel when I got there, only this time it was somebody I recognized.

'I hope you don't mind my dropping in on you like this,' a harried looking Sylvia Nuez said, standing before the door to my room, 'but I've been calling you for hours and you haven't been answering your phone.'

She was right. I'd turned my cellphone off at the request of the Sheriff's detectives who had questioned me out in Carson, and I hadn't given it a second thought since.

'Sorry. I've had a rather rough day.'

'I know. That's why I was calling. You've been all over the news.'

'Ah, yes. I guess I would have been, huh?' I gave her a smile to show her that, if nothing else, the day's events had not cost me my sense of humor.

'Are you OK?'

'I'm fine. Physically, anyway. Would you like to come in?' I started to put my key in the door.

'Actually, I was hoping you'd let me take you out somewhere. Just for drinks, or even to eat if you like. Have you had dinner yet?'

I hadn't. In fact, it had been over six hours since my last meal and I was famished. She drove me out to Manhattan Beach, where we just beat closing time to do seafood on the pier and empty a bottle of fine Chardonnay, agreeing early on to avoid all conversation that would darken the mood of the evening. To fill the void, she talked about her two grown sons and the abusive ex-husband who had fathered them, and I talked about my daughter Coral, telling her nothing close to everything there was to say, but far more than I'd ever shared with another soul. Though the subject pained me more than I could hide, reminding me as it did of the devil's bargain I had made with Coral the day before, Sylvia Nuez didn't push me for details. She just let me speak my piece and listened attentively, her occasional notes of commiseration genuine and unforced.

Overall, the lady was a good listener who only laughed to suit herself, not me, and she knew when to let a subject drop and move on to something else. I liked her, which was no small thing for a misanthrope such as I, and in the flickering wash of candlelight at our table, her edgy, unconventional beauty was becoming more obvious to me by the minute.

I paid our bill and we walked along the pier for a while, the churning water out beyond the pilings beneath us nearly as black as the starless

264

sky above. We were alone, save for a handful of homeless people swaddled in multiple layers of old blankets, and young, paired-off lovers too enchanted with each other to notice anything else.

'This is stupid, isn't it?' Sylvia Nuez asked.

'What's that?'

'What we're doing. Seeing each other like this. We met two days ago. What am I doing here?'

I'd been wondering the same thing myself, and had yet to come up with an answer that made sense from every angle.

'You have someplace better to be?'

She thought about it, then smiled and shook her head. 'No. And that's sad, isn't it?'

'It is what it is. We aren't the first two lonely people to hook up without having good reason, and I'm sure we won't be the last.'

'Yes, but what's the point? Why bother taking the chill off like this if it's never for more than a night or two?'

'You want me to tell you this is bigger than that? I can't. I won't.' I reached out to stroke the side of her face, nudging a strand of hair away from her eyes. 'So we're acting like a couple of clueless kids. So what? Stupid and pointless as this may be, it feels good. Doesn't it?'

I had to ask her again to get an answer: 'Doesn't it?'

'Yes. It feels good.'

'All right, then. It's been a long time since I last found the need to stop all my self-pity and get close to somebody, anybody, for longer than five minutes. And for two nights running, I've done that for you. That may not make you the answer to all my problems, no, but it does make you somebody I'm happy as hell to have run into. For whatever that's worth.'

She tilted her head back, came up on her toes to give me a soft, generous kiss on the mouth. 'It's worth a lot.'

We made love in my motel room in the dark, and afterward she insisted we turn on the TV to hunt for news coverage of my narrow escape from death in Harbor City. I tried to talk her out of it, only to realize I was curious enough about the way the news people would portray me to acquiesce.

It was well after eleven and most of the late-night newscasts were deep into their lead stories, but we did manage to catch the tail end of one report that featured some video of Darrel Eastman's body being removed from his mother's house by people from the coroner's office, and a pair of Linda Dole's neighbors offering their observations of the mayhem that had occurred there. I was nowhere to be seen, though the perky young Asian woman filing the remote dropped my name at least twice, referring to me as the 'suspect' authorities had taken into custody and then released.

At the conclusion of this stirring bit of enter-tainment, Sylvia gave me a kiss, laughed and promptly went to sleep. I started to do the same, until the reel-to-reel tape recorder on the lone table in the room caught my eye and beckoned me to its side. On my way into Bellwood to see Jessie Scott, I'd stopped at an electronics supply shop and picked up a new drive pulley, a reel of tape and a cheap condenser microphone, and I'd been anxious to break them out of the bag ever since.

Twenty minutes in, working in meager light to avoid waking my guest, I had the Sony moving tape in all three modes – play, fast forward and reverse – but it wasn't playing back sound. It recorded just fine – the needles of its VU meters did the proper dance when I whispered into the mic – but all I heard on playback was silence.

One step forward and two steps back. Repair or detective work, it seemed to be all the same.

I was going to pursue matters with the recorder further when the phone in my room rang, finally drawing my attention to the red message light flashing on the instrument. I still hadn't turned my cellphone back on, and upon my return to my room, had been too preoccupied with taking Sylvia Nuez to bed to even glance in the direction of this one. My first thought was that it might be Coral calling, having learned of my stabbing a man to death earlier in the day via the Internet or some national newscast back home, but it wasn't my daughter on the other end of the line when I picked up.

It was Toni Burrow.

'Thank God,' she said upon hearing my voice.

She told me she and her mother had heard about Darrel Eastman's death, and my significant role in it, late that afternoon, and like Sylvia Nuez, Toni had been trying to reach me ever since. Not unexpectedly, and despite the late hour, she wanted a full report, certain that the story the media was disseminating was rife with false truths and inaccuracies. I gave her the shortest version possible, both tired of reliving a bad day and uncomfortable talking to R.J.'s daughter with a woman he'd been having a casual affair with lying naked right beside me, awake again now and listening in.

When I was done, I asked Toni Burrow if she had shared everything I had told her that morning with her mother, unable to ask the question in a way that would imply I had no great interest in her answer.

'No. And right now, I doubt that I ever will,' she said.

She sounded ashamed of the deception. I promised her I'd come see her and her mother in the morning to discuss Eastman's death in greater detail, then begged her forgiveness for being too tired to say much more than goodbye, anxious to get off the phone.

'But wait,' she said, before I could hang up. 'There's something I need to tell you.'

'Yes?'

'I got an answer back from Pelican Bay this afternoon. Your request to visit Paris McDonald has been approved.'

TWENTY-THREE

O' would never tell R.J. and me much about what he'd done in that house out in Simi Valley after we'd left him there. 'The less you niggas know about it, the better,' he kept saying, growing increasingly tired of being asked.

I'd been right about the fire, however, and once the story hit the news, everything else about O's actions that night became painfully evident. Prior to torching the place, and after having stripped it of any trace of our presence in it, he had manipulated all the evidence in the bedroom – the bodies of Excel Rucker and Paris McDonald's woman, the weapons that had killed them, etc. – to infer that McDonald had at least murdered one of them, if not both.

And the cops bought it.

From all indications, a four-year-old girl had been snatched from her home, brutally beaten and her body done away with, and nobody much cared to hear anything the man responsible had to say about being innocent of the three murders he was eventually charged with. They had found him unconscious and stinking of booze at the scene of the Simi Valley fire, sprawled out on the grass in the backyard like a fallen scarecrow, and swearing he couldn't remember how he'd gotten there didn't dissuade anyone from thinking they already knew: He'd crawled out there after setting the house aflame, then passed out before he could finish off his escape. The man had a long record of criminal brutality, both in and outside the ring, and if that didn't exactly prove he was a murderer, his lack of short-term memory almost certainly did.

As for the thieves who had allegedly made it impossible for the child's father to meet McDonald's ransom demands, we ultimately became little more than a distraction the police and the D.A.'s office chose to only half-heartedly pursue. If a couple of hoods – or three, depending on which unreliable witness was telling the story – had in fact complicated the girl's kidnapping by ripping her father off only days before, this was judged at best an insignificant aside to the central issue of McDonald's culpability in three homicides. Why worry about us when the only purpose that would serve would be to muddy the waters of an otherwise solid case against a suspect already in custody?

Not that we would have been easy to find had the police made a greater effort to look for us. For days after O' put a match to the house of the dead woman we now knew had gone by the name of Noreen Phillips, we went back into the three shells we had created for ourselves immediately following the Inglewood safe house robbery. I stayed put in my crib while O' and R.J., holed up together, did the same out at O's, where they had been since the night Excel Rucker died. It was O' who nursed R.J. back to health, following the instructions for treating a gunshot wound he found in a book he'd checked out from the library: apply pressure to stop the bleeding, clean the wound with hydrogen peroxide, then dress with a dry cloth and do the last two steps all over again, three times a day for at least a week. In the end, it worked, but none of us ever had any illusions about why: R.J. had been damn lucky. Another inch closer to his liver and the bullet that tore right through him would have left him with a hole too big for a layman like O' to heal.

Unlike R.J., however, there was no putting our lives back together the way they had been before we ripped off Excel Rucker. That ill-fated decision had taken the world we knew and changed its shape forever, making it impossible for us to assume our old places in it. O' and R.J. were slower than me to understand this, but I was convinced of it from the moment O' returned to his apartment from Simi that night, three hours after we'd last seen him, and our collective guilt began to shred us to pieces.

'What the hell're we gonna do?' R.J. kept asking, weeping like a widow at a funeral from where he lay on O's living room couch. I'd gotten his bleeding to stop and redressed his wounds once already, but he was still in a lot of pain. 'We killed that little girl.'

'Shut the fuck up! We didn't kill anybody!' O' snapped.

'You know what he means,' I said. 'We may not have killed her ourselves, but we're the reason she's dead. There's no way of getting around that, O'.'

'Bullshit. For all we know, she's been dead since the day McDonald snatched her. That ain't on us, that's on him.' When I shook my head at the vacuity of his argument, he grabbed me by the front of my shirt and, snarling into my face, said, 'Besides, nigga, you're the last one who ought'a be cryin' about what we've "done", seein' as how this whole thing was your goddamn idea in the first place. Or have you forgotten that?'

I broke his grip and threw him off me, wanting to do more to shut him up but knowing I had no right.

'What's done is done,' O' said. 'It all turned to shit and, yeah, I feel bad about it, but there isn't anything for us to do now except chill and wait for McDonald to take all the heat.'

'It's not that simple,' I said.

'He's right,' R.J. agreed.

'We've got a man over there who might be dead tomorrow. But even if he pulls through, and McDonald does take all the heat, how the hell are we supposed to go on hanging together without somebody finally doing the math and connecting us to the robbery?'

'They won't,' O' said. 'Not if we play this thing the same way we've played every other job we ever pulled.'

'Except we've never had a job go this wrong before. Until tonight, we'd never hurt anybody, and that's all changed now. This is a whole new ball game, O'. We've killed one man and caused the death of at least two other people, including a little girl.'

'We didn't *touch* that little girl.'

'Playing it smart and keeping a low profile isn't going to cut it this time. We aren't just thieves anymore, brother. If you haven't figured that out yet, there's no point in my even talking to you.'

'All right. So what do you suggest? How do we make things right?'

I looked over at R.J., apologizing for what I knew he would take harder than any of us. 'We've gotta go our separate ways. All three of us. After this thing winds down, assuming it ever does, we can't ever be seen together again.'

'Say what?' R.J. said, breaking into a coughing jag.

O' started to chuckle. 'That's wack.'

'It's not wack,' I said. 'It's the way it's gotta be. What we did tonight isn't going to go away just because we don't get hemmed up for it. Whether we get busted or not, we're gonna carry this shit around for the rest of our lives, and it's only gonna be that much harder to live with if we go on kicking it with each other.'

R.J. shook his head. 'Naw...'

'We're a team, Handy. We've always been a

team,' O' said.

'Word. You brothers have been like family to me, and I'm not ever gonna forget it,' I said. 'But that doesn't change the fact that every time I look at you after tonight, and every time you look at me, we're all gonna be thinking about the same thing.' I glanced over at R.J. again. 'Aren't we?'

The look on his face said he knew I spoke the truth, but he wasn't up to admitting it. 'It don't matter,' he said, eyes finally beginning to flicker from exhaustion. 'What O' said ... is for real. We're a team, Handy. Without you niggas ... I ain't got *nobody.*'

And that was also true; we were all the poor bastard had. But my sympathies for him were not going to be enough to change my mind. Though it would be tough on all of us, separation – *permanent* separation – was the only way I could see us surviving the long-term nightmare we had bought for ourselves.

'I don't like it any better than you do,' I said. 'But this is it. We either split up right now, for good, or we're fucked. Maybe not tomorrow, or a year from now, but somewhere down the road. It's inevitable.'

'Ain't nothin' inevitable,' O' said, still unconvinced. He was in that zone of his in which nothing you said to him was going to penetrate his intransigence.

'You brothers can do what you wanna do. Me, I'm gone.'

'Gone where?'

'I don't know yet. Maybe Cleveland or some-where down in Minnesota. It's gonna take me a while to decide.'

'Uh-huh. And let me guess: You're gonna need a little taste of Excel's dope for extra seed money.'

'I don't want anything that belonged to Excel. We're gonna flush that coke just like we plan-ned. Only thing different now is, we're gonna burn the cash, too.'

He grinned at me like I was a circus clown who'd just challenged him to a fight. 'Say again?'

'You heard me. We're gonna burn it. I don't want a dime of that bread, and neither do you. It's blood money.'

He shook his head, tickled, said, 'R.J., are you listenin' to this fool? Can you believe this shit?'

But R.J. *wasn't* listening. He had dozed off, head cocked to one side, mouth open wide like a hatchling waiting to be fed.

'We're gonna have to watch him carefully,' I told O'. 'Make sure he doesn't slip into a coma or something.'

'Only person in a coma around here is you, Handy, if you think I'm gonna set fire to my share of a hundred and forty Gs.'

I glared at him, then moved over to the couch to check on R.J. He was sweating like a fat man in a sauna and his temperature felt a little higher to me than normal, but his breathing was even and his bandages gave no indication that his bleeding had started up again.

'And what do you think he's gonna say about it?' I asked O'.

'I suspect he'll side with you for a change. Hard as homeboy is in some ways, he's a soft-hearted fool in others. But I don't give a shit. This ain't no democracy, Handy, it don't matter if the vote's two or a thousand to one. I'm not burnin' up forty-five grand just 'cause you and R.J. ain't got the stomach to spend it.'

'And you do?'

'Goddamn right I do.'

'No.' I shook my head. 'You don't. You've got a conscience, same as us, and makin' a profit off that little girl's death would haunt you till the day you died.'

I'd finally said something he couldn't dismiss out of hand.

'We've got to walk away, and we've got to walk away clean,' I said. 'All three of us, to-gether, the same way we've always done every-thing.'

I had him thinking now. He made no sound, but you could look in his eyes and see his mind working away behind them just the same.

'I don't know, Handy,' he said at last. 'Maybe there's somethin' we can work out...' He tipped his head in the direction of R.J. ' ... just you and me.'

He waited for me to catch his drift. It wasn't hard.

'I don't think so, O',' I said.

Three weeks later, we all stood around an old

black barbecue drum in O's mother's garage and watched a pile of green paper burn down to nothing. R.J. had been against the idea initially, but as his injuries healed and his will grew stronger, so too did his guilt over the death of Sienna Jackson and his need to wash his hands of it. As for O', all his talk about my opinion and R.J.'s holding no sway over him eventually dwindled down to nothing, R.J. having threatened to stick a foot up his ass if he continued to bitch about having to relinquish his share of Excel Rucker's 140 grand.

Convincing both men that we needed to split up for good, on the other hand, continued to be a hard sell for me right up until the morning we actually did, two days after we put a match to the dead dealer's money and flushed all his coke down the commode. My friends thought severing ties was an overreaction. Everything we were reading and hearing about the Paris McDonald murder investigation seemed to suggest it was going to begin and end with McDonald, just as O' had planned. Why throw away four years of friendship with men I had loved like brothers when, by all indications, we were in the clear?

'Because I want to *stay* in the clear,' I said.

Whether or not R.J. and O' ever completely bought into that argument, they ended up agreeing to terminate our limited partnership. For R.J., our every minute together had become a constant reminder of the nightmare he wanted desperately to put behind him, and O' simply grew tired of trying to hold something together I was bound and determined to dismantle. By the time we all met that cold February morning in Leimert Village Park to say our final good-byes, each of us was quietly resigned to a future that did not include the other two.

Unlike O' and R.J., I wasn't going to test my commitment to our dissolution agreement by remaining in Los Angeles. I needed more distance from what we had done, and from things I had done without them, than the mere length of a freeway could provide. So I had decided to run off to the Twin Cities of Minnesota, because I'd heard more good things than bad about that part of the country, and because that was as far as I thought my old Ford could carry me. I loaded the car up like a four-wheeled pack mule, bid my brother Chance a brief and somewhat cruel farewell, and then met R.J. and O' at the park, not even bothering to kill the Fairmont's engine.

'You're really goin', huh?' R.J. asked.

'Yeah,' I said, shaking first his hand, then O's. 'Any need to go over the deal again? Or do we all have it down?'

'No more contact after this. We get it, Handy,' O' said.

'Guess that's it then.'

I couldn't think of anything else to say, and neither could they. O' was having enough trouble just standing there without throwing a punch at somebody. I turned to get in the car.

Just before I could jump in, O' called out,

'You know it didn't have to be like this, Handy. Running scared is for babies and old women.'

For years afterward, I would wonder why I didn't answer him. He was out of line, and his final words to me should have been better chosen. But I let them pass without comment, just sat down in my car, pulled the driver's side door closed behind me and drove away.

I couldn't get to St Paul, Minnesota, fast enough.

TWENTY-FOUR

All throughout my flight from LA to Crescent City, I kept wanting to glance over my shoulder, certain that somebody seated behind me on the plane was eventually going to flash a badge and place me under arrest. It was a crazy thought, of course, but when you kill a man one day and ignore a police order not to travel the next, paranoia is both the fair and natural price of the ticket.

I would have avoided the trip given an alternative. I had no desire to test the patience of the law, and was not anxious to confront the man I was coming here to see. But I had run from Paris McDonald long enough. He was waiting for me now, Toni Burrow having moved my

279

pending visitation request forward by lending it the authority of her private investigator's license, and I could think of no one other than McDonald who might have the answers to the few open questions that remained about R.J.'s murder.

Situated just over twenty miles south of the Oregon border, Crescent City was a picturesque little jewel on the California coast that hardly resembled a fitting home for a state penitentiary. From the airport, where the Pacific spread out to the west like a sun-dappled sheet of blue ice, to the peaceful, bucolic heart of downtown, the prison city was a visual salve for the soul, as far removed from the bleak world inhabited by the convicts at Pelican Bay as heaven itself. And yet, as I soaked it all in from the back seat of a taxi early on a bright, clear Thursday morning, I could see nothing but a beautiful, ornate gateway to my doom. Even the trees standing along both sides of the highway leading out to the prison struck me as ominous, emerald sentries someone had placed there solely to ensure my arrival.

Based upon everything I had read about the man in recent years, McDonald was no longer the short-tempered, brutal thug I remembered. At some point during his incarceration, he had turned his life over to Jesus Christ and declared himself born again, taking his redemption so far as to become an ordained minister. If the reporters who wrote about him were in the habit of portraying him accurately, he was something just short of a harmless, soft-spoken teddy bear now, quick to warm up to strangers and next to impossible to ruffle. I had never heard him speak, but as in the letter he had written to R.J., whenever he was quoted directly, he sounded surprisingly articulate and kind.

Still, he scared the hell out of me.

I had been rehearsing what I would say to him for years and yet, even as my taxi pulled up to the prison's outer gates, I had no idea where to start. My friends and I had framed this man for two murders he did not commit, and arguably, by way of our interference in Excel Rucker's affairs, positioned him to commit a third. How could I look the man in the eye, let alone ask for his help in putting R.J.'s murder to rest?

Security check-in was just a blur to me; I answered questions and filled out paperwork without conscious thought. My head cleared only after I'd taken my seat in the visitation room of the PBSP Security Housing Unit and McDonald entered the cubicle opposite me. Wearing the same full-length, long-sleeved white jumper as the other inmates here, he sat down on the other side of the glass and nodded in greeting, smiling as if he were certain that only good things could possibly come from my visit. His body had gone soft since the last time I saw him, and his hair had turned to a mere wisp of white fuzz growing on the back and both sides of his head, but in size and overall mass, he was still an imposing giant worthy of the nickname 'the Tower'.

He picked up his telephone handset and waited for me to do the same.

'Errol White?'

I nodded. 'Thanks for agreeing to see me.'

'Not a problem. My door is always open – so to speak.' He grinned, casting a sideways glance at one of the guards stationed nearby. Then he added: 'Especially for friends of Brother Burrow.'

'Excuse me?'

Both my visitation request, and the follow-up telephone call Toni Burrow had made to the Department of Corrections to try and move it along, had indicated I was a freelance reporter seeking an interview for a profile piece, that was all.

'I've become a very popular man up here at the Bay,' McDonald said. 'Seems like I meet a new reporter wantin' to write about me every week. So I kind'a know one when I see one now. And you?' He shook his head.

'And that makes me a friend of "Brother Burrow"?'

'It does if the Lord has graced you with clarity of vision, as he has me. I look at you and what do I see? A man roughly the same age as Brother Burrow, with the same sad, hangdog look in his eyes. Could be just a coincidence, but I don't think so.'

We both sat there staring at each other.

'Tell me what I can do for you, Brother White,' he finally said.

There was no point in continuing to be coy.

'You can tell me who might have killed him. You did know he was dead?'

'I read about it in the newspaper. I was very sorry to hear.'

'Do you have any idea what happened?'

He produced a small shrug, said, 'I imagine he just lost faith. Coming correct with the Lord can be a frightening thing for some people; they can't believe their sins will really be forgiven, so they just give up and go back to doing all the unrighteous things they did before. I see it happen in here all the time.'

'And what sins was R.J. hoping to have forgiven?'

'There were quite a few, as I'm sure you know. He said he was a thief and a drug user, just for starters. But what seemed to bother him most was what he said you and he, and another brother he didn't name, did to me. Or "for" me, depending on your point of view.'

He smiled.

'I don't understand,' I lied, the telephone handset feeling like an enormous lead weight growing larger in my hand by the moment.

'Well, he talked in riddles, of course. But as near as I could understand, he said you were all responsible for the murders I've been accused of committing. It was your fault my cousin couldn't pay me the ransom I wanted for his daughter, so you were also to blame for every-thing else that followed.'

There was no animus whatsoever in the tone of his voice. The expression on his face was completely devoid of anger and ill-will. I had made this trip to Crescent City half-wondering if McDonald's conversion in Christ was genuine, or simply a show of some kind intended to draw the sympathies of an ever-gullible public – and now I thought I knew. He was the real deal.

'He was right,' I said. A maelstrom of diverse emotions was threatening to send me stumbling out of the room like a wounded drunk, and it was all I could do to remain in my chair.

'He wanted to tell me how sorry he was,' McDonald said, 'and to ask my forgiveness. But I told him the same thing I'm about to tell you: You don't need my forgiveness because you already have it. Mine *and* the Lord's.'

I shook my head in disbelief. 'No. We're talking about almost thirty years of your life here. You telling me you were willing to just let that go?'

'Yes, I am. I'm telling you I can let it go because whatever you brothers did or didn't do, it was all part of God's plan for me. Before they put me in this place, I was a disciple of Satan. An animal full of rage and hate. I was capable of any act of evil, including murder, and what I did to that little girl should be proof enough that I would have done much worse if I hadn't been stopped. But I was stopped. By the grace of Brother Burrow's and your intervention – accidental or not – my soul was saved. The only thing I owe all of you, if I owe you anything, is my thanks.'

'Your *thanks*?'

'I know it sounds crazy to you. It did to Brother Burrow, as well. But I promise you, I mean what I say. The only person you and Brother Burrow's friend have to make peace with now is the Lord Jesus Christ. Not me.'

'What about getting out of here? If I went to the police now—'

'No,' he said sharply, cutting me off. 'The time for all that has passed. Even if I thought I could get a new trial, I wouldn't want one. Because *this* is my home now. It's where I'm meant to be, where I need to be to do the work the Lord wants me to do. And I'm not ever gonna do anything to interfere with His designs on my life again. Never.'

It didn't seem possible, this measure of mercy and self-sacrifice. But it was. The harder I tried to spot some crack in his veneer, some suggestion, no matter how small, that what I was seeing was all just an elaborate front for a bitter, vengeful liar, the more convinced I became that his words were genuine. I had seen renewed faith make profound changes in people before, but this was something well beyond my experience. This was one of those rarities in life men pray to see, then claim do not exist when we look right past them: a minor miracle.

Having been discouraged from any more talk about helping him win his freedom, and with time winding down on my visit, I asked him if R.J. had ever said anything to him about a man named Darrel Eastman.

'No. Not that I recall.'

'What about Cleveland Allen?'

'No. Brother Burrow was only here for a short time, I'm afraid, and he didn't say much more than I've already told you. Except for the good news he brought me about the little girl, of course.'

Somewhere off in the distance, I heard a voice that sounded much like my own ask, 'What little girl?'

'Excel's daughter. Sienna.' McDonald beamed, his euphoria impossible to contain. 'It was a great blessing for me to learn she's still alive.'

On the taxi ride back into Crescent City, my only thoughts were of my daughter.

'Coral' was not the name her mother gave her. That was something I came up with to satisfy my own selfish needs. Specifically, I was trying to give the two of us a fresh start, a life together separate from the one she might have had with the woman who gave birth to her, and it seemed to me a new name was the only place to start. Like every other critical judgment of mine at the time, it was a decision only a deaf, dumb and blind man could have made.

My excuse? I was desperate to do something right, to perform some heroic act of self-sacrifice that might make up for all the lives to which I'd laid waste. Assuming the role of single parent to a child who had already been dealt a terrible hand was my way of trying to turn back the clock, to return to a point in time in my life when my first sensation upon waking every morning was something other than shame.

I had been a good father to the girl. I had made mistakes, both of omission and commission, and there were things I could have done differently that might have spared her some of the suffering she eventually came to bring upon herself. But I had given her all that I had to give. She was my masterpiece, the recipient of everything I knew about love and repair and reclamation – and it wasn't going to be enough. I could see that now. For some, the past is an unstoppable force, a shaft of burning light that can only be imprisoned in the dark for so long.

It was coming for Coral and me both.

TWENTY-FIVE

The next flight out of Crescent City to Los Angeles wasn't until Friday morning, so after I left Paris McDonald at Pelican Bay, I checked in to my motel room and waited several hours before calling Sylvia Nuez at home to ask her a few questions about Doug Wilmore. I'd been trying to put all the pieces of R.J.'s murder together since McDonald had dropped his bomb on me about R.J. and Sienna Jackson, and the man Mike Owens had said was R.J.'s best friend at Coughlin Construction was the one person my attention kept coming back around to.

'I seem to recall you telling me something about him having trouble with women who told him no. Were you speaking from personal experience?'

'Sure. Doug used to hit on me all the time, early on.'

'Early on, meaning before you and R.J. started seeing each other?'

'Yes. Way before that. But once I set him straight, he was fine.'

'Describe "fine".'

'Well, he sulked for a while, of course. In fact, now that I think about it, he didn't speak to me for months afterward. But you don't think—'

'Is he married?'

'No. He's divorced.'

'Kids?'

'I don't think so.'

'You happen to know if he's scheduled to work tomorrow?'

'He isn't. Fridays are his day off. Handy, where are you? Why are we having this conversation over the phone?'

'I'll explain all that to you later,' I said. 'Right now, I need you to tell me everything else you know about Wilmore. Starting with where I might be able to find him in the morning.'

It rained all day Friday, a hard rain that dropped out of a cold black sky like a wall of three-penny nails. It reduced busy intersections to wading pools and drenched pedestrians from head to foot, regardless of what they used – umbrellas, newspaper, jackets pulled up over their heads – to fend it off. You could turn on the wipers in your car full blast and still see nothing but gray in front of you; the blades just beat ineffectively against the torrent like a pair of frantic, over-wound metronomes.

It was all a perfect match for my mood.

'It was a terrible thing, what happened to R.J.'

'Yes, it was.'

Silence.

'But that man you killed the other day, I forget his name – he was the one done it, right?'

'Darrel Eastman. He's the one the police think did it, yes. Me, I'm not so sure.'

'You're not?' O's sister Brenda gave me a surprised look. 'How come?'

I shrugged. 'Just a feeling I get.'

For someone who hadn't seen me in over twenty-five years, she was treating me with unexpected hospitality. I'd shown up at the door of her West Adams home completely unannounced, Toni Burrow having traced her to this address for me only hours earlier, and she'd asked me in out of the rain with only a small measure of noticeable discomfort. R.J. and I had shared enough meals at her mother's table to develop a certain affection for her, and it was

289

good to see that time had not been unkind to her. She was a big, heavy woman now, as her build back in the day had always foretold, but beyond the extra weight and a little gray in her hair, she looked like the same gentle soul I remembered.

'Are you still a registered nurse?' I asked. 'Or did you finally become a doctor?'

'No, I'm still a nurse. I work the night shift over at Queen of Angels.'

I walked over to the fireplace in her living room, drawn to a photo displayed prominently on the mantel.

'This is your daughter Iman, isn't it?'

'Yes.' She moved quickly across the room to join me, as if I'd just reached out to touch something she was afraid I might break.

The photo was a full-color wedding portrait. The groom was a stranger to me, but the radiant bride was the aide I'd seen O' confer with in Bellwood City Council chambers Monday morning. There'd been more curls in her hair on her wedding day than there were now, and the portrait left no doubt about her most striking feature, something I'd been too far away from her to notice four days ago: Her eyes were the color of molten gold.

'O' tells me she's really your stepdaughter. Your first husband's child, I think he said.'

'No. She's Herman's daughter. My second husband.' She hadn't raised her voice to make the correction, but the distinction was clearly one she thought important. 'Would you like some coffee, Handy? I was just about to make some coffee.'

'Coffee would be nice,' I said.

O's sister smiled and quickly headed for the kitchen.

'And Brenda, if I could ask a favor,' I said, before she could vanish from sight.

She stopped, turned. 'Yes?'

'When you talk to O', could you tell him something for me? Tell him that before I came over here to see you this morning, I went to see a man named Doug Wilmore, and we had a very interesting little talk.'

'Doug Wilmore?'

'The name doesn't mean anything to you, I know. But O' will understand.'

She stared at me, thoroughly unsure of herself now. 'You want me to call Neal?'

Seeing no point in embarrassing her further, I just said, 'If you could. I'm sure he'd appreciate it if you did.'

Whatever Bellwood city business he had to bring to an utter standstill to do it, it took O' all of thirty minutes to drive to his sister's home, shortly before noon.

For both Brenda and me, it had been a long, awkward wait, a charade of calm and small talk in the face of mounting fear and foreboding. I didn't ask her any more questions about Iman, and she didn't volunteer any more answers.

The young woman was there in the house all around us, in the form of graduation photos, sports trophies and notices of academic achievement, yet both her adopted mother and I treated her like the proverbial elephant in the room we could not see.

'What the hell are you doing, Handy?' O' asked, after Brenda had gone to the door to usher him in. He was wearing a long black overcoat on top of his expensive blue suit, but he must have walked from his car to the house through the still-raging downpour without bothering with an umbrella, because he glistened with rainwater from the crown of his head to the tips of his shoes. He had his anger in check for now, but his control of it looked tentative at best.

'Getting to know you better, O',' I said, without getting up from the armchair I was sitting in.

He didn't ask me for an explanation; my meaning was clear to him. He turned to look at his sister. 'Handy and I are gonna need to be alone for a while, BeBe.'

It wasn't a question, and she didn't treat it like one. 'OK. How long—'

'I'll call to let you know when it's all right to come back.'

Brenda nodded. She retreated to a back bedroom, returned with a coat and umbrella of her own. We watched her throw the coat on hurriedly and go to the door.

'I didn't tell 'im nothin',' she said softly, by way of offering an apology, then she disappeared without waiting to hear how her brother would respond.

In her wake, the house fell deathly silent, save for the sound of the rain shaking the nails loose from every shingle on the roof. O' glared at me for a long minute, wanting to make sure his sister had time to get in her car and drive away, before he sat down in the chair opposite mine, giving no thought to removing his coat first.

'You always were a pain in the fucking ass,' he said.

'Yeah. That's what R.J. always thought, too.'

'I didn't think you'd gotten that good a look at the girl. What, you go back to see her again at the office or something, before I got her the hell out of Dodge?'

'No.' I told him about my visit with Paris McDonald on Thursday, and what McDonald had said R.J. told him about Sienna Jackson still being alive.

O' lowered his head, shook it from side to side. 'Fuck. That goddamn fool...'

'He only knows the girl didn't die that night out in Simi. R.J. didn't tell him anything else.'

O's head snapped upright again, his eyes damp and on fire. 'That was enough! And for what? What good could it have possibly done McDonald to know after all these years?'

'The poor bastard never killed anybody, O', least of all Sienna Jackson. If finding that out twenty-six years after the fact did nothing but ease R.J.'s conscience a bit, that was reason enough to tell him, seems to me.'

'Yeah, well, you can say that because neither

of you niggas saw what that motherfucker did to the child that night. If you had seen her face, her little arms...' He tried to shake the memory out of focus. 'Just 'cause he didn't kill her doesn't mean he didn't try.'

A single tear escaped from the corner of his right eye and slid down the side of his face. He let it be.

'Tell me what happened,' I said.

'What, you don't know? Mr "Undercover Brother"? Why don't you tell *me* what happened?'

I'd been trying to put it all together for days now and I still couldn't do anything more than speculate. 'You and R.J. were lying when you told Excel and the woman that the girl wasn't in the house. She was either still in the bedroom where you'd found her, or hidden somewhere else, maybe out in R.J.'s car; Excel and I hadn't stopped to look on our way in. McDonald came back from wherever he was after R.J. and I left—'

'No,' O' said, his voice a jagged knife of irritation. 'R.J. didn't know anything about it. Up until about a year ago, he thought the girl was dead, too.'

'Then you were alone when you found her?'

'No. No! It wasn't like that.' He scrubbed his face dry with both hands, let out a long, heavy sigh. 'McDonald and Sienna were gone, just like I said. I'd searched the place myself and the only sign of either one was all the blood on the bed where she'd been sleeping. I thought sure the child was dead.

'But then McDonald came back to the house, just before I put a match to it, and he had her with him, all wrapped up in a sheet like a mummy. He'd gone out looking for either a hospital he couldn't find, or a place to bury her like we thought, till he realized she was still breathing. I never talked to him, so I can only guess. But wherever he'd been, he brought her back. Alive.'

'When the fire department showed up, they found him unconscious out in the yard, bleeding from a nasty knot on his head. You?'

'I heard him coming in through the front door and caught him with the butt of my gun before he had time to hit the lights. When I saw what Sienna looked like, I almost killed the sonofabitch right then – but then I realized that would be a mistake. I couldn't frame his ass for Excel and the woman, and the fire I was about to start, if the man was dead.'

'So you dragged him outside, went back for Sienna, and then torched the house and split.'

'Yeah.'

His voice had a tinge of disgust in it now, but I couldn't tell for whom it was meant.

'How long, O'? Did it come to you right away, or did it take a while?'

'What?'

'The idea that the girl could be worth a lot more to you dead than alive.'

He bristled at the accusation. 'Go fuck yourself, Handy. I may not be the altar boy you've

295

always thought yourself to be, but I'm not the calculating piece of shit you like to think I am, either. When I left the house that night, my only thought was of Sienna. I was gonna take her to the first hospital I could find and drop her off out front.

'But then she came to in the car and started crying, and it freaked me the hell out. I figured I might have a shot of leaving an unconscious kid in a hospital carport without somebody seeing me, but a hysterical one? So I stayed on the freeway until I could calm her down and talk her back to sleep. It took a long time.'

'And then?'

'By then I realized something I hadn't before: She wasn't as bad off as I thought. She was bruised and in a lot of pain, but she wasn't dying. It occurred to me that maybe a hospital was an unnecessary risk. Brenda was a nurse, and I could trust her to treat the girl without saying anything to the police.'

'You still haven't answered my original question,' I said.

He let several seconds go by, just to keep me writhing on the hook. 'It was a long ride back from Simi. I had a lot of time to think, to go over everything that had happened that night. I remembered how you and R.J. had been acting earlier, before we'd even driven out there to try and find Sienna. Both of you were already talking like her father's money was tainted, like we'd all burn in hell for eternity if we touched so much as a penny of it. And now you thought

296

the girl was dead for sure. There was no way you were gonna want to keep that bread.'

'Unless we found out she was still alive.'

He nodded, clearly taking no pride in the memory. 'The money was right there with me in the car, 140 grand, and the more I looked at it, the more ways I could think of to use it. I had plans for my life, things I wanted to accomplish, and it was all gonna take money to get done. Forty-six thousand would've been enough to get started, but 140 would've put me on a whole new timetable.

'And hell, Handy, what were you and R.J. gonna do with forty-six Gs? You never wanted the money in the first place, and R.J. would've pissed his share away inside of six months, no matter what we told him about spending too much too soon.'

'So you took Sienna to BeBe and asked her to take care of the girl for a while.'

'Yes.'

'And she ended up doing it for the next twenty years.'

'More or less. She fell in love with the child. After a week, I couldn't have taken Sienna from her if I'd wanted to.'

He told me the rest of it in fits and starts, how all the paper we'd burned that day in his mother's garage was mostly prop money he'd bought off some brother who worked on the lot at Columbia Studios, mixed in with just enough real cash to sell the illusion. Then, after I was gone, he and his sister gave Excel's little girl a new name and the phony papers to go with it. They cut her hair to change her appearance and sent her to schools out in the Valley where R.J. was unlikely to ever come across her, all the while raising her to believe that Brenda and her late husband Herman Evans were her biological parents.

'She didn't remember her real mother and father?'

'She didn't remember anything prior to that night in Simi. The traumatization of her kidnapping and beating had wiped out her memory completely.'

'What about now?'

O' got up from his seat, walked over to a bookcase to lift a photo from a shelf: a pre-teen Sienna/Iman in a green and white soccer uniform, beaming into the camera with a soccer ball as a prop. 'As far as she knows, her name is Iman Evans. BeBe's her moms and I'm her Uncle 'Neal. And you know what? She's happy, Handy. We gave her a life she would've never had otherwise. Blow this thing up now, and you throw that all away.'

'And her real mother? Excel's woman? What kind of life did we give her, O'?'

'Vicky Jackson? A drug dealer's ho' with two other kids, and from everything I ever heard about her, a crackhead to boot. With Excel around, she might've still found a way to be a good mother to Sienna, but without him, she would've been no better for her than McDonald himself. I wouldn't waste a whole lot of time

298

trying to raise my sympathies for her, Handy.'

'OK. How about your sympathies for R.J., then? Not only did you cheat him out of his share of a hundred and forty grand, you let him go twenty-six years thinking he had the death of a four-year-old girl on his hands.'

'I thought he could handle it. It was a mistake.'

'But a mistake you were happy to live with until he found out Sienna was still alive. After that, I guess, all bets were off.'

'I smell coffee. You want some coffee?'

I looked at him like he'd lost his mind, the thought only now occurring to me that that could in fact be the case.

'Sure.'

He went out to the kitchen. I could hear him rummaging around in his sister's cabinets, searching for clean cups. 'How do you like it?' he asked.

'Lots of sugar, no cream,' I called back.

He returned a few minutes later, two steaming mugs in hand. He passed one to me, then sat back down with the other, and somewhere in between, he found a blue-steel semi-automatic that he set down easy on the right armrest of his chair, nozzle turned more or less in my direction.

'That isn't really necessary, is it?' I asked, blowing on my coffee to cool it down.

'You just accused me of being a murderer, Handy, so your state of mind's a little questionable. Let's just say the hardware's only there to discourage you from doing something we might both be sorry for later.'

'You want to set my mind at ease, O', try convincing me that what happened to R.J. wasn't done on your orders.'

This time, judging from the mayor's expression, I was the one who was crazy. He shook his head, said, 'Jesus, man. Talk about leaving police work to the professionals. You've been pokin' around this thing for what, almost a week now, and you're just as ignorant today as when you started.

'I didn't kill R.J., Handy. Hell, I did everything in my power to keep him alive! I got him his job at Coughlin. I loaned him money when he said he was strapped. Ever since you tucked tail and hauled ass to Minnesota, I've been trying to keep that nigga from puttin' a bullet in his head, or throwing himself in front of a goddamn train. But not for the reason you think. That's something else you're wrong about.'

He glanced at his coffee cup and gently set it down, hand shaking too much now to risk dropping it at his feet.

'Sienna was foremost on his mind all that time, of course. But she wasn't the only thing ridin' him.'

He paused to see if I could go the rest of the way without him.

'What are you talking about?' I asked, feeling the hairs at the back of my neck come alive with dread.

'I'm talking about the second big mistake I made, after deciding to let that damn fool go on thinking Sienna was dead. I split the money with him. I didn't think I had a choice.' He finally looked away from me, affecting the mannerisms of a man squirming in the cramped confines of a confessional booth. 'Burning up a pile of phony money was a trick I might've got R.J. to believe, but you?' He shook his head. 'You would've never bought it.'

I let my mind drift back to the day in question, sifting through the details. 'Unless I saw somebody else check the cash first.'

He nodded.

All these years later, my memory of that day was as vague as a ghost, but there were some things I could still remember distinctly: the smell of tar from across the alley; the suspicion R.J. kept voicing that O' was looking to run a game on us; the bundle of bills he tossed for me to look over personally while he inventoried the remainder of the bag, until I, like an idiot, called him off...

'Goddamn,' I said.

'If it makes you feel any better, it took a while to talk him into it. For all the bitching he used to do about you, he really held you in high esteem. But once I reminded him that every-thing that had gone down and gone wrong had started with you, and the fucking, inexplicable hard-on you had for Excel Rucker, he came around to seeing the justice in it. You had the shit coming, Handy. If not for you, there would've been nothing for any of us to feel guilty about.'

I wanted to take his words and ram them down his throat. He was telling me that I had earned every sleepless night I'd ever endured, that all the tears I had cried and self-loathing I had suffered were nowhere near the actual punishment I deserved. Paris McDonald was in prison for life because of me. Linda Dole lived her days and nights in a wheelchair because of me. Excel Rucker and Noreen Phillips, Darrel Eastman and the three people Rucker had killed himself, they all were dead because of me.

R.J. Burrow was dead because of me.

I tried to move from my chair, to lift my hands or turn my head, but I couldn't. I could only sit there and sink, farther and farther down into the empty hollows of my conscience.

'I'm not completely blameless myself, of course,' O' said. 'What we did, I allowed to happen, there's no gettin' around that. But while you were off in St Paul making a new life for yourself, I was here trying to make up for my part in what we did, spending damn near every minute of the last twenty-six years looking for ways to keep R.J.'s guilt from ruining us all. But it just wasn't possible.'

O's eyes flared, suddenly enraged. 'It was like trying to save a drowning man who keeps taking you both farther and farther away from shore. First it was the armed robbery that landed him in the joint, then it was his goddamn crack habit. He went back to the safe house in

Inglewood and made a project out of "saving" Linda Dole's son, hangin' out with the boy and counselin' him like a parish priest or somethin'. There was nothin' I could do to stop him, Handy. Talking was just a waste of time.

'So I finally did something desperate. Something I thought would bring him down, but only made things a thousand times worse.'

For once, he didn't have to wait for me to understand. 'You introduced him to Iman Evans.'

'I was a fool. He lost his mind. I didn't know until you told me that he'd written to McDonald in prison, but I wasn't surprised to hear it. He was that far gone. So, naturally—'

'Get up.'

He'd been too preoccupied with his confession to notice that I'd left my chair. I stood over him, rocking on the balls of my feet, unable to see anything else in the room but the man seated before me.

'Oh, what – you're gonna kick my ass now?'

His right hand made a move for the gun on the armrest and I kicked him in the face with the heel of my right foot, sending chair and occupant both tumbling backwards to the floor. He tried to roll to his feet before I could get there, the semi-auto in his fist, but I surprised us both by reaching him in time to kick the weapon from his grasp. As it clattered off to some unknown corner of his sister's living room, he barreled into me waist-high, reducing the left I threw at his face to a mere gesture of a punch.

Legs churning, head down, he drove me backward into a credenza against one wall, then hit me with a right hand across the bridge of my nose that instantly flooded my eyes with tears.

Amid the spray of knick-knacks and mementos flying off the credenza shelves behind me, something heavy tumbled down my right arm and, half-blind and spitting blood, I instinctively snatched it out of the air to swing it at O's face. The crystal swan lost part of a wing as it slammed against O's left eyebrow, stunning him just enough to stagger him momentarily. I tried to follow up with what was left of the glass bird in my hand, but he threw up his left forearm to block the attempt and swung another anvil-like right that landed just under my jaw. I stumbled backward, feet flailing away for balance, left arm reaching behind me for something to latch on to that might keep me upright – a wall, a floor lamp, anything.

But O' wouldn't wait for me to find it. As I glanced off the armchair I'd been sitting in only moments before, he launched himself toward me to hit me again, this time with a left that seemed to cave in the whole right side of my face. I went down like an old woman, taking an end table and everything on it to the floor with me, and all at once I could see us reverting to form. This was how it had always been when I was foolish enough to try O'Neal Holden. The superior athlete versus the more righteously indignant. It was like trying to stop a moving forklift with willpower alone.

I came up on my hands and knees, dog-like, and tried to catch my breath, staring down at the carpet I was staining forever with blotches of dark red. O' kicked me under my right arm and rolled me over again, then stood there watching as I tried to gather the nerve to go on fighting. The crystal swan had opened a deep cut over his left eye, which was half-closed and bathed in blood, but compared to me, he looked as fresh as a daisy.

I could have easily quit right then. Pressing on seemed to hold no other promise but more of the same – humiliation and pain. Left alone to decide, I think I would have just closed my eyes and let O' do as he pleased, unable to recall what motivation I could have possibly had to ever care this much about R.J. Burrow.

But then O' put a sharp, needless spear into my side: 'Get up, you stupid old fool.'

So I did. I came up quick, caught his right foot with both hands when he tried to kick me down again and torqued it to the left, hard, like a frozen water valve I was trying to force open. O' let loose a scream and went down without any further help, clutching at his leg as if I'd snapped it in half and tossed him the pieces.

I got to my feet, prepared to do the man more damage if he required it, but I could have been a painting on the wall for all the attention he was paying to me now. He was in that much pain.

'Manual versus Dorsey, homecoming game our senior year,' I said, spitting a wad of blood on to the floor near his head. 'You ran for a hundred and eleven yards in the first two quarters, then tore up your right knee just before half-time. Doctors weren't sure you'd ever walk again. Funny, the shit an "old man" remembers, isn't it?'

'Goddamn you, Handy!' He had to pause before going on, sweat rolling down his face in wide rivulets from all the effort it was taking just to remain conscious. 'I need a doctor,' he said, anger slowly dying to a mere ember, because anger, too, required energy he no longer had to burn.

I looked around for the gun he'd lost and found it on the carpet a few feet away. I brought it back to where he lay, loaded a round into the chamber and aimed at the center of his face. 'How much you want to bet this one will work when I pull the trigger?'

'I did that for your own protection, you dumbass. I didn't want you shooting somebody who meant you no harm.'

I laughed. 'That right?'

'I'm talking about Fine, not Eastman! I had him watchin' you, just like you thought. But only to have your back, not to kill you.'

'Just like Doug Wilmore was supposed to have R.J.'s back. Is that what you mean?'

Wilmore hadn't confessed to anything when I'd visited his home that morning, but in his clumsy, liquor-impaired refusals, he had said all I'd ever need to know about his relationship with O'Neal Holden, and the feelings of resentment he had toward Sylvia Nuez and the co-worker she'd chosen over him to have an affair with.

'Who the hell is Doug Wilmore?'

'Come on, O'. I dropped his name to get you over here, remember? He was gonna be your new boy at Coughlin, somebody who could keep an eye out for you for the next Cleveland Allen so the back-door construction deals you'd been cutting for the city of Bellwood wouldn't have to stop just because Allen was no longer around.'

'Is that what Wilmore told you?'

'You bet on a horse that can't run, O'. His crib's a minefield of open whisky bottles and he's in love with a woman R.J. was seeing on the side. Putting him to work tailing R.J. for you was no different from killing R.J. yourself.

'Or maybe you already knew that,' I added.

'I never told that goddamn fool to tail any-body! He was supposed to watch R.J. at Cough-lin, that's all.'

If he was telling the truth – and I had the sense that he was – he'd given a sick man a job to do and Wilmore had run too far with it. Which still made O' the reason Wilmore had been at the pier that night to see R.J. and Eastman get high – and to stumble upon the perfect opportunity to take R.J. out of Sylvia Nuez's life forever. The gun, the drugs, Darrel Eastman...

'It doesn't matter what you told him,' I said. 'What matters is that the man who murdered R.J. worked for you.'

O' shook his head, grimacing. 'I'm not gonna fuck around arguing with you, Handy. You wanna believe I've got a bullet comin' to me, shoot my ass and get it over with. Bad as this leg hurts, you'll be doin' me a favor.'

I didn't move.

'Go on, nigga, shoot!'

I was trapped in a bad dream, the kind in which your only chance of survival is to run – and your feet won't work. I tossed the gun to the floor where O' would have no trouble reaching it.

'I'm supposed to pick that up now, right? 'Cause all I gotta do is kill you to be in the clear.' O' threw his head back and laughed, the old back-in-the-day laugh of his that used to crack me up one minute and boil my blood the next. 'You just don't get it, do you? I'm not the bad guy in this thing, Handy. My hands are clean. Excel killed McDonald's woman and the three brothers from the safe house. R.J. killed Excel. According to you, Doug Wilmore killed R.J. And you—'

'I killed Darrel Eastman,' I said, seeing the perfect symmetry of his argument for the first time, when it had always been sitting there, right in front of my face.

'That's right. Me? I haven't killed anybody. I told some lies and made a few dollars. Took a little girl who would've either died or been raised by a crack dealer's widow and gave her a loving home and a college education. And I turned a hick town named Bellwood into a city people can be proud to live in. But you wanna blow me up, put all our business in the street just so you can sleep at night, knowin' I got my just deserts.

'Well, fuck it. I've got lawyers, just like Doug Wilmore will get one. And you know what? We'll probably both walk.' He adjusted his position on the floor, grunting with grave discomfort, then chuckled.

'How's that for irony, Handy? You go through all this shit tryin' to get justice for R.J., and only end up fixin' things so that the man who actually whacked him goes free.'

He laid his head back, fading, and asked the ceiling, 'Ain't that a bitch?'

A few minutes later, during a lull in the winter storm a pewter sky promised to unleash anew, I drove my rental car around the block and jerked it into an empty space at the curb, pulling my shirt open like a man whose skin was crawling with leeches. Frantically, I stripped off the wide bands of medical tape glued to my skin, first to free the tiny voice recorder pinned just beneath my ribcage, then the microphone wire snaking up the side of my torso to the middle of my chest. I didn't want the shit on me anymore.

As near as I could tell, neither the recorder nor the mic had suffered any ill effects from my brawl with O'Neal Holden. I'd gotten the setup and a lesson on how to use it from Toni Burrow earlier that day, having called her the night before from Crescent City to see if she could provide me with such specialized equipment on extremely short notice. Now that she had, all the questions I'd been able to put off last night regarding my intended use of the gear had come due. Assuming the conversation I'd just had with O' had been successfully recorded, it wouldn't be hard to satisfy her curiosity. All I had to do was hand the tiny recorder back to her and urge her to give its contents a listen.

Or not.

It may have been an easy decision for some to make. The difference between doing what is morally right and that which is simply less personally intolerable. But there was nothing easy about it for me. My choices seemed to be equally inadequate and unjust, mere bandages on a wound that ran bone-deep.

I was not God; judgment was not my purview. Yet I had made this trip to Los Angeles in search of nothing if not someone to hold accountable for the brutal murder of my friend R.J. Burrow. Exacting vengeance on only one of the two people responsible for the crime – either the man who'd actually committed it, or the one who'd set him up to do so – would be a sham. But that was the latest devil's bargain I was left with.

O' had been right. I could make him pay for all the evil he had done to me, or Doug Wilmore for having taken R.J. Burrow's life. I could not do both.

'If I pretend I don't know what I know and go home right now – what happens to Wilmore?'

I'd asked O', just before leaving his sister's home.

'What do you think? Now that you just told me he's the one offed my boy?' O' asked, a small spark of rage igniting behind his eyes. It seems, in his way, he did love R.J., after all.

'Fine?'

O' smiled, looking ahead to the next assignment he would give his friend with the Bellwood City Police Department. 'My pal Hymie can sometimes be a very good man to know.'

On my way out the door, I couldn't get over it. Hell if Walt Fine didn't know O'Neal Holden better than I ever had myself.

TWENTY-SIX

I never did fix the reel-to-reel tape recorder I found in Culver City. I ran out of time and motivation. The last time I saw it, it was waiting for the cleaning crew at my motel to discover its limitations and put it back in a trash bin somewhere. I guess some destinies can be deferred, but not completely avoided.

As for my own destiny, the Los Angeles authorities put me on a plane to St Paul this morning and told me to never come back.

That's not the way the order was worded, but that was the gist of it. It took every LA cop I crossed paths with last week the entire weekend, plus Monday, to decide they preferred me gone to still around.

My brother and Sly saw me off at the airport, the only people in the world who now know every secret I have to keep – save for one. I called Sylvia Nuez 'Sly' today for the first time. Something is happening between us, we aren't quite sure what. We only know we aren't ready to pull the plug on it yet. We've made tentative plans for her to spend a few days with me up in Minnesota over the summer. That'll be a big test. I've fucked up lesser chances at happiness before.

Doug Wilmore had an accident at a Coughlin construction site late Saturday afternoon. The site in Gardena had been shut down for the weekend and he was there alone, making a routine check for signs of vandalism. The stories in the paper said he was killed instantly when the brakes failed on a cement truck parked on a grade and he got pinned between the truck and a retaining wall. Nobody saw it happen, and the driver who'd parked the truck insisted he'd both set the brakes and wedged blocks in front of its wheels. Whether he had or not, company officials were still at a loss to explain how its first fatal accident in nineteen years could have occurred even as I was boarding my flight to St Paul two hours ago.

From what I understand, R.J.'s daughter Toni

Burrow is scheduled to fly back to Seattle tomorrow night. We're on speaking terms, but only barely. She thinks I'm holding out on her. She'd aided and abetted my every effort to determine the circumstances of her father's murder, trusting I would be honest with her when the time came to issue a final report, and I had reneged on my promise to do so. My insistence that Darrel Eastman had killed R.J. for the very reasons the police had given his widow rang hollow to her, as did the feeble explanation I'd offered for failing to return the surveillance recorder she'd loaned me: I'd lost it in a fight with O'. A silly, childish, schoolyard fight that in the end, I said, had only served to prove that the mayor of Bellwood had had nothing to do with our mutual friend's murder.

If Toni Burrow saw through my lie, it was the one true thing I told her afterward, and the genuine conviction I had brought to it, that seemed to dissuade her from ever pursuing the matter again: 'The man who killed your father is dead. I swear it.'

Frances Burrow will never believe it, of course. Her illusions about R.J. are just too strong to accept the true tawdriness of the circumstances behind his demise, and the substantial role he himself played in it. But she, too, will let his murder go in time, because it is either that, or live with an open wound that will never heal.

I promised her there is nothing more to be done.

What little I know about O'Neal Holden since I last saw him at his sister's house is only what I've seen in the news. The one-car auto accident that supposedly put him on crutches and tore up his face didn't get a lot of media coverage, but to O', I'm sure, any press is good press. I suspect he would feel differently if I ever decide to mail the little micro voice recorder packed away in my luggage to my brother's friend Jessie Scott at the *Bellwood Carrier*, but I could be wrong. O' is almost as hard a man to comprehend as he is to hate.

In any case, I've done all the worrying about O'Neal Holden I intend to do. My account with the past is closed for good, boarded up and shut down like an old, rotted storefront. I might give a thought to Paris McDonald now and then, unable to do otherwise, but that's it. I have the future to be afraid of now, and it's going to take everything I have to build one designed to last.

I will start with my daughter Coral.

I have promised her the truth about her mother, and I will keep my word. I will tell her how, not long after arriving in St Paul, I met and fell in love with a woman named Susan Yancy. We were engaged to be married. But Susan had a little sister, Denise, a wild and self-destructive siren who reminded me of someone else I once loved, someone who'd only recently died, and one night, like a fool, I drifted too close to her flame and she became pregnant with my child. Betrayed, my fiancée left me, and when Denise – shot full of heroin and wasting away – died nine months later, only weeks after giving birth to our daughter, I was left with nothing to do but raise the baby on my own, already determined to tell her nothing but lies about how she had come into the world.

It will be a terrible admission to make, but it will only be part of a much larger story. Coral will need to hear everything, and I will need to share it, in order to help her understand how her father – a man who has always made his living fixing things others cannot – could have ever made such a tragic mess of both our lives.

It is the story of a man who once took a girl who did not belong to him to a dance party and, in so doing, brought a world of hurt to a great number of people, not the least of all himself.

I pray Coral will find it in herself to forgive me.

Just as I pray I will someday learn to forgive myself.